DRAKE UNWOUND

BOOK 2 IN THE DRAKE SERIES

S. E. LUND

ACADIAN PUBLISHING LIMITED

S. E. LUND'S NEWSLETTER

If you would like updates on new releases and sales, special promotions and other news, sign up for S. E. Lund's newsletter. She hates spam and so will never share your email with anyone!

S. E. Lund's Newsletter Sign Up

CHAPTER 1

THOUGHTS of the delightful Katherine McDermott, my new submissive and rapidly becoming my obsession, was distracting me from taking care of business.

I sat at the Foundation, a document in my hand, and tried to concentrate. Dave Mills, my old friend and manager of the Foundation's Africa desk, sat across from me, briefing me on the latest projects. Something about a clean water initiative that was tied to better health outcomes for mothers and babies but I couldn't keep my mind focused on what he was saying. At one point, his lips were moving, but I honestly didn't hear a word he said.

My mind was occupied elsewhere, particularly on one lovely and disarmingly responsive Kate, whom I couldn't wait to ravish once I had finished meeting with Dave.

He said something important, for I could tell he was waiting for my response, but I couldn't for the life of me remember what he asked. I'd been tying Kate up in my mind, imagining her dressed in her black lace garter belt and fishnet hose. Her black pushup bra that made me hard just thinking of how her breasts spilled out over the top. How I'd bind her hands to the headboard, spread her thighs wide with a spreader bar, and blindfold her with a black silk scarf.

How her generous lips would be wet and parted while she waited for my cock.

"Drake..." Dave raised his eyebrows at me, half a grin on his face.

"I'm sorry," I said and blinked rapidly, trying to pull myself back into the present. "What was your question?"

"Where are you? Or do I even have to ask? Inside the thighs of the lovely Ms. Bennet?"

I frowned and shook my head. "I have so many loose ends to tie off before we can leave for Africa. Sorry..."

He shrugged. "I asked you whether you wanted to fund the clean water campaign as part of the mother-baby program."

I remembered reading about the project. It was a worthy cause, but there were so many. How could you possibly decide? Every time I turned down one project, I felt bad for denying the people there much-needed funding.

"Yes, by all means, if you think this fits with our new direction, go ahead and draw up the papers. I'll sign. Was there anything else? I have plans for this afternoon."

"We just started..."

"How many projects do we have to get through?" I said as I flipped through the file, disappointed that I wouldn't be able to sneak out and enjoy Kate the way I had been imagining.

"Twenty applications," Dave said, shaking his head. "Drake, I told you that you couldn't put this off any longer. Kate will just have to wait."

He grinned at me and finally, I sighed and resigned myself to concentrate on matters at hand.

It was the least I could do. I was paying Dave's salary after all...

We talked about the projects for a solid hour, with Dave going through each one before offering his opinion.

I really did pay attention but when I checked my watch, I realized I had to call Kate and let her know I'd be later than planned. I still had to drop by the Corporation to sign some papers. "Let me make a phone call," I said to Dave. "This will just take a moment, if you don't mind."

Dave left me alone in my office and went to the staff room. I took out my cell and pulled up Kate's number. She answered after the second ring.

"Hi," she said, and I could hear the pleasure in her voice. "I was just going to call you."

"Kate, I'm sorry," I said. "Something came up and things have taken longer than expected. I'm going to have to put our meeting off until later tonight."

"Is everything okay?"

"Everything's fine. Just some business to wrap up before we leave."

"My dad called and wants to take us out to dinner tonight. He said the restaurant was our choice. Do you feel like joining them for dinner? Is there somewhere you'd really like to go?"

I considered. I really wanted to eat *her* for dinner, but I knew Kate was really going to find it hard to say goodbye to her father for our trip to Kenya. Dinner with Ethan and Elaine would be enjoyable and give Kate more quality time with her father now that the two of them were on better terms.

"Of course," I said. "How about we all go to the Russian Tea Room one last time?"

"Only if you agree that we don't sit in a booth."

I laughed, remembering very fondly the first time I took Kate there. When Dave returned sooner than I thought he

3

would, I kept my voice as quiet as possible. "Don't *tempt* me, Ms. Bennet. You've got my mind working overtime thinking of ways to enjoy you while we're in public."

"*Drake...*"

"*Katherine*," I said, my voice firm. "Hold on a second." I stood and thanked Dave for the meeting and told him I really had to go. He laughed good-naturedly and left my office once more, closing the door behind him.

"Sorry," I said. "I had someone in my office."

"Drake, we could *never* do anything when my father's there..." she said, although I knew the very idea of me playing with her under the table would arouse her despite her good-girl tendencies. Kate wanted to be debauched. She just wanted someone who loved her to do the debauching. Someone she could trust.

Someone who knew what he was doing and wouldn't go too far.

Me, in other words.

"Of course not," I said. "But we could arrive a bit early..."

She said nothing and I knew she was imagining it. Probably smiling to herself. "What time would we meet them?" I asked.

"The usual time. Seven-thirty."

"Tell your dad it's my treat and that I insist," I said, using my best authoritative voice. "I'll reserve the fourth floor at the Russian Tea Room. Now, as for you, Ms. *Bennet*, I'll pick you up at your father's at six-forty five and we'll arrive a half hour early. Remember my rules for going out in public. I want you wearing that black dress you wore at the fundraiser and your stockings and garters. Nothing underneath. Put your hair up so I can see your collar and get at that neck of yours. You'll be so wet when we get to the restaurant, I imagine I could make you come very easily."

"If you really want this," Kate said, her voice breathy and hesitant at the same time.

"I *really* want this, Katherine. I'm getting hard thinking about slipping my fingers inside of you while we're sitting at the table. I'm going to have to do some serious meditation and deep breathing to get rid of my not so little problem before I go to my next meeting..."

"I wish I could help you with that problem, Doctor Morgan."

I laughed. "I do as well. You'll help me later."

"See you and it at six-forty five," she said.

"That's my good girl. I love you."

"I love you, too."

I ended the call, imagining having Kate at my disposal. It would be hard to sit through another meeting, but I'd give it my best.

After another hour of sitting and listening to staff brief me on the performance of my father's company for the fourth quarter, trying to keep my focus on the matter at hand, I was able to slip out early and make my way to the 8th Avenue apartment. Kate texted me to say she was ready earlier than planned and would use her father's limo service and meet me at the apartment. I arrived before Kate once more, kicking myself because I knew Kate wanted to be waiting for me the way I had outlined in my letters to my subs, but life, apparently, had other plans for us. I had a very quick shower, dressed in a dark suit appropriate for the night at The Russian Tea Room, and poured two glasses of Aniso-vaya. I waited only slightly patiently for my beautiful submissive in training to arrive. I stood at the large multi-paned window looking out over the street below and watched the traffic, searching for the limo that would bring

Kate to me. The sun had already set and the streetlights caught the soft flakes of snow as they fell to the street.

Since New Year's Eve, my life had been in complete turmoil. I never thought I wanted or needed a partner but I was wrong and it was only when I had her to myself that I felt truly happy. Not only was she submissive sexually, she was intelligent and socially aware, even if her politics were left of center. She was delicious, with a body meant for sex and a mind meant for submission.

I broke all my rules for her. Every single one. I was, perhaps, the happiest I had been in a long time in spite of it.

I saw the limo and immediately felt a surge of adrenaline, smiling at the prospect of seeing her pretty face as she stepped out of the vehicle. My cell chimed and I looked at my messages.

I'm on my way to the apartment.

I knew she'd be disappointed I was there first once more but there was no helping it.

I'm already here.

There was a pause but then she responded.

I'm outside.

I texted her back, a smile on my face as I watched her stand on the sidewalk and look up at the building.

I'm waiting for you...

When she opened the door, I was waiting for her, two glasses of Anisovaya in my hands.

"Ms. *Bennet*..."

"Dr. *Morgan*," she said, trying to be formal but failing due to her barely hidden smile. "I see you've got everything well in hand."

"Always," I said, smiling back. "I hope to have *you* well in hand all evening." I watched as she removed her boots and stood before me, waiting for my commands. "I hope you obeyed my orders about your manner of dress."

"Do you doubt it?"

"Of course not, but you have quite a will. One I intend to tame."

"Tame?" she said, matching my mock stern tone, enjoying this little game. "What could you possibly mean by that, Doctor?"

"*Tame*," I said, handing her the glass. "To make docile, tractable, obedient. To domesticate. To harness, to *control*."

We shot back the Anisovaya, and I sighed as the liquor burned in the nicest possible way in my throat and stomach. I associated it with sexual pleasure and so enjoyed the burn.

"You like your women tame?" she said, tilting her head to one side. There was a playful look in her eyes so I knew she wasn't offended by my choice of words.

"No," I said, taking the glass from her hands and placing them on the table by the door. "After meeting you, I realized I like them quite the opposite. I like them wild, willful, self-prepossessed. What I love is *taming* them. I love the battle of wills." I helped her off with her coat and hung it over the chair in the entry. I took her in my arms, pulling her against my body, brushing a lock of hair from her pink cheek. "I love the planning, the reconnaissance, the approach, the first engagement, the attack, the resistance, the eventual surrender."

She examined me from the corner of her eye. "But do you lose interest once you've conquered?"

That was a surprise and I frowned, wanting her to explain.

"Once your adversary has surrendered," she said. "When there's nothing left to tame?"

I shook my head. "The wise general never totally destroys the spirit of the conquered. What good is a razed and barren landscape?"

She leaned her head against my chest. "Will you go off looking for new lands to conquer once you've subdued your current target?"

I pulled away and looked down at her, surprised she was so insecure.

"*Kate...*"

"Well, when you put it that way, it got me thinking."

I led her over to the couch in the living room and sat down, pulling her down to sit on my lap, the way we sat that first night in November. I wanted to remind her that I was the Dominant and she was supposed to not think. Especially not overthink, which she had a tendency to do.

"I was just playing around."

She nodded, but I knew that wasn't enough.

"Kate, you're not merely a submissive to me," I said. "I *love* you. I want to be with *you*. Not only as your Dom but as your partner. I'm old enough to know when I've found what I need to make me happy. I *have* found it." I stroked her cheek with the backs of my fingers, searching her face for under-standing. Acceptance that I was telling her the truth. "I'm not going to grow bored with you. I want you to stay who you are. I don't want a footstool. I thought you understood."

"I do, but it's every woman's insecurity." Her cheeks were pink and it wasn't the cold. She was embarrassed by her inse-curity. It made my heart melt even more.

"Shh," I said, a finger against her lips. "*You* are completely everything I want and need. You're beautiful, intelligent, warm, loving and submissive sexually underneath all the questioning and resistance. You don't have to worry."

"We hardly know each other," she said, still not convinced.

I knew that words weren't enough. I had to show her. She had to feel it, but that would take time.

"I *know* you, Kate," I said, kissing her cheek. "You don't easily hide your emotions. You question everything, so I know where your mind is. I know *you*."

She sighed and leaned her head against my shoulder, giving in just a bit. She said nothing for a while and we sat there in each other's embrace, the warmth of our bodies mingling. But I knew she was still doubting everything. I knew her mind was going somewhere it shouldn't.

"*Stop*," I said, tilting her chin up so that she had to look into my eyes. "I know what's going on in that mind of yours. This is a big commitment, but don't you feel the way I do? That this is exactly what you want and need?"

"Yes," she said and she said it without hesitation.

"Good." I kissed her softly, my gaze moving over her face, her large green eyes, her smooth skin, her lush mouth. I stroked her cheek, and touched the choker I gave her as a Christmas present, before letting my fingers drop to her cleavage. "I want us to be happy and enjoy ourselves tonight, with your father and Elaine but also as a couple. Until they arrive, we're in scene and I want your total submission to me. No questions. No more doubt."

I ran my hand along her leg, from her knee to her thigh. I slipped my hand under the hem of her dress, searching out the tops of her seamed stockings to the clasps of her garter belt.

"Mmm," I said, murmuring against her throat, my cock thickening at the feel of the lace against her creamy skin. "Just what the doctor ordered."

She smiled and closed her eye. "Your wish is my command."

I pressed her down on the couch, lying between her thighs. Could there be anything better than that position? A beautiful woman beneath you, her eyes closed, her mouth open, ready, waiting for you to kiss her?

I reached down and ran my fingers over her garters and the tops of her stockings, loving the contrast between the lace and her milky thighs. My fingers found her pussy, slipping between her folds and inside her warm wetness, my cock jerking in response. Beneath me, Kate moaned and pressed her hips up, against my fingers. I kissed her deeply, searching her mouth, sucking in her tongue. I pulled back, and my eyes moved over her from her face to her breasts to her pussy, my fingers penetrating her.

"Nice and wet already," I said approvingly. "It'll be hard to last through the night with you like that."

She lay with her eyes closed. "All you have to do is talk to me and I'm ready. In fact," she added. "I only have to *think* of you."

I bent down and kissed her neck, smiling at her admission.

"That's an awful lot of power," I said playfully. "I like it, being a Dom and all." I grinned and abruptly sat up, pulling my hand from between her thighs and beneath her dress. I stood and helped her up and she was a bit unstable so I steadied her.

"So, what are your plans?" she asked. "Are you going to make me so aroused before dinner that I can't focus and I sit there like a rag doll in front of my parents?"

"Oh, I have *so many plans*, Ms. Bennet," I said and pulled her to the entry, where I picked up her coat and held it out. "You'll just have to be a good submissive and wait to find out." I opened my eyes wide at that, reminding her that she was supposed to be in sub mode.

"I'm still learning what being a good submissive means," she said and slipped the coat on. "I'm always questioning everything."

I wrapped my arms around her from behind. "That's how I knew you and I would be so good together. You want to know, to understand. I love to teach. We're perfect together."

She smiled and leaned back against me.

We *were* perfect for each other.

CHAPTER 2

WE TOOK my car and drove through the early evening traffic to The Russian Tea Room, which was busy when we arrived. I took Kate's hand, rubbing her skin with my thumb affectionately as the hostess escorted us to the fourth floor Hearth Room, which I'd reserved for the evening. In the elevator, I stood slightly behind Kate, my arms around her, pressing my already-semi hard erection against her while the hostess made pleasant conversation.

We emerged into the Hearth Room, with its ornate décor, the wallpaper dark brocade, the fixtures gilded, mirrors and glass, silver, white tablecloth and crystal glasses. I loved the place and imagined sitting in a café in St. Petersburg before the revolution, where there was lively conversation about art and music and politics.

I led Kate across the room to the sofas. Displayed on the coffee table was our blini, caviar and vodka. As soon as the hostess left, I pulled Kate down onto my lap and began to feed her blini smeared with caviar, sour cream and minced red onions.

On her part, Kate gave in completely, lying across my lap,

her arm around my shoulder. She seemed to really enjoy the blini and caviar, her eyes widening with pleasure as she ate. That sent my thoughts to her face while I pleasured her, which I planned to do once we made a toast. I handed her a shot glass of vodka.

"Za vas!" I said.

She held up her glass and responded, then drank down the vodka. When she lay back in my arms one more, I slipped my hand beneath her dress to caress her thigh and her lace garters, unable to get enough of them. After we enjoyed a few more blini, I left Kate on the couch, and closed the double doors, so that we had privacy from the other rooms. Kate stood up, adjusted her dress and turned towards another door that lead to the restrooms.

"Where do you think you're going?" I said, frowning.

"Just to freshen up before my parents get here."

"You look beautiful just the way you are." I went to her and fixed her with my gaze. "I want you," I said, my voice hoarse. "*Now.*"

I grabbed her and pulled her close, pressing her against me, one hand at the small of her back, the other tangled in her hair.

"*Drake,*" she whispered. "My parents are supposed to arrive..."

"Not for at least fifteen minutes. That gives me plenty of time, so relax, *Katherine,*" I said, trying to make my voice commanding. "I gave the establishment strict instructions that we aren't to be disturbed until your parents arrive. When they do, they'll call my cell first, and won't send them up until I say."

I tilted her head up and kissed her, pressing my erection into her to let her know how she affected me. She moaned when my tongue found hers, and I sucked it into my mouth, while I squeezed her ass, pulling her even closer.

She ran her fingers through my hair, grabbing it and pulling me down to her. Heat built in me and I kissed her more deeply, my heart racing, my cock so hard and in need of her tight warm wetness. When she ground her hips against me, I growled, surprising even myself with the strength of my response. I inhaled deeply when I felt the top of her stockings, the clip of her garter, the naked skin of her pussy.

"Fuck, I need you, right *now*." I lifted her thigh and ground myself into her.

I pushed her down on the couch so that she lay beneath me, my hips between her thighs. I kissed her deeply once again, pressing against her, grinding my hips, and my erection, into her. I slid down her body and lifted her dress, baring her lower body before kissing her all over, her belly, her inner thighs, her mound.

"*Drake*," she said, her body stiffening.

"*Shh*," I said sternly. "Comply."

She bit her lip and closed her eyes but when I slipped my fingers inside her body, she gasped, her thighs trembling. She moaned when I covered her with my mouth, unable to stop from thrusting her hips against me. Soon, as I licked her labia, and stroked her clit with my tongue, she was writhing under my mouth. I thrust two fingers inside her, sucking her clit between my lips, my tongue circling it.

When I pulled away, she opened her eyes and I held her gaze, enjoying the expression of desperate need I saw on her face. I leaned over her, my arms on either side of her head.

"I'd love to fuck you from behind right now. Your dress hiked up over your back, your body over the back of the couch, me standing behind you, watching my cock slide inside of you, but we have only a few minutes. Instead, I think I want you to stand in position for a while so I can imagine it."

15

I lifted her up and turned her around, pulling up her dress so that her nice round creamy ass and legs were on display. Her black sheer stockings with the seam up the back, and black lace garters and garter belt contrasted beautifully with her fair skin. As I admired Kate's luscious curves, I bent her over the couch and then I sat on the opposite couch and watched her, knowing it would arouse her to be on display, coupled with the risk of being discovered by the serving staff or worse – her parents.

We remained like this, Kate in position before me, for a few more moments, and when my cell chimed Kate startled and tried to stand up, but I placed one hand on her back to stop her from getting up just yet.

The hostess said Ethan and Elaine had arrived and asked if I wanted her to bring them up.

"Yes, you can bring them up," I said, totally in control. "But give me a couple of minutes first. Show them the new ice sculpture. Introduce them to the chef."

I ended the call and Kate tried to stand up straight again but I stopped her once more.

"*No.*" I ran my fingers down the small of her back, between her ass cheeks to her pussy, my fingers teasing the entrance to her body, my thumb stroking over her clit, which was nice and hard and swollen.

"*Drake...*"

"The more you resist, the longer I'll take."

She said nothing while I stroked her clit more firmly, and soon her breath was coming in short gasps. Finally, I pulled her dress down, turned her around and stroked my hands over her hair, adjusting her dress to make sure everything was presentable.

I ran a hand over my erection and buttoned my jacket to cover it. I dipped my fingers in my glass of vodka and licked them off, smiling at Kate when I did. I dipped a corner of a handkerchief into the vodka and wiped my mouth.

"My two favorite things – your pussy and vodka."

Kate couldn't help but smile back, although her cheeks were flushed red and I knew she was anxious about her parents finding us. "How am I going to get through this dinner?" she said, her voice breathy with unmet desire.

"You'll manage. Keep imagining what I'm going to do with and to you when we're alone later."

I went to the double doors and opened them when I heard their voices coming from the direction of the elevator. I welcomed them both, taking them off the hostess's hands.

"There you are," I said, smiling, reaching a hand out to Ethan for a shake.

"Glad to see you my boy," Ethan replied.

I bent to Elaine and kissed her cheek.

"Please bring up more caviar," I said to the hostess, and ushered them into the room.

Kate kissed Ethan's and then Elaine's cheeks. "I'm so glad you suggested this," Kate said. "I never thought I'd say it but I love caviar."

We sat around the coffee table and I poured them both a shot each of vodka.

"To your health," I said. They all responded in kind and downed the vodka. Ethan seemed especially pleased to be here and smacked his lips in appreciation, reaching for one of the last blini to follow his shot.

We caught up with each other's days and I asked Ethan about his campaign. Elaine asked me about the job in Africa and so I described what I'd be doing to help Michael at the hospital and told her about the Medical College. Kate took my hand, squeezing it, smiling up at me.

I smiled when I saw the expression on her face – she was

clearly happy. I leaned over and kissed her briefly before turning back when the cocktail waitress brought more blini and caviar.

I held up my glass. "*Za vas*," I said, looking at everyone in turn. "To us."

"To us," Ethan replied. He held up his glass, as did Elaine and Kate. Together, we shot back the vodka and turned to the blini and caviar once more.

I ordered a sample menu, enjoying the savory specialties of the Chef on the line that night. When each course came, I described it and where each dish came from in Russia, familiar with the most popular dishes.

I turned back, picked up my glass of wine, and toasted us once again. I knew that my father would be pleased to see me with his old friend and especially with Kate, probably imagining that she'd moderate my political conservatism. Instead, it would be me who encouraged her sexual liberalism. Whatever the case, Kate and I were happy together and I hoped I had learned enough about women and life that I didn't make the same mistakes he made with my mother.

I was determined not to let that happen. Kate's happiness was everything to me.

After our coffee and dessert, and following our goodbyes to Ethan and Elaine, Kate and I were back in my car and headed to the apartment on 8th Avenue. The streets were less busy and huge snowflakes fell lazily from a cloud-covered sky, the lights of the city reflecting on the cloud surface, lighting up the streets.

Once we were back in the apartment, I could barely wait to ravish Kate, and after I removed our coats and threw both onto the chair by the door, I pushed Kate into the living room, guiding her with hands on her hips, biting playfully at her neck.

"Now, my lovely *Katherine*," I said, pulling her hair out of its clip, smoothing it with my hands. "It's time to do your duty for your Master."

I pushed her to the couch so that she stood in front of it and leaned over, her arms on the back, her knees spread wide. I pulled up her dress so that her bare ass was once more there for my enjoyment. And enjoy it I did – her ass was perfect, round, full, soft. Her pussy peeked out from beneath her buttocks, and I could barely wait to push myself inside of her.

I unfastened my belt buckle and unzipped my fly, letting my pants and boxer briefs fall to the floor. I leaned over her, one hand sliding around her waist to her pussy, fingers spreading her until I found her clit, which I began to massage. With the other hand, I brushed her long hair out of the way and pulled down the shoulder of her dress.

I kissed the back of her neck and shoulder, biting the muscle softly, nibbling at her ear as I cupped her breast through the fabric of her dress. Finally impatient, I pulled down the zipper on the back of her dress and drew down the entire side so that her breast spilled out. I grabbed it and squeezed, her nipple between my fingers and thumb. I tweaked it, and Kate gasped in response.

I rubbed the head of my cock over her folds from behind, aching to slide inside of her wet tightness, but wanting to build her up so that she would come very quickly.

Finally, I entered her, sliding my entire length inside right to the hilt, my hands on her hips. She groaned, her body clenching around me. I stayed in that position for a moment, breathing in deeply as I relished the pure pleasure.

"You look so *good*," I murmured, stroking her ass, my

fingers tracing her garter belt, my cock all the way inside of her. "So damn *beautiful...*"

I began to thrust, the fingers of one hand brushing her clit, while the other hand played with her breast. When I glanced up, I caught her eye in the mirror and her expression was one of pure desire.

She came very quickly, as I expected and wanted. Usually, I'd tease her and tease her, denying her orgasm to make it even more powerful but tonight I wanted her to come and come fast. I didn't want to wait.

"Oh, *God*," she gasped. "*I...*"

I grasped her hips and thrust hard and fast and that sent her over, her body convulsing around my cock, her legs shaking. She gasped as she came, her face a mask of pleasure. I stopped, wanting to feel her body convulsing around my cock, the spasms delighting me. I kissed her shoulder for a moment and began thrusting once more, watching our bodies where they joined, watching her face as I fucked her hard, until finally, I felt the exquisite pleasure in my balls as I started to ejaculate and slammed into her, grunting in plea-sure with each thrust.

I collapsed against her, breathing fast in her ear. We remained in that position for a moment and I turned her head and kissed her. "Stay like that," I said as I withdrew slowly. "I want to watch."

I withdrew and stepped backwards, sitting down on the chair across from the couch and examined Kate, watching as my semen dripped out of her.

"Tomorrow, after I'm finished with a few things at the hospital, I want you waiting for me here, naked except for your garters and stockings, blindfolded, kneeling beside the bed. We'll do a scene from my letters."

Kate nodded, but said nothing, for I expect she was a little shy about having me watch her so intently.

"Does that please you, Katherine?"

"Yes," she said, her voice soft. "It pleases me very much."

"You're going to let me tie you up and have my way with you tomorrow. I'm going to enjoy you exactly as I want to."

"Yes," she said. "You will."

"Good girl." I went to her, pulling her upright, turning her around and embracing her, our mouths finding each other in a passionate kiss.

CHAPTER 3

THE NEXT DAY I spent my last few hours in the OR, finishing a few cases that required my expertise. That night, after I drove Kate to her apartment to pick up an extra charger for the laptop that she'd forgotten to pack, I was going to drop her off at 8th Avenue and make a brief run to the hospital to check in on the last of my surgical patients. After I was finished, I'd join her there and we'd do our scene.

"Will you take me to your apartment in Chelsea instead?" she said, out of the blue. It startled me but I tried to take it in stride. So far, we hadn't gone to my place. I preferred to stay at the apartment on 8th Avenue.

I quirked an eyebrow, trying to stall for time. "Curious, are you?"

"I showed you mine. I think it's only fair to show me yours." She turned to me, and I could tell from her expression, that this was some kind of test. I finally smiled, amused at her attempt to get me to break another one of my rules. "Trying to figure me out are you, Ms. Bennet? Sometimes a little mystery is a good thing. You might be disappointed when you see it."

"Why?"

"It's not really all that interesting. Just a nice old apartment in a nice old apartment block. My broker recommended it and I bought it sight unseen. It was decorated professionally so there's not much of my personality in it."

"Still, I'd love to see it," she said. "The *Sanctum Sanctorum*."

I laughed. "It's not the holiest of holies. It's just an apartment."

"If you really don't want to take me, we don't have to go but I will feel slighted."

"No, *no*," I said and shook my head. I glanced at her as we stopped at a stoplight, trying to sound unconcerned. I wasn't sure what I had against taking Kate to my place. "If you really want to see it, we can drop by there now. In fact, if you want, we can do our scene there. I have quite a few *toys*…"

"I'm sorry," she said and now her voice was full of reluctance. "It's just that I'd like to see how you lived before you met me."

"No, it's fine. As to how I lived before I met you," I said and cracked a grin. "I lived like a monk most of the time. I worked at the hospital. I gave lectures at Columbia. I attended fundraisers. I played racquetball at my club. And, when I had a submissive, I went to her apartment and tied her up and fucked her. Sometimes, I went to a dungeon party or one of the local munches. That was pretty much it. I lived a bachelor's life, Kate. The Chelsea apartment is where I eat and sleep. 8th Avenue is my *place*. My refuge. When I think of us, I see us there."

We drove along in silence for a few moments, and I could almost feel her mind working.

"How many submissives have you had?"

I was actually surprised she hadn't asked me before. "Eight with signed contracts."

"*Eight?*" she said, turning to me, a frown on her face.

I smiled, a bit guilty given that it had only been five years since my divorce. It worked out to quite a high rate, especially when you added in the subs that were one-offs when I'd gone to dungeon parties and took part in scenes.

"That doesn't include the subs I topped at play parties. I don't know how many there were. Maybe another six or so. You have to remember," I said, forming my words carefully. "Lara trained me and introduced me to a number of different subs. She was helping me learn what kind of Dom I was, so I went through quite a few in the first couple of years. It's not easy to find compatible people."

Beside me Kate nodded, but there was this look on her face. I reached over and took her hand, lifting it to my lips to kiss her knuckles.

"You don't have to be jealous. I never felt anything for them other than a desire for bondage and to dominate them sexually. They were a more rewarding way of having an orgasm than jerking off. You're completely different."

"I'm *not* jealous," she said, but I didn't believe it for a moment. I didn't even want to hear about her past – not anymore.

"I'm curious," she said. "And intimidated."

I smiled. "Good," I said. "A Dom is supposed to be a bit intimidating. It helps get the sub in the proper submissive state of mind, but when you think of me as your partner, you should feel my equal."

"I'm really *not* your equal." She glanced at me, her gaze moving over me like she was sizing me up. "You're a neurosurgeon. I haven't even had a real job yet."

I laughed. "*Kate...*" I leaned over and kissed her on the cheek briefly. "I'll let you in on a very well-kept secret." I focused back on the road. "Take away all the trappings of power, the accomplishments, the money, and underneath

25

every mogul, however successful, is just a flesh and blood man. We all want the same thing, deep down."

"What?"

I glanced at her, smirking. "Hot sex with a really great-looking babe."

"Drake!" She pulled her hand out of mine and punched my shoulder playfully.

"Just kidding," I said, laughing. I grabbed her hand back and threaded my fingers through hers. "No, seriously. Men fall in love more easily than women. When I finally met you, before our meeting with Lara, I wanted to ask you out, even thought I knew it would probably only be vanilla. I'd already plotted out a way to seduce you and initiate you into my depraved ways and so learning you were the sub I was supposed to initiate into the secret world of D/s..."

"You really *were* going to try to seduce me, you bad man," she said, her voice lightly scolding. "I *told* Lara that the relationship would be purely research."

"Lara thought you needed a bit of encouragement. You know," I said, grinning. "Find your 'inner sub'. I was more than willing to try because I'd already thought of it. I do love a challenge. I just had to find out how to push your buttons, so to speak."

"That sounds so," she said, hesitating as if to find the right word, "Machiavellian."

"Oh, it's *completely* Machiavellian. I can't lie. I *wanted* to conquer you, Ms. Bennet." I smiled to myself. "I thought I'd have you totally under my control in no time flat. How wrong I was..."

"What do you mean?"

I didn't answer. I was not going to let her know just how much control I'd lost in this relationship. She wanted me to take control. If I slipped, if I became too relaxed and loose with her, she'd go somewhere else and find someone who offered her the control she craved. I couldn't let that happen.

"You look like the Cheshire Cat," she said, looking at me from the corner of her eye. "The Cheshire Cat who swallowed the canary, to mix metaphors."

"Oh, I *ate* the lovely little canary. " I glanced over at her, unable to stop grinning. "I had her for breakfast and lunch and dinner."

"Don't get too smug." She took her hand back, her arms folded across her chest, smiling. "You're the one who came to me in the end, professing your love. Not wanting to be parted from me ever *again*."

Of course, that was right. I did come to her to profess my love. And I did love her. Too much for my own good. I reached over and took her hand once again. "You don't have to remind me about that. I thought I'd lost you for good. I was serious when I said I don't want us to be parted again."

"And yet, you were going to leave me, leave Manhattan and go to Kenya without even a goodbye?"

"Kate, remember what happened to me the last time a close relationship ended." I said nothing for a moment, thoughts of my divorce sobering me up a bit. Finally, I sighed. "After you said it was over, I tried not to feel *anything*. I shut down emotionally so I wouldn't over-react. I went through the motions of my life, hoping that going to Nairobi would distract me enough to keep the emotions locked away. Luckily, Elaine called me to tell me you'd fallen in love with me and were miserable, or right now, I'd probably be in some bar in Nairobi with a colleague, drowning my sorrows in a bottle of cheap vodka."

"You'd probably be looking for a new submissive. Lara would be busy sorting through her list of hopefuls."

"No. I'd have been overly invested in my work and my

27

music. After you?" I shook my head and turned to her. "A relationship with *just* a sub would feel hollow."

She smiled, seemingly pleased at my confession. We drove in silence for a few moments and I thought about how empty my life would have been if Elaine hadn't called.

"I'm so glad she *did* call," Kate said, her voice a bit choky. "I haven't thanked her enough."

I kissed her knuckles again. "We had a lot of people behind the scenes trying to get us together."

"And one determined to pull us apart."

We cruised to a halt at a traffic light. "She can't hurt us now," I said and glanced at Kate, at her sweet face, her large eyes and lush mouth.

After we drove on a few more blocks, she turned to me again. "Does anything *ever* faze you?"

I frowned and searched her face for her meaning. "Does anything ever *faze* me? Does anything ever faze me. Let's see..." I turned my attention back to the road, chewing my bottom lip for a moment. I was admittedly a very calm and controlled person. "You." I glanced at her. It was the truth. She fazed me.

"Me? You control me so well. How could I faze *you*?"

"I *don't* control you so well, in case you didn't notice," I said, reluctant to admit it, but we were in confessional mode and I thought, what the hell. This is the woman I love. "With you, I'm a terrible Dom. I'd be laughed out of a dungeon if other Doms saw how much I'm wrapped around your little finger."

"What?" she said, laughing. "You're not wrapped around my finger. The other way around, *Master.*"

"*Ha*," I said and shook my head. "I'm convinced you call me Master to keep me happy. Kate, I'm usually much more firm with my subs than I have been with you. Other Doms would punish you far more than I have. They'd demand absolute obedience by now. No questions. No hesitation." I smiled sheepishly and turned to look her in the eye. "I'm a lousy Dom."

"You're not happy with how things are between us?"

Of course, it was the wrong thing to say. "Yes, of course I'm happy. Remember? Meat and potatoes all smothered in gravy?"

"I think you control me quite well."

I chuckled, thinking what Lara would say if she saw what a bad Dom I had become, letting Kate get away with so much. "I *can* control you *sexually* fairly well, so far. But you made me break all my rules, Ms. Bennet, despite all my efforts to keep the parts of my life safely separate. You *totally* fazed me. I never thought I'd say it, but I enjoy you too much, especially when you resist me, question me. I'd do anything to keep you." I turned to her and smiled. "Love does that to you."

She smiled softly and squeezed my hand.

We arrived at my apartment building on 10th Avenue and West 23rd Street, a few blocks from the Hudson. I parked in my spot in the parking garage and we walked to the building. I saw it again as if for the first time, imagining it through her eyes. She was accustomed to wealth, so it wouldn't impress, but there was something really grand about the old building. My apartment was worth a couple million on the current market and it had all the bells and whistles in addition to being in a historic building.

The concierge greeted me, holding the door open for us. We took the elevator to the top floor and before we entered, I stopped.

"Here," I said and slipped an arm under one of hers, picking her up. I wanted to re-establish control over her, and

I knew one way was to make her feel helpless by picking her up. It worked and she tensed, resisting me.

"What are you doing?"

"You should be carried the first time you enter my apartment."

"Drake!" She tucked her head into the crook of my neck while I carried her inside. We stood in the entryway that had doors leading off to other rooms. I turned to examine her.

"So," I said, my eyes narrowed. "What's your first impression?"

She wriggled in my arms. "Are you going to put me down?"

I nuzzled her neck, needing her to let me lead, but she was still so independent.

"I don't know…" I murmured in her ear. "I kind of enjoy holding you like this. It brings out the Dom in me."

"But I want to *see* it!"

"You can see *it* anytime you want, Ms. Bennet," I said, unable to resist the double entendre. "All you have to do is ask."

She glanced at me and when she saw that I was smiling, she did as well. I let her slide out of my arms and threw my keys onto a plate on a circular table in the center of the room. Kate walked into the living room, which looked out onto the red brick building across the street.

"It looks just like you," she said, turning in a circle. "Sleek, high end, rich, dark, cultured."

I glanced around. The place was crowded with musical instruments, a baby grand, my guitars and amps. On the walls were my father's posters from the 60s and 70s of all his favorite bands.

"Are these your father's?"

I nodded and watched as she walked around and examined my possessions.

"He collected old photographs of the musicians and the bands he saw."

She stopped in the center of the room and glanced around before her gaze came to rest on me. Then, she came to me and slipped her arms around my waist, leaning her head against my chest. She caught me by surprise once more. I was unused to being shown affection by my subs. I didn't have that kind of relationship with them and was used to being the one to initiate everything. Still, I enjoyed her show of affection and embraced her back. She snuggled against my body, her arms slipping under my coat.

"I *like* this Drake Morgan," she said, looking me in the eye. "I'm seeing him a bit more clearly now."

"Oh?" I said, my eyebrows raised. "And what have you seen?"

"You seem so self-contained."

I sighed and squeezed her more tightly. "My mother had me after my brother died, so I was an only child."

She pulled back. "I never knew you had a brother who died."

I nodded and ran my fingers through her hair. "We've never talked much about personal things."

"*Tell* me."

I exhaled, for I didn't talk much about Liam – to anyone. He was this mythic creature who died before I was born. I was just the replacement. Not the original. "He died before I was born from a very rare and aggressive form of leukemia. My mother never recovered, even after she had me. I *had* to be independent after she left. I think I was a little too independent for married life and that's one reason why Maureen and I split. I was also reluctant to have children because of the chance of passing on the mutation that caused my brother's leukemia, and that was a sore point between us. As soon as she left me, she had a child with her new boyfriend."

"Oh, Drake, that's so sad." She squeezed me and I knew she was feeling sorry for me. It was a sentiment I did not want to cultivate. Pity. "What was your brother's name?"

"Liam, after my father."

"How old was he when he died?"

"Five."

I thought about my dead brother, who I never knew, but who loomed so large in my life as a child. My mother had a shrine to him in the spare bedroom. A collection of his baby pictures, his pictures in pre-school, of him as a sickly little boy, his head bald from chemo, an IV in his scalp.

I sighed and ran my hands over her hair. "I don't want to think about the past," I said gently. "Right now, I only want to think of me inside of you."

"I thought you had a patient..."

"I'll go later," I said and picked her up once more, carrying her into the bedroom at the back of the apartment, flicking on the light switch as we entered. I let her slide back out of my arms and took off her coat, leaving her standing beside the bed in my room while I went to the closet in the entry.

After I hung up our coats, I went to the server in the dining room and removed two shot glasses, then went to my refrigerator for the bottle of chilled Anisovaya. I returned to the bedroom with them, coming to an abrupt halt just inside the door to the bedroom.

Kate was standing by the closet doors, flipping through my photo album, which contained a variety of photographs of my subs in various bondage poses.

"*Oh*," I said, shocked. "I see you've found my book."

CHAPTER 4

SHE DIDN'T SAY A WORD, and kept turning page after page. I came to her side and looked over her shoulder, wondering what she thought of the pictures. They were artistic images taken by a friend who was a professional photographer.

In one photo that was taken from the side of the bed, I straddled Leah, one of my subs from a few years back. A blindfold covered her eyes and her hands and feet were tied to the bed frame. She sucked my cock while I leaned against the wall, my hands spread wide.

The photos depicted several of my former subs. I'd had the photos taken as a gift for them and provided each with their own personal album. None of them revealed my identity.

She closed the book when she came to a photo of me fucking Nikki, one of my wilder subs, who had sleeve tattoos and several piercings, my cock up her ass. I knew anal was a sore point with Kate. She was afraid of it. I put the vodka down on the table and turned her to face me, taking her chin in my hand, forcing her to look in my eyes.

"Are you OK?" I said, my voice soft. "That's quite... *personal.*"

"They're beautiful," she said, her voice cracking a bit. "The pictures are gorgeous and erotic at the same time. I'm sorry. I shouldn't have opened it. I feel like a voyeur."

I smiled. "I wanted them beautiful rather than porno-graphic. To me, D/s is an art. Photographs should convey that."

"Do you use them to, you know," she said, shrugging one shoulder. "Get off when you don't have a partner?"

"No," I said, and smiled. "I mean, I *have* before. I'm not going to lie. But they're meant more as a tribute to my former submissives. I don't want to have any photos out there that directly identify me. I gave them all copies of their photographs in a special book."

I handed her one of the shot glasses. She sniffed it, prob-ably wanting to see if it was Anisovaya.

"You've hardly done anything with me, have you?" she said and glanced up at me.

I shook my head. "Don't want to go too fast with you. Besides," I said and held up my glass to her. "All this messy love stuff got in the way."

She smiled at me, giving me a look.

"Drink up," I said.

She did, shooting back the vodka when I did. When I finished swallowing, I leaned down and kissed her, wanting to taste the vodka on her tongue, sucking hers into my mouth. When I pulled back, I brushed a lock of hair from her cheek.

"What's going on in that mind of yours?" I asked because I wanted to get her talking so I could see how she responded. If she liked them, I'd get pictures of us together one day. "You must feel something about those pictures."

She turned back to the images and considered.

"Why does bondage excite you?" She examined one in which Leah was suspended off the ground, bound, gagged, blindfolded.

"Bondage puts a sub in a certain headspace. Unable to move or escape, she's also unable to resist. It's liberating," I said, examining the photograph. "She can't help but feel what I make her feel. She can respond even more than normal to what I do because she has no other choice. Her body is mine. Her *mind* is mine. She's no longer responsible and as a result, she can feel everything without guilt."

Kate nodded, but said nothing else. I took her empty shot glass and placed it on the table beside the photo album. I took the album and led her over to the bed, sitting on the edge and pulling her down onto my lap. I opened the album to the first page.

"Tell me what you feel when you see these."

She inhaled and examined that first one. "They're very artistic. Did you set them up yourself or did you have a professional photographer do them?"

"A professional photographer who specializes in BDSM."

"Were the poses your ideas or his?"

"Mine." My chin rested on her shoulder as she sat on my lap. Kate turned a few more pages. "What do those make you *feel*?" I said once more, wanting her to open up.

She hesitated. "Jealous." She flipped the page. "Envy. Aroused."

I nodded. "What arouses you the most?"

She said nothing while she flipped through the photos, back and forth, and came to rest on one of Leah on her back, blindfolded, gagged, her hands bound, her feet bound. She wore nylons and a leather corset, her breasts spilling out over the top. I knelt between her knees, naked, splitting her labia with my cock.

She pointed to it. "This."

I leaned closer and examined it. "Interesting…"

"Why do you say that?"

"It's the most submissive," I said. "She's the most helpless. Unable to move at all, unable to see, or speak. Trusting me completely. Totally under my control."

Kate examined the photograph for a moment before flipping the page.

"What else do you like?" I said, squeezing her, slipping my hand beneath her sweater to cup a breast.

She stopped at one of Leah on her knees before me. I was dressed in black leather pants. One hand was on her head, her long hair caught up in my fist. She had my cock in her mouth, her lips taut around the head.

"This one."

"I like that one, too. Why do you like it?"

"It reminds me of your letter," Kate said thoughtfully. "She's on her knees, her hands tied behind her back. Blindfolded. You're controlling her, guiding her by pulling her hair."

She flipped to another one that featured me performing anal sex and seemed to linger over it.

"Do you like that one?" I said, my voice soft.

"I'm ambivalent about it," she said.

"Do you want to try these positions and acts?"

"The other ones, yes. This one?" she said, pointing to the anal. "Maybe some day. When I'm ready."

I closed the book and put it on the bed beside us. I turned her to face me so that she was straddling my hips, her hands resting on my shoulders. I wanted to remind her of that first night and how she wanted me to take the lead. How it excited her, despite being fearful. She fiddled with my tie, tightened and loosened it again, and tried to avoid looking me in the eyes.

"What?" I said, tipping up her chin so that she had to look in my eyes. "What are you thinking?"

She shook her head, shrugged one shoulder, and I knew she was embarrassed. Finally, she exhaled and leaned in close to me, her lips beside my ear.

"I want you to put your book away," she said, her voice barely above a whisper.

I pulled back, searching her face, until finally, our eyes met. Her cheeks were red.

"You don't need to be jealous," I said, amused. "I didn't love them."

"I know," she said. "But they mattered to you."

"I only want to be with you." I tucked a strand of hair behind her ear. How could she doubt how I felt for her? I couldn't stand to be apart from her. I wanted her every moment of the day. Everything else was a diversion.

"I don't want reminders of all the other submissives you've had," she said. "I don't want you looking at those photos."

I watched her, wondering what I could do to make her feel more secure. I reached down and touched her bottom lip. "Do you want us to make some photographs like those?"

"Yes."

"We will. Once we've explored more. I'm sorry that I've never done the whole scene with you. It seemed like I was always waiting for you at 8th Avenue instead of the other way around. And you always seemed to throw me off my game with your seductive ways..."

She smiled innocently. "What do you mean?"

"You have a way of disrupting my train of thought, Ms. Bennet. My plans all crumble when that happens. I *planned* on giving you exactly what you read about in my letters, but I failed."

"I know," she said, smiling. "I felt very cheated. Like false advertising..." She pouted. For a moment, I took her seriously but then I laughed when I realized she was teasing me.

"I better get it together."

She nodded, smiling at me. "I'd like that. Finally get what I paid for."

I grinned. "One of these nights, we could meet at 8th Avenue. You have a key. I'd want you to wait for me," I said, running a finger across the tops of her breasts, making her shiver. "Naked except for your stockings and garters and a blindfold. I want you kneeling on a pillow by the bed, your lips parted. I want you nice and wet for me, waiting."

"When?"

"*Shh*," I said, holding a finger to her lips. "That's for me to decide. I'll text you and let you know."

I pulled her into my arms and kissed her neck, my lips trailing down her throat to the swell of her breasts. I had to teach her to just submit, and stop asking when and what and how. It was hard for her – like she said, she'd been independent for quite a awhile, and as much as submission appealed to her, she fought it out of fear of what it meant about her. If I let her, she'd keep peppering me with questions and hoping for reassurances. I had to take control and not let her question my decisions and plans.

The best way to silence her was to take over and kiss her, arouse her, stop her talking. So I kissed her, my kiss soft, my fingers in her hair. Her mouth was so inviting, her lips soft and lush and parted willingly when I explored her with my tongue, finding hers, the touch of hers on mine making my cock jump.

I unbuttoned her sweater and ran my tongue along the top of one breast. She shivered, her skin all gooseflesh. I couldn't get enough of her breasts, and rolled down the fabric of one cup, squeezing it, my thumb and finger tweaking the nipple to a hard point. She inhaled when I covered it with my mouth and sucked, my tongue soft against the hard nub. She groaned, and that sound made me even harder.

I had enough of her clothed and so I pushed her down on the bed and began to undress her, impatient to have her naked beneath me, struggling with her buttons before pulling the sweater off over her head. I pulled down the other cup and sucked on her nipple, and she gasped when I drew my teeth over the hard nub.

I didn't want to hurt her. I wanted to titillate her with the idea that a tiny bit of pain followed by pleasure could heighten the experience. I unbuttoned her jeans and unzipped them, pulling them off her hips slowly. Underneath was a matching pair of cream lace bikini panties.

"What are you going to do?" she said.

"*Katherine*," I replied, frowning for effect. "No questions."

She grimaced. "Sorry. But when we started all this, Lara picked you because you love to teach. I was supposed to be a student..."

"School's out." I kissed her again, silencing her with my mouth, one hand squeezing a breast while the other cradled her head.

I ran my hands over her body, my fingers grazing her erect nipples, my palms sliding over her belly. I slipped one hand under her ass, pulling her up on the bed and I lay on top of her, grinding my erection hungrily against her groin. She whimpered, and thrust her hips up to meet me.

I kissed her again and traced a line from her throat to her shoulder and down to one breast, circling her nipple, before moving lower over her belly. I spread her thighs and slipped my fingers between her folds to the entrance to her body. She groaned and writhed under my touch and her responsiveness aroused me even more. I slid two fingers inside of her body and received a gasp in reward, her body trembling.

I left a trail of kisses and licks on her belly and lower until I was between her spread thighs, her body open to me completely. I kept her like that, enjoying the sight of her pussy spread out for me to see, keeping her open with a hand on each of her knees.

I left the bed and went to my closet and my bondage cupboard, which I had locked. I removed a key from a shelf and opened the lock. Inside the cabinet, I sorted through a selection of leather ties, straps, some thin nylon rope, several dildos and butt plugs and several long spreader bars.

I selected several leather cuffs, some longer straps, a small butt plug, a bottle of lubricant and returned, my hands behind my back.

"Lie with your head at the top of the bed. Close your eyes, Katherine."

She said nothing in reply, closing her eyes, biting her lip.

"Don't be nervous," I said firmly. "Nothing I do will hurt."

She nodded and took in a deep breath, moving further up on the bed, lying with her hands over her head close to the headboard and her eyes closed.

I climbed onto the bed and straddled her hips. First, I tied a soft cloth blindfold around her head, covering her eyes. I knew she'd be too curious to keep her eyes shut, especially when I used the butt plug, so I had to use the blindfold. It would heighten her anticipation, and focus her so that she paid attention to her body and what she was feeling instead of what things looked like. Next, I attached leather cuffs to each of her wrists before fastening them to the headboard. She pulled on them and was able to move an inch or two, no more.

I left the bed and went to the fridge, wanting to use some ice to introduce her to different sensations, the burn of ice something that would help her get over her fear of new experiences. I returned with a glass of ice and as I sat on the bed, I took an ice cube and pressed it against the skin of her neck. She gasped as I trailed the ice cube from the base of her throat below her collarbone, down between her breasts, circling each one, her skin all goose bumps. I held the ice against one nipple and then the other, each one tightening to hard points. The chill from the ice would be intense, almost bordering on pain. I held it on her nipple as long as I could and covered it with my mouth, my tongue circling it, stimulating it further.

She writhed beneath me as I repeated this on the other nipple, the alternating sensation of cold and warm would intensify her pleasure.

"Oh, *God*," she groaned. I squeezed her breasts together and pulled each nipple with my teeth, softly, just enough pressure to border on pain. When I sucked them, one after the other, she gasped and arched her back, pressing up against my mouth so I knew she was enjoying the sensations.

I left the remaining chip of ice between her breasts, where it sat and melted into a cold pool of water. I slid another ice cube down her ribs, over one hip and across her belly to the other hip, circling her navel in the process. She squirmed, biting her lip. I slipped the ice between her labia, pressing it against her clit, and was rewarded with a gasp, moving her hips in response.

"Be still," I said, my voice firm.

I kept the ice on her clit until she groaned out loud, and covered her with my mouth, my tongue swirling against the swollen bud. She moaned in response and ground her hips. I slipped the ice just inside her body, following it with my tongue. She clenched around me and so I knew she wanted more. I slid a finger and then two inside as I sucked and stroked her, and she was completely focused on what I was doing. Now was the time to try some anal play so I lubed up one finger on my other hand and press it against her, softly, barely detectable, but she tensed.

I pulled my mouth away. "Relax. I promise if you relax and trust me, you'll enjoy this. Do you trust me, Katherine?"

She nodded, but said nothing. When I pressed my finger inside a bit more, she gasped and clenched instinctively to keep me out.

"*Relax*, Katherine. Take in a deep breath."

She did, inhaling deeply and my finger slid inside a bit more.

"Good girl."

I continued to stimulate her with my mouth and fingers, my other finger slipping in a little further past her resistance and soon, she was trembling and I knew that despite the anal contact, she was ready.

"I think I..." she said, her voice hoarse.

I stopped licking her and slipped my finger inside her a bit deeper. I continued, waiting for her to come close once more. In this way, I prepared her and when she was coming down from the next peak, I slipped the lubricated plug inside her a bit, past her remaining resistance. I covered her once more with my mouth, knowing that the combination of sensations would be even greater, more arousing if she could get past the concept of being anally penetrated.

Soon, her thighs were shaking and she thrust her hips up against my mouth.

"Master, *I*..."

This time, I didn't stop and continued my motions, my mouth covering her pussy, my tongue stroking incessantly over her clit, my fingers inside her, stroking, and the combined pressure pushed her over. I let her come this time, wanting her to feel the pleasure of orgasm while the plug was inside of her and was rewarded by her body tensing, her flesh clenching around everything.

"Oh, *God*," she cried out. I didn't stop, wanting to keep her at the peak as long as possible, my mouth insistent, my fingers stroking.

Finally, I stopped as her orgasm began to wane. I could feel the convulsions against my fingers in the aftermath, and I enjoyed this proof of her pleasure. Finally, I pulled my fingers out and lifted my mouth from her flesh, but I left the plug inside.

"There," I said, as I rose up and loomed over top of her, my hands on either side of her. I kissed her deeply. "One more barrier down."

"Thank you," she said, "for breaking down one of my barriers."

"You were afraid."

"Yes."

"Does this show you that you can trust me to know what will give you more pleasure?"

She nodded. She had to learn to trust me, but that would only come by showing her that nothing I did would hurt her. Everything I did was designed to bring her pleasure. I had more experience than her and knew what a woman could enjoy if she was open to it.

She could let me take her where I wanted her to go, knowing it was all about getting the most pleasure for us both.

I covered her nipple with my mouth and sucked hard, wanting to keep her level of arousal high so she would come once more while I fucked her. I unfastened her cuffs and flipped her over onto her knees, the blindfold still in place. I leaned over her, one hand around her waist so I could play with her clit, while with the other, I cupped a breast, tweaking her nipple, squeezing it.

I wanted to build her up once more so she was ready for me. I slid the head of my cock against her labia, stimulating her with long slides of my shaft against her pussy, before pushing inside her just a bit. I kept up the stimulation on her clit while I slowly pushed inside further and further with each thrust. I wanted her to adjust to the plug and my thickness before thrusting with any real intensity.

Satisfied that she was more than ready, I began to fuck her, thrusting slowly in and out, keeping my fingers on her clit as I leaned over her back.

"Oh, *God*, I'm going to..." she said, unable to finish her sentence. I didn't stop thrusting, and soon, I felt her body tense beneath me as her orgasm started. She cried out, her small cries of pleasure spurring me on, so that I thrust harder and faster, and soon I came as well, my hands gripping her hips, pulling her tightly against my body with each deep thrust, the pleasure blinding as I ejaculated deep inside of her.

When the pleasure subsided, I leaned over her, collapsing against her, my mouth on her shoulder.

I was pleased that she responded so well to the anal training with the small plug. I knew that she could respond if she let herself and so it would be my goal to slowly show her exactly that.

CHAPTER 5

I PULLED OUT SLOWLY, relishing the sight of my semen drip-ping out of her well-used and pleasured pussy. It was a kink of mine, one that was tied up in some unconscious notion of impregnation, completely male, although I always took measures to ensure my subs were on the pill and could not get pregnant. Still, it was an interesting kink, considering how I was the loner type who was far too busy for emotional entanglements.

I removed the plug and helped Kate lie on her side before going to the bathroom for a washcloth so I could provide her with aftercare.

I washed the plug off and my hands, then returned to the bedroom and washed Kate with a warm washcloth, tending to her needs.

"I think I want to stay here tonight," I said when I was done, my arms around her, my face nestled in the crook of her neck while she sat on my lap. "You should call your father and let him know."

Kate nodded and slipped out of my arms, going to where she'd dropped her bag to retrieve her cell. I watched her from across the room while she dialed her father's number. After a few rings, he answered.

"Hi, Daddy," she said, her face transforming to a sweet little girl talking to her beloved father. "We're going to stay at Drake's place in Chelsea tonight."

There was a pause while Ethan responded and then she replied. "It's really nice. He's converted the dining room into a music room."

"Just a bit more packing but yes, we're almost ready."

"Good night, Daddy."

She ended the call and quickly checked her messages. I watched from the bed, wondering what kind of mail she received. She sat on the bed beside me and bit her lip as if concerned.

"What is it?" I said, reaching out to squeeze her arm.

"An email from Dawn."

I exhaled heavily. "What trouble is she trying to raise now?"

She shook her head and read silently.

"What is it?" I said, leaning closer, my chin on her shoulder as I looked over it to her cell.

She closed the email program and turned to me, her face a strange mixture of wonder and fear. I lay back on the bed, resting on my elbow, prepared for bad news.

She took in a deep breath. "Tell me about Sunita."

Fuck.

I inhaled deeply. "I knew it," I said, shaking my head. I lay back on the bed and ran my fingers through my hair. What the fuck could I say about Sunita?

"Tell me, Drake. Dawn said I should ask you what happened with her."

I frowned. "What did Dawn tell you about her?"

She shook her head. "She said I should ask you about her. That's all. Nothing else."

I closed my eyes. Of all the subs Kate should learn about, Sunita was the one I did not want to have to talk about. It wasn't that I was ashamed of our relationship. It was just that Sunita was a problem. A mistake.

"Sunita was one of my first subs. You have to understand," I said, rising up on my elbow. "Lara didn't believe I wasn't into pain. She thought I was being gallant, so she thought Sunita might help bring it out. Sunita was a bit of a painslut. Lara was trying to see if I was into pain."

Kate frowned.

"I *tried*, Kate," I said, needing to make her understand. "It did nothing for me so I didn't do it with any conviction. Sunita had a bit of a crush on me. She was upset when things didn't work out between us and tried to stir up trouble."

"What did she do?"

"She tried to force me to do what she wanted," I said. "Lara finally hooked Sunita up with a new Dom, but she's always made me know how she felt. I've seen her a few times at dungeon parties and she's tried to get back with me. I've always refused her politely."

"Then you intentionally hurt her."

"Only as part of my training," I said in protest. "Once I discovered my own hard limits, I never did S&M again. What is it with Dawn?" I said, leaning over to kiss her shoulder. "Why can't she understand?"

"She was traumatized as a young girl. It's her blind spot."

"You're very generous with her." I shook my head. "If she were my friend, I'd have ended it with her by now."

"She's only trying to help. She really believes I'm in danger from you."

I pulled her onto my lap, so that her arms threaded around my neck and her face was level with mine. I needed to look in her eyes to see if she could understand. "I hope you know you're not. I'd never purposely hurt you, Kate. I love you."

"I know," she said, avoiding my eyes.

"Look, if you doubt me, Lara can tell you."

"No, that's all right," she said, her voice sounding apologetic. "I don't need to call her. You've never done anything to make me question you. I've never been afraid of you."

I nodded. "We have to trust each other for this relationship to work."

"I know. But maybe before we leave, I'll meet with Dawn and have it out. Try to reason with her."

"Why?" I said, frustrated with her that she kept trying to be friends with someone who clearly was unhinged about us. "What do you owe her? She tried to break us up. She tried to harm me professionally."

"She did." She cupped my cheek with a hand. "But she's like family. I've been her friend forever. I owe her one last chance to make her understand. Or at least, accept."

I sighed and pulled her closer, my face in the crook of her neck. "You're too good."

"She's been there for me through so much of my own stuff. When my mother died. Flyboy. Problems with my father. Africa. I *can't* throw her over without one last try."

I nodded, pushing her hair away from her shoulder, which I bit softly then kissed.

"Sweet, forgiving Kate." I pulled her down on top of me, her head resting on my chest. "If you really want to see her, go ahead, but at some point, you'll have to decide if keeping her as a friend is worth the aggravation." I slipped out from under her and tucked her into the bed. I bent down to kiss her. "You go to sleep. I have to zip to the hospital and check on a case."

She nodded and watched as I dressed. I left her alone in the apartment and went to the hospital with extreme reluctance, but I'd put it off too long. I hated leaving Kate at that precise moment and knew that while I was gone, her mind would be going over the whole thing with Sunita. Without me there to comfort her, I was afraid she'd make too much of it.

I went to the hospital and checked on my patients, reading over their charts to see how they had been doing post-op and going in to see them personally. I spoke with the nurses who cared for them and was satisfied that everything was going as expected. The cases were complicated and required close observation for the first day after surgery, but so far there were no complications. On my drive back to the apartment, I thought about Sunita and was angry that Dawn had been snooping around looking for dirt on me so she could try to convince Kate that I was dangerous.

There was no convincing Sunita otherwise. I had hurt her, using a flogger, riding crop and finally a cane, but it was consensual and I didn't enjoy it. It didn't make me erect, and all it did was make me consider the damage done to the tissues in a non-erotic and solely medical way.

I finally stood up to Lara and said that I was definitely *not* a sadist, did not respond sexually to inflicting pain, and that I wanted to find a sub who was more appropriate to my own tastes. In other words, not into pain. I had nothing against those whose tastes ran to S&M but it wasn't for me. I tried it and I didn't like it.

End of story.

Except the story was coming back to haunt me, potentially destroying the one relationship I'd had for years that actually made me feel love.

I arrived home a few hours later and Kate was fast asleep, her hair a mess on the pillow, the covers tucked under her chin.

I crept in beside her and didn't wake her, falling asleep within moments, the comfort of her warm body next to mine a wonderful sleep aid.

In the morning, I woke up and slipped out of bed early, deciding to run a bath for us both. When I returned to the bedroom, naked, I saw that she was awake, and was lying on her back, rubbing her eyes.

"Would you like a nice bath? I feel like a soak."

She smiled and that was all the answer I needed.

She crept out of bed, still a little shy with me despite our relationship, and quickly brushed her teeth. I joined her at the sink and when we were finished, she slipped into the bath.

I took a moment to enjoy her as she did, her soft skin, softer curves, the angle of her cheeks all becoming so familiar to me. I felt as if I was imprinting her onto my memory as protection in case Dawn's attempt to separate us was successful. I'd do everything I could to stop that, but I had learned the hard way that there was no controlling someone who didn't want it. If Kate was going to listen to Dawn, it was because she preferred to hear her version of the story instead of mine.

Kate was the best thing that had happened to me since Maureen and I divorced. If I could keep her, make her mine, I would use every tool in my romantic and sexual toolbox to do so.

I stepped into the tub after she had submerged herself, noting a narrowing of her eyes, a contemplative expression on her face while she watched me.

"What's that look, Ms. Bennet? What's going on in that mind of yours?"

She smiled. "Drawing you naked. Or photographing you naked."

I made a face at that as I sat down, the water rising, threatening to overflow the rim.

"I don't want photos taken of me, but you could draw me, as long as you kept my face out of it..."

"If you want," she said. "I'd love to draw or photograph that delicious body of yours. I've never drawn a male nude before or photographed one. I might get so aroused doing it that I'd need you to..." she said and raised her shoulder, her cheeks pink.

"Need me to *what?*" I grinned and leaned forward, pulling her onto my lap in the water. "I'm always up for giving you a good fucking, Ms. Bennet, if that's what you need..."

I kissed her and ran my hands up and down her back. I pulled back and looked at her, tucking hair behind her ear. "I know you're always horny in the morning. How would you like to be fucked today? Tell me what that big heart of yours desires. I don't have much time, but I'm sure we could pull something off."

She shrugged a shoulder in her characteristic way. "I don't care, Drake. Whatever you think. Whatever you want. I know I'll enjoy it."

I nodded. "I'm considering."

I did consider. She was so delicious with her bright eyes and nicely pink skin from the heat of the water that I wanted to watch her pleasure herself. I wanted to watch her masturbate purely in a voyeuristic manner but I knew I'd be pushing it to ask her this now. Instead, she could use me as her Big.

"What I *want*," I said, my voice low. "What I want is for you to use me like an object. I'd like to watch you use Big some day, but using me to get off would do fine as well. To watch you do yourself using my body... I think *that's* what I want."

Her eyes widened at that and I knew it was a bit risqué

for her shy sensibilities, and I wasn't usually into passivity, but I wanted to remove every bit of shyness in her. I wanted her to be a lusty wanton woman, seeing my body as her playground.

I helped her up and poured clean tap water over her to rinse off the bubbles. She stepped out of the tub and started to dry off. While she did, I felt her eyes on me, and that look of lust and anticipation made me hard. Her eyes were glued to my groin, watching my body respond, my cock thickening, slowly starting to rise. She smiled to herself and that made me even harder.

I poured water over myself to rinse off then ran my hands through my wet hair, deliberately trying to entice her. I knew I had a good male physique, and worked out regularly so I had some definition in my abs and arms and thighs. Although not a body builder and so not cut, I was lean and my muscles were visible. She seemed to enjoy my little display of masculine nakedness. When I stepped out of the tub, she took a towel and started to dry me off, starting at my shoulders and working her way down. I stood still, smiling, my eyes on her, watching her face as she moved the towel over my body.

My cock twitched when she dried it, and she couldn't keep from smiling. I wanted to comment, but decided to let her take the lead in this, at least as much as I could given my nature.

She took my hand and led me through the door to the bedroom and the large four-poster bed, the sheets and coverlet rumpled.

"Here," I said, and sat with my hands behind me on the bed, my thighs spread, my rapidly hardening cock laying lazily to the side. "Lick me."

So much for giving over control.

Kate knelt down and moved between my thighs, licking

me, her tongue and lips sliding up and down my shaft to the head and back down again.

When her lips circled the head and took me fully inside her mouth, I groaned. She sucked and licked me until I was rigid, breathing fast, my heart racing. I stopped her, pulling her off me. I could have come if she kept it up, and didn't want it to end so quickly. I wanted to watch her fuck me until she came first.

"That's enough." I moved back onto the bed so that I leaned against the headboard with my arms spread out on either side. "Come here," I said. "Fuck me." I waited while she straddled my hips, tilting her head like she was wondering how to do this.

I sat up a bit more, helping position her. She moved closer and rubbed herself against my shaft, her labia sliding along my erection, up and down. She closed her eyes and I could see that she enjoyed the sensation. I leaned forward, trying to catch one of her nipples with my mouth, knowing that nipple stimulation would arouse her even more. She stopped her motions so that I could, letting me suck her nipples, one after the other. I grabbed one breast and squeezed it while I sucked her nipple, grazing it with my teeth. I leaned back and caught her eyes.

"Sit on me."

I held my cock so that it jutted out. She started to move again, and this time, she sat on the head, rising up high enough so that it penetrated her a bit, before sliding along the shaft once more. After a few moments of sitting deeper and deeper onto me, she finally took me in completely, sitting on me with her full weight so that I filled her up. She gasped, her eyes closing in pleasure.

"That's what I want to hear."

Her cheeks were pink, her eyes closed, her lips parted in

pure delight and that is what I wanted – for Kate to finally lose her inhibitions, to pleasure herself.

She moved slowly with my cock inside of her, resting her hands on my shoulders. She rode me this way for a few moments, every now and then withdrawing completely to rub herself against me before sitting on me again.

It didn't take long before she was ready and I had learned to listen and watch her body for the signs – her sexual flush on her chest and neck, her nipples hard, her breath fast.

"Open your eyes," I said, wanting our eyes locked when she came so that there was nothing between us. No shyness, no shame. Just pure bliss. She did, her eyes half-lidded, her mouth open.

"Oh, God, oh, *God…*"

"That's it," I said. "*Come* for me."

Her whole body tensed as she came, her eyes closing despite her best efforts to keep them open.

"*Look* at me," I commanded and she struggled to open her eyes. "That's so *good*, Katherine."

When she finished, she collapsed against me, her arms around my neck and her face pressed against my shoulder. I let her recover for only a moment. She sat up straight again and met my eyes.

"So?" she said, licking her lips. "Was that what you wanted to see?"

"*Exactly* what I wanted to see, Ms. Bennet. I believe I might make this a regular part of our lovemaking."

"*Lovemaking?*" she said, as if she were surprised I used that word. "That wasn't lovemaking. It was me fucking you until I came."

I leaned closer and kissed her. "Whatever you say."

She laid her head against my shoulder again, then she started to move on me, but I stopped her.

"My turn," I said and lifted her up. I turned us over, remaining inside of her.

She smiled. "We're really a very vanilla couple," she said while I positioned myself above her.

"We are." I agreed, a laugh escaping me. "We'd be booed out of the dungeon." I leaned down and kissed her shoulder softly. "Now, be quiet Ms. Bennet. You talk far too much, like your namesake." I silenced her with a kiss and that was the end of our playful banter.

I pulled her to the edge of the bed so that her feet rested on the side. I grabbed hold of her hips and began to thrust, watching as my cock slid inside of her and enjoying the sight of it. I reached up to squeeze a breast, then leaned down to suck a nipple, my hands running over her body, hungry to touch her now that I was the active one. I needed to feel her skin beneath my hands, to squeeze her delicious breasts, to suck her nipples, to hear her little gasp of pleasure when I did.

I took her feet in my hands and held them, spreading her thighs wide, all the time watching as I fucked her, my thrusts increasing in tempo until finally, my own orgasm started, the pleasure blinding in intensity as I ejaculated deep inside of her.

"Oh, fuck, oh, *fuck...*"

I thrust slow and deep, my eyes closed despite my own best attempts to keep them open and on hers.

When I was finished, I collapsed onto her and she wrapped her arms around my neck and pulled me closer.

I dressed quickly after we finished washing up and left the apartment with a promise to return later after several meetings I had at the hospital, wrapping up my work before we left.

Once I arrived in my office, I called Lara on my cell.

"Hey, Drake," she said, sounding a bit distracted. "What's up?"

"Complications," I said. "Kate's friend found Sunita and brought it up to her. I had to spend quite some time calming her fears that I'm a closet sadist."

She sighed. "I told her you weren't, multiple times, Drake."

"Tell her again, okay? I told her a bit about our time together during training but it might be a good idea to tell her in your own words."

"Okay, if you think so." There was a pause. "You really, really like this girl, don't you?"

"I really, really do."

"Okay then," she said. "But seriously, Drake. I'm going to have to put out a sexual therapy and couples therapy shingle and start charging. You two…"

I laughed at that. "You should. I'd owe you a fortune."

I hung up and smiled, glad a million times over that I met her. I sat staring at the phone, thinking about Sunita and the harm she could still do to me if she really wanted to. What Dawn could do to me.

I pulled on my lab coat, hung a stethoscope around my neck and made my way to the neurosurgery ward to check on my patients.

CHAPTER 6

DURING THE REST of the week, both Kate and I spent our time finishing off our own individual plans before leaving for Kenya. I had to wrap up my cases, handing off new patients to my colleagues who were taking over for me.

I practiced with Mersey on Wednesday as usual, and spent some time afterwards with Ken and the guys, drinking and talking about the time I'd be away.

"Bring this girl to Sunday dinner," Ken said and put his arm around me in a brotherly manner after we were done. "I know Mom is dying to meet the one girl who captured Drake's heart. Plus, I'm curious as hell, too."

I smiled. "Maybe someday. We're still pretty new, and I don't want to overwhelm her with family so soon."

"What?" Ken said and punched my shoulder playfully. I held up my fists and we sparred for a moment. He always thought of me like his little brother, in size and in age even though we were the same age. "You've spent time with her family, right?"

"That's different."

"No, it isn't. Bring her over before you go."

"I'll think about it," I said, conceding nothing. "If we're still together when we come back, for sure."

Ken sighed and I knew he was disappointed. "You gotta let people into your life, Drake. You can't keep everything perfectly segregated forever."

"I know," I said and nodded as I pulled my coat on. "I'm learning. I'm trying."

"Good. Will we see you at least for Sunday dinner?"

"Sure," I said. "I'd like to say a proper goodbye to your mom."

Ken waved as I left the pub and walked to my car, which was parked a half-block away. He was right. I did have to let people into my life. I was letting Kate into my life, bit by bit, but it was still difficult.

I was learning.

The next day after spending the afternoon at the Corporation, I arrived at Ethan's apartment to pick Kate up, waking her up from a nap. I had taken my coat off and was unbuttoning my jacket as I stood over her.

"Sorry to wake you. I tried to be quiet."

She sighed and stretched, watching me as I removed my jacket.

"That's OK. I'm a bit under the weather. I think it's the Malarone I had this morning."

I sat on the side of the couch and bent down and kissed her.

"Mmm, I love it when you're all warm and sleepy," I said, smiling. I ran my fingers down from her cheek to the swell of her breast. "I want to ravish you every time I see you after we've been apart."

She smiled back as I leaned down to nuzzle her neck.

"I feel the same way. Except I want you to do the ravishing."

"That's my little subbie." Then, my lips followed my fingers, traveling down to her chest. I unfastened the top button of her sweater and pulled down the fabric of her bra to expose one nipple. When I took it in my mouth, and laved the hard nub, she gasped.

"I think I want you in your bedroom."

"Drake, my *father*..."

"Shh," I said. "Your father's old enough to know not to enter your bedroom in the middle of the day when both of us are home and nowhere to be found. *Relax...* He's probably in the middle of one of his meetings and isn't likely to come in anytime soon. Where's Elaine?"

"She's out for the day. I have to talk to you about something."

"Later." I silenced her, kissing her forcefully. "Submit, *Katherine*."

I bared both her breasts, my mouth moving between her nipples. I knew Kate was anxious about her father coming in, but I wanted to see how far she would let me take control, even when it was something she didn't want to do.

She submitted but only just. Satisfied, I returned her bra to its proper position and helped her up, adjusting my erection in case we ran into Ethan on the way back to Kate's bedroom.

I led Kate out of the den and down the hallway to her bedroom. We passed Ethan's office but he was deep in conversation with his advisors and didn't notice us. I pushed Kate ahead of me into her bedroom and closed the door behind me. I pushed her up against the door, pressing my erection against her.

"I need you, *Katherine*. I've been imagining fucking you all day."

She sighed as I kissed her neck, restraining her hands above her head. I kissed her deeply, my tongue finding hers.

She smiled when I picked her up, carrying her over to the bed.

"What are you smiling at? You should be all weak-kneed by now, not amused..."

"You like to carry me," she said, threading her arms around my neck.

I grinned. "Imagine that I'm a conquering warlord, and you're my spoils of war. What would you do?"

"You want to role play?" she said, her expression innocent but with a hint of excitement.

"Why not? It would be fun."

"If you were a real conquering warlord, I'd have to resist you," she said, all breathless.

"I like what turns *you* on," I said, grinning. "A little resistance would only add to the excitement."

She blinked as I stood beside the bed with her in my arms, our eyes meeting.

"I'm not sure. I didn't like it when..." she said, and I knew where her mind went without her even having to tell me. Flyboy. The issue of mock rape.

"*Shh*," I said. "Do you trust me?"

She looked in my eyes. There was only a second or two hesitation. "Yes."

I kissed her, silencing her once more. When I pulled back, I held her eyes.

"Sometimes, it's the things that scare us the most that excite us the most as well," I said and sat on the side of the bed, with her lying across my lap. "Trust makes all the difference, Katherine. All you need to know is that you'll get fucked hard, fast and a bit roughly, with no preliminaries. I'll let you know which day it will be, but you'll have no idea when. I suspect that the anticipation will make you so wet, you'll probably come very quickly, although I won't do a thing to help."

"Dawn would freak if she thought—"

I held a finger to her lips. "*Shh*," I said, frowning. "Forget what Dawn thinks. She doesn't understand and probably never will so you shouldn't waste time trying to convince her. What do *you* think?" I paused for a moment, my gaze moving over her face. "Kate, does the prospect of me taking you by force, a bit roughly, without thought to your own desires or pleasure – does that excite you in any way?"

She took in a breath and held it, but I knew that deep down, this excited her.

"Yes."

I nodded. "I'm safe. You can try things with me that you could only fantasize about. If I do the things that scare you, you can experience them without being hurt or truly scared. Role-playing is fun, especially when I know it will push your buttons." I slid a hand between her legs. "And it's your sweet little tasty little buttons I want to push, and eat, and suck..."

She didn't respond to me the way I planned, her forehead furrowed. "I'm meeting with Dawn later to try to sort things with her."

I closed my eyes and exhaled. "*Kate...*" Frustration filled me that she was so intent on making amends with Dawn. "Why? You're wasting your time and hers, and probably messing things up between us." I snuggled more closely, my face inches from hers.

"Kate, you have to make a choice between your own happiness and pleasing others. Are you going to try things that excite and fulfill you or are you going to settle with less in order to please the people who don't really matter? Whatever you want, Kate, whatever you need, I want to give to you."

"I want *you*. I want you to do what you think I need, whatever that is. You've been right so far."

I kissed her, softly. "Thank you for admitting that. Don't

waste your life trying to live to please others. Do what makes *you* happy," I said and sighed. "Life's too short. People die."

She nodded in agreement, but I knew this was something she would have to learn through experience.

"Think of a scenario that arouses you. I'll do whatever it takes to make it happen the way you want, the way you fantasize."

"What do *you* fantasize about?" she asked, and I knew she was avoiding answering.

"Kate of a million questions." I shook my head and cupped her cheek, stroking her skin with a thumb. "I fantasize about you letting me fuck you any way I want, any time I want, anywhere I want and making you cry out my name in pleasure." I smiled and kissed her, my fingers threading through her hair. "Right now, I want you to stop with the questions and let me *fuck* you, *Katherine*..."

She bit her lip and closed her eyes. I knew that she still needed a blindfold to submit fully. I kissed her deeply and insistently, taking her clothes off, spreading her thighs and rubbing my cock all over her. It took barely two minutes of thrusting, my fingers on her clit, to bring on her first orgasm.

I smothered her cries of pleasure with a kiss.

CHAPTER 7

THE JAM SESSION with the guys went well, but it was a sad night for us because it would be the last one before Kate and I left for Kenya.

Even Mrs. O came out from her office and sat in the audience, listening as she worked on her receipts for the night. The small crowd of regulars even listened with a bit more attention than usual, because Ken announced that I'd be leaving in a short while and the band would be taking on a new member while I was in Kenya.

I felt a tinge of regret that I was leaving my life in Manhattan, and would miss Ken and the guys. I'd miss my music, although I could still practice as much as I felt like it in my time off. Of course, now I had Kate, and would have Kate full-time, so I knew my life was changing – for the better.

I would rather have fewer hours playing with the band if it meant I had Kate with me.

Later, when I got back to the Chelsea apartment, Kate lying on the couch in the living room with a blanket around her. I'd given her a key earlier in the week, but wasn't expecting her. She looked happy to see me.

I smiled at her when I came in, and after taking off my coat, I went right over and kissed her before I did anything else. I wanted her to know she was my main focus. When we were together, I pledged to myself that I would put her first, and ensure my other responsibilities took second place. I wasn't going to lose her the way I had Maureen.

"I'm beat," I said, flopping down on the couch beside her. "Can we just snuggle? I don't feel like doing anything."

She moved closer to me. "Fine with me."

"Oh," I said, remembering that she had been planning on meeting with Dawn. "What's up with Dawn? How did your meeting go?"

"Terrible," she said and frowned.

"What happened?" I ran my fingers over her cheek and waited. She took in a deep breath and exhaled, like she was steeling herself in order to talk about her meeting with Dawn. That woman frustrated and angered me. Most of all, I was upset that Kate was so determined to mend their relationship. However, it did show how loyal Kate was and that was not something to view lightly. My previous experience with women and loyalty was somewhat tainted.

"I tried to explain things to her, reason with her," Kate said, her voice sad, "but she wouldn't listen to me. So, I asked her to pretend we weren't together, but everything came back to you. I had to walk out on her and give up. She can't accept that we're together and that you're not a danger to me."

I shook my head. "I'm sorry. I know you two have been friends for a long time. Maybe when she sees that you're still the same person, only happier, she'll come around."

She sighed. "I hope so."

We spent the rest of the evening on the couch, watching

an old Bogart movie on television, and eating microwave popcorn.

I woke the next morning to snow falling outside the window. Kate snuggled closer beside me and as much as I would have loved to roll over and have sex with her, I couldn't. I had an early meeting, so I leaned up on my elbow to check the clock radio on the nightstand. I slipped quickly out of the covers and sat on the side of the bed.

"Good *morning*," Kate said. She crawled up behind me and kissed my shoulder and then my neck. "I love waking up with you beside me. What are your plans for the morning?" She slipped her hands around my waist and felt my morning erection. I groaned when she took me in her hand, but I didn't have time to properly fuck her so I moved her hand away.

"I have a meeting," I said. "I'm late. Didn't the damn clock radio go off?" I glanced at the settings on the clock radio beside the bed. "Crap. I have to run. My appointment's in half an hour."

Kate lay back down and said nothing but I knew she'd be disappointed.

I started the shower, intending to have a quick wash and get ready as fast as I could. Kate followed me and pulled back the shower curtain a crack to watch. I felt her eyes on me and knew she probably would have liked to come in but it would delay me. I lathered up and began washing, trying to do so as fast as I could.

"Can I join you?"

I felt bad but couldn't encourage her. "I'm in a hurry, so we can't do anything this morning."

"That's OK," she said, and stepped back to close the curtain. "I'll wait until you're done."

I took hold of the curtain and stopped her, catching her eyes with mine.

"I'd love to fuck you, but I'm really in a rush," I said and shook my head. "But later, I want to watch you make yourself come for me." There. That would arouse her and excite her. She'd be wet all day in anticipation.

"What?" She made a face.

"*Katherine*," I said and furrowed my brows in a sad attempt to look stern, fighting a grin the whole time. "I enjoyed watching you fuck me so much, I want to see you get yourself off. No objections. Masturbation was part of the agreement, in case you forgot."

She bit her lip. "I've never done it in front of anyone. I don't know if I can, you know," she said, raising a shoulder. "Relax enough."

That excited me. I'd be the first to watch her pleasure herself to orgasm. I'd be semi-hard all day in anticipation. It wasn't just the visual of her masturbating that aroused me. It was the thought that she'd let go of all her own inhibitions and be open enough to make herself come in front of me.

That required complete intimacy, and that's what I wanted. It's what I craved.

"I want to see you use Big, but for today, I'll let you use your own fingers," I said. I finished rinsing off and stepped out of the shower, grabbed a towel and dried off. Kate leaned against the doorjamb and watched while I brushed my hair. She was still naked, her arms crossed around her waist.

"You look entirely edible, Ms. Bennet," I said, my eyes roving over her body. "I don't know how I'll make it through the day, thinking of what I'll get when I return tonight."

"You're going to be gone all day?"

"Meetings and more meetings," I said. "But when I get back, I want you freshly showered and waiting for me, naked, on the bed, your legs spread. I want you already wet, thinking of me."

She smiled reluctantly. "If you really *want* to watch..."

"I *really* want to watch," I said, knowing that she'd be both aroused by it and shy. "I want you looking in my eyes as you make yourself come, thinking of me watching you."

"I'll feel like a wanton woman," she said, biting her lip as if she was trying not to grin.

"That's exactly how I want you to feel, because there's one inside of you if you'll let her out." I went to the bedroom closet and pulled out my clothes for the day – a dark suit, white shirt and dark tie. After I dressed and pulled on socks, I stood before her, trying my best to look stern and dominant. I wasn't used to moving between being a normal boyfriend and a Dominant. Doing so would take some finesse.

"I want you to perform for me on command. I want you totally focused on me, your eyes on mine. I'll be so hard, I'll have to fuck you immediately after."

"Oh, *God*," she said, closing her eyes. "How will I last until tonight?"

I stood in front of her and tilted her chin up, staring in her eyes. "You are *not* allowed to even touch yourself until I'm watching you, except to wash, do you understand?"

"I love it when you're all bossy," she said, smiling.

"Katherine, you need a spanking for that grin." I shook my head, unable to hold back a smile. "You can think of me," I said, stepping closer. "You can *imagine* what will happen, but don't touch yourself until I'm with you."

She nodded. "OK," she said. "I won't."

"Good girl." I bent down to kiss her. "I'll call you from the street and let the phone ring twice so you'll know to be ready and waiting for me. When I unlock the door, I want to find you on the bed, naked, your legs spread."

She smiled, a flush spreading on her cheeks.

"Do you have time to eat?" she asked and followed me to the entrance.

I grinned. "Ms. Bennet, you know I *love* to eat you, but I *told* you I have to run..."

She laughed. "I meant food."

I opened the closet. "No. I'll pick something up at the cafeteria after my appointment." After I pulled on my coat and boots, I bent down and kissed her once more. "You are *so* delicious looking, all naked and beautiful. I hate to leave you, but think of me while I'm gone. Imagine it."

Then, I left, pulling the door closed behind me.

CHAPTER 8

MY DAY WENT QUICKLY, despite the slate of business meetings I had at the Corporation, the Foundation and the hospital, wrapping up the small details that would allow me to hand over both my cases and business matters to others.

I didn't like giving up control, but I had to do it. There was no way I could keep things going at a distance, even with the conferencing software on the web. I'd have a teaching load, a surgical load – and Kate – to keep me busy in Nairobi. I had to give them all my total focus because Michael Owiti was relying on me to help him out at the college and hospital. Kate would be relying on me as a partner and lover.

I enjoyed being responsible and in control. In truth, I knew nothing else but being in control. I'd been responsible for myself for so long that I couldn't remember a time when I felt out of control – except when Maureen left and again when my father died. Luckily, both times I had someone to help me stand up straight and get back in control. Lara supported me when I got divorced and Ethan befriended me when my father died.

Being out of control was something I didn't want to experience again.

It was late in the afternoon when I was able to stop for a moment and take a breath before heading to the hospital for a quick check on my patients recovering on the main neuro-surgery ward. I sat in my office and read over my files, my mind wandering to Kate and what she'd be doing at that moment. I expected she'd be waiting in anticipation of our scene, excited and slightly dreading the prospect of mastur-bating in front of me. I had to insist that she do so, for I wanted there to be no boundaries between us – no sexual boundaries. I wanted to be as deep into her libido as I could get, to understand every little kink and explore every nook and cranny of her desire. Watching her touch herself, make herself aroused, would give me incredible knowledge of her sexually, in addition to making me hard as a rock.

As I sat there imagining it, my cock thickened, a pleasant ache in my groin in anticipation of seeing her naked on the bed, her thighs spread wide, her pussy open and on display for me.

Making her masturbate to completion in front of me was just one more step in possessing her completely.

As per my instructions to her when I left that morning, I rang the apartment when I was on my way from the parking garage where I kept my car. I let the phone ring twice and hung up to signal her to be ready and in position. My own body responded to the thought of her lying on the bed naked, waiting for me and how delicious it would be to watch her make herself come. Doing so would break down one more wall between us. Soon, there'd be nothing left.

I ran up the stairs, eager to get inside, and slipped the key into the lock, knowing she'd be listening for the sound of me opening the door. I entered the apartment and removed my coat and boots, then I went immediately to the bedroom to check and see if she was as I had specified. I put on my best stern taskmaster expression and stood in the doorway.

She was there on the bed as I had directed, naked, her legs spread.

"Good *girl*," I said as I strode to the side of the bed, pulling off my suit jacket, and loosening my tie. I removed it and threw it on the chair against the wall and unbuttoned the cuffs of my shirt. "Let me see how wet you are, Katherine." I bent down, resting a hand on the bed between her thighs, my face close to her pussy. I examined her, making a big show of it, unable to keep from smiling as I thought of how aroused she'd be. I frowned up at her, trying hard to keep in stern taskmaster mode.

"Did you touch yourself?"

She shook her head, her voice barely above a whisper. "Only in the shower and to wash myself."

I nodded, but didn't let up the guise of Dominant inspecting his sub. "Good. I want to watch the first time you do touch yourself for pleasure."

She moved her hand down but I shook my head. "Not yet. I want to look at you like that, all open and waiting."

She quickly pulled back her hand and let it fall beside her head on the pillow. I removed the rest of my clothes and stood naked by the bed, my already stiff erection jutting out, the head shiny with fluid.

"Touch yourself. Watch me the entire time. Imagine it's my tongue touching you."

She slowly touched herself while I watched her intently, my eyes riveted to her pussy, watching every move. I dragged my eyes away to check if she was watching me as I commanded.

"Yes," I said. "Exactly like that. Tell me what you'd be thinking if you were masturbating alone."

She didn't say anything, frowning a bit.

"Tell me what you'd do if I wasn't here and I told you to masturbate and make yourself come."

She took in a deep breath. "I'd think of your body," she said. "How nice and thick you are. How good you feel inside of me. How good your mouth feels on me, your tongue like velvet."

"Yes?" I said, urging her on, curious about how her mind worked when she pleasured herself.

I grasped my erection and began to slowly stroke my hand over its length while I watched her fingers on her clit. She pressed lightly on it, circling slowly at first. I glanced back up at her face and noted that she was busy staring at my cock and not my face as I demanded. She bit her lip when she realized I caught her.

"Keep your eyes on my face, *Katherine*," I said.

"Sorry, Master," she said, contrite.

I knew she wanted to watch me masturbate as badly as I wanted to watch her, but I had to insist she keep her eyes on my face. I wanted that intimacy that watching my face would bring when I chose to look in her eyes. The gaze was such a powerful force to break down boundaries. Still, I enjoyed her curiosity and was aroused in turn by her eyes on my cock as I stroked my shaft and palmed the head, squeezing it to remove some more fluid to act as lubricant.

When I caught her eye, she was unable to suppress a guilty smile.

"Katherine," I said, trying my best to stay in role. "I want you focused on my face, my eyes. I want you to know I'm watching you. I'm seeing inside of you."

She held my gaze for a few seconds, but I was drawn back

to her fingers on her clit, and how she stroked them over herself, faster.

"Slip two fingers inside of your pussy while you stroke your clit," I said, wanting to see her penetrate herself.

She complied, wetting first one then two fingers, slipping them slowly inside a couple of inches.

"Good girl," I said and the sight of her made my cock even harder. I caught her eye and nodded appreciatively. "Move your hips while you fuck yourself with your fingers. The way you do when I do it."

She obeyed, thrusting her hips softly. Still, she couldn't keep her eyes on mine and glanced down once more to watch me pump my fist over my cock more rapidly, while I cupped my balls with the other hand.

She looked like she was getting close, the telltale flush spreading up her chest to her neck. "Tell me when you're going to come, Katherine. You know the rules."

She was barely able to speak. "I'm so close…"

"Fuck yourself with your fingers," I said, my voice shaky, so close myself. "Think of my cock inside of you, filling you up. Think of my tongue on you, stroking your clit. Think of me sucking your nipples."

She closed her eyes as she began to lose control.

"Open your eyes, Katherine," I said. "Look in mine."

I moved closer, kneeling on the bed, bending over to watch her fingers on her clit, the others moving more rapidly inside of her.

"I think I…" she gasped and I knew she'd come right away.

"*Come* for me, baby," I said, my voice shaky, right on the edge of my own orgasm. "Open your eyes. Look in mine."

She did, forcing them open. "Oh, *God*." she gasped, her body tensing. "*Ohhh*."

I climbed further onto the bed between her knees and

leaned over her, stroking fast, and aimed my cock at her pussy.

"Take your fingers out. Spread yourself for me."

She complied, spreading her lips. Then, my orgasm started and I tensed, as my fist pumped over my cock. Finally, I ejaculated, my semen spurting out onto her labia and belly. To my delight, she spread it over herself, rubbing it into her pussy, using it as lubricant, her fingers slipping over her clit.

I collapsed over her, lying directly on top of her, my face beside hers, panting.

"Fuck, that was *good...*"

She wrapped her arms around me while I groaned into her neck. "You know how many times I jacked off thinking of you doing that? Before we got together, I was so desperate to fuck you. Just fuck you plain old vanilla."

"You didn't imagine us in scene?" she said, her voice sounding surprised. "Me all tied up and blindfolded?"

I shook my head and kissed her chin, her cheek and her forehead as I rested on my arms, my face above hers. I nestled my body between her thighs, which she wrapped around my hips.

"I wanted you any way I could get you. Vanilla, D/s, kink. *Anything.* I was like a teenager wanking while dreaming of his favorite girl," I said, surprised at how honest I was being. "I knew you'd been alone for a year after Flyboy and I used to imagine you masturbating. Then, when I knew you wanted to experience D/s, I figured I'd better give you what you wanted. But damn, it was hard not to fuck you plain old vanilla."

"Drake *Morgan*, what kind of Dom are you?" she said playfully. "I heard all these rumors about Dr. Dangerous. Master D. Were they all just clever marketing?"

I laughed out loud at that. Yes, it did help to have bad boy rumors about me floating around. "*Very* clever." I kissed her, long and tender, my fingers threading through her hair. I felt almost overwhelmed with emotion as we lay together, our bodies entwined, and had to pull away, kissing her face, her chin, her throat.

"I couldn't stand the thought that someone else would introduce you to D/s. That someone else would be the one to bring out your submissive side and enjoy you. It *had* to be me," I said, remembering how I felt when I saw her at the café with Lara and realized my sub was Katherine. "Once I knew you were interested, I hatched my Machiavellian plan to overwhelm you with pleasure."

"You have." She ran her fingers through my hair, pushing it out of my eyes. "I'm glad it was you."

I kissed her again, unable to get enough of her, wanting to devour her. She pulled me more tightly against her body.

"Dawn tried to warn me off you but she couldn't have known that it would draw me to you instead," she said, her voice confessional. "When I saw you at the bar and she said you were another bad boy like Kurt, controlling, trouble, I wanted you. I wanted someone like you. When you turned out to be the Dom who would teach me, you were what I was looking for. I was already gone. I had no chance."

"Both of us were goners," I said and smiled. "I'm not letting go of you, Ms. Bennet. I hope you realize that."

She slipped her arms more tightly around my neck and kissed me deeply, and I felt at that moment as if all the pain I'd gone through in my life had been washed away by her love.

CHAPTER 9

THE NEXT MORNING, I woke up to Kate snuggling closer beside me. Unlike the previous morning, I had no meetings planned and so I hopped out of bed, went right to the bathroom for a shower.

After I turned on the faucets, I peeked my head around the door and caught Kate's eye.

"Join me?"

She smiled and got up, only too happy to do so.

We showered together and if Kate wanted to have sex, she didn't do anything to initiate it. I watched while she washed herself, and took hold of her hips when she bent down to wash her feet.

"Ms. Bennet you look entirely edible this morning. You're giving me ideas..." I pulled her up and against me, my hands sliding up her body, cupping her breasts, tweaking her nipples.

"You're hungry."

"I'm always hungry for you," I murmured against her neck. I turned her around and kissed her deeply as I lifted her off the floor. I slipped my hand between her thighs.

"Mmm," I said as I kissed her neck, running my lips over her skin. "I'm getting so many ideas..."

I quickly dried her off, but didn't want to waste any time, pushing her back into the bedroom and onto the bed. I devoured her with my mouth and hands and eyes as she lay beneath me.

"Spread your legs wide," I said, pulling her thighs apart. "We're going to do each other at the same time. I want you to come with my cock in your mouth, my mouth on you."

We lay in sixty-nine position, pleasuring each other. When Kate moaned around my cock, I groaned in response, trying to keep my focus on pleasuring her. She writhed under my mouth; I writhed under hers.

When her orgasm neared, I felt her tense. She knew she needed permission but I didn't make her ask.

"*Come* for me, baby," I said, my fingers thrusting inside of her body.

Her body convulsed around my fingers and under my tongue, her breath coming in short gasps. I kept my mouth on her throughout her orgasm and while she recovered. I licked her still-swollen clit softly, making her shudder.

I said nothing, waiting for her to start stimulating me and soon, she was once again stroking my shaft and sucking the head of my cock as if eager to feel and hear my release. I kept licking her, hoping to make her come again. She tried to focus on my cock, stroking it, sucking the head, taking me as deeply into her mouth but I was also unrelenting.

"Stop," she gasped when I slipped my fingers inside her again. "I can't focus when you do that."

"I want you to come again," I said, greedy for more.

"I can't do both."

"Let yourself come," I said. "Then I will. I'm so close..."

After a few moments while I built her up once more, her second orgasm started as I sucked and stroked her clit, my fingers thrusting inside of her. She groaned with the head of my cock in her mouth and I began thrusting into her fist, trying to come as well. Soon, I felt that sweet sensation starting in my balls, the pleasure blinding me, my cock so hard as I ejaculated into her mouth. I continued to thrust into her, my whole body shuddering, my mouth on her sweet clit, my fingers deep inside of her.

Finally, she pulled slowly off and swallowed, licked my length, her tongue playing gently with the sensitive head. I had to groan and pull away from the sensation, which almost overwhelmed me.

"Oh, *God*," I said, gasping. "That was so *good...*"

I crawled around and lay facing her, pulling her into my arms, one thigh thrown over her possessively. I kissed her deeply.

"I love you, Kate," I said when I pulled away, brushing the hair from her face. "I *love* you."

"I love *you*," she said, and crawled more closely into my arms.

This was bliss.

After we both recovered, we lay in each other's arms. I stroked my hands over her body affectionately, cupping her breasts, threading my fingers through hers, unable to get enough of her.

"That was delicious. I think I'd like to do that at least once a week."

"It wasn't too vanilla for you?" she asked, smiling at me coyly.

"In case you didn't realize, I like vanilla ice cream, too," I said and smiled. "Besides, my kink is control, with a bit of leather thrown in for good measure."

"You can't let me come only once, can you?"

"Sacrilege!" I said and laughed. "My evil plot is to keep you so thoroughly aroused and then satiated that you can't imagine looking at another man."

She wrapped her arms around me. "Other men don't even exist."

Although I would have loved to stay with her and laze away the day, I did have a meeting scheduled in about an hour and some reading to do beforehand so I rose up on my elbow and ran a finger down her body from her chest to her hip. "As much as I'd love to lie here all morning, I have work to do."

"You're leaving?"

"Foundation work to wrap up." I leaned down and kissed her. "I'll be home later this afternoon. I'm going to play one last game of racquetball after lunch with a colleague. We'll have a nice dinner and spend the evening together."

"Sounds good."

"I love you," I said and kissed her again, hating to leave her but having no choice.

"I love you," she replied.

My morning went quickly, and after reading over some briefing material before hand, I met with the board overseeing the Foundation and discussed plans for the coming year while I was gone. Lunch was brought in as usual and after signing some papers, I left for my club and a game of racquetball with a colleague from NYP.

Finally done all my duties, I went back to the Chelsea apartment and found it empty. There was no message from Kate so I texted her.

Where are you? I'm home and you're not here.

She texted right back.

I needed some air so I went for a walk and stopped in at 8ᵗʰ Avenue. I'm going to take a taxi home.

I could just as easily pick her up so I texted back.

Let me come by and pick you up. I'll be there in ten.

OK. See you outside.

I didn't like the thought of her waiting outside on the street so I responded.

Wait inside and I'll text you when I drive up.

I'm a big girl, Drake. I can take care of myself...

That made me smile. I knew she was a big girl, but I loved being able to care for her. It was my thing.

Let me take care of you, Kate. It makes me feel all Dominant...

I could almost see her smile.

Yes, Sir.

Once I arrived outside the apartment, I texted her once more.

Ms. Bennet, your chauffeur awaits...

She responded immediately.

Ha ha! Should I start calling you Mr. Darcy? Or was it Heathcliff?

There are a few voice messages on your phone and while I was here, a woman called and said you should call her before you leave. Should you come up and listen to your messages?

I sat in silence, not responding for a moment, trying to figure out who it could have been. I didn't give out my number to any of my subs. It had to be Maureen... That wasn't a pleasant surprise.

Hmm. Maybe I should pop up and check. Let me park and I'll be right up.

I parked the car in a no-parking zone, figuring it would only take a moment to hear the message. I ran up the stairs to the apartment and entered, smiling when I saw Kate standing by the window.

I went to her and wrapped my arms around her, pulling her into an embrace and kissing her. I wanted her to know she was the first thing I thought of. Then, I turned to the answering machine and looked at it with reluctance.

"If you want, I can wait downstairs in the entry while you listen," Kate said softly.

I shook my head and hit the play button to listen to the messages. After a few messages from people wishing me a successful trip, I heard Maureen's voice asking me to call her as soon as possible before I left for Africa.

"Maureen," I said after a moment. I sighed and ran my fingers through my hair in exasperation. I did not want to talk to her and couldn't imagine why she was contacting me after almost five years of radio silence. "I should call her, see what she wants to talk about."

"I can leave if you need privacy..."

I shook my head. "No, you don't have to leave."

I dialed her number and as I waited, I stroked my fingers over Kate's cheek, smiling to calm her fears – and mine.

Finally, Maureen came on the line.

"Hey," I said. "It's me. What's up?"

Maureen sounded distracted, upset.

"Drake, I don't know how to tell you this, but I have a son. *We* have a son. I thought he was Chris's as you can imagine. I wanted him to be Chris's but when we had him tested, he wasn't a match. He's yours. I need to talk to you in person as soon as possible."

I felt adrenaline surge though me, making my heart pound. I turned to stare out the window, listening to Maureen as she told me about the boy. Five years old. Born eight months after we split and she moved to California with Chris. I felt a bit weak and so I sat on the edge of the couch, holding my head in my hand.

"Why didn't you *tell* me?"

"I didn't know until just a few days ago. There was no reason to think he was yours. I'd been seeing Chris for weeks before we split and we'd only had sex once or twice... I thought I was safe. None of that matters, Drake. I need to see you."

"Why?"

"I can't tell you but you have to come and meet me. That's all I can say."

She hung up and I threw my cell across the room at the wall.

"Let's go," I said and turned to the door, not meeting Kate's eyes. I was too angry and shocked to know what to say to her.

Kate followed me out of the apartment and down the stairs. I couldn't think. I knew Maureen had a son, but I thought it was Chris's. We'd had sex only a few times in the final month before she left. It meant she had been fucking Chris while she was still with me.

I could barely believe Maureen never bothered to check to see if he was mine or Chris's, giving that she was fucking us both.

"*Drake*," Kate said when we arrived in the lobby. "Tell me what's wrong." I stopped in the entry, but said nothing, my mind still in a whirl over what I'd just leaned.

"Tell me!"

I shook my head, opening the door for her. I was so upset that when I got to the car, I dropped my keys before disengaging the locks.

"*Fuck*," I growled as I bent down to pick them out of the snow, wiping them off on my coat.

Kate got in the passenger side and I closed her door, then came around to the driver's side and got in. I sat for a moment, and stared at the console.

"Drake, you're scaring me." Kate reached out and took my hand and squeezed. "Tell me what's wrong."

Finally, I turned to her and exhaled heavily.

"I have a son."

CHAPTER 10

I DROVE THROUGH THE STREETS, struggling to focus on the road and not on Maureen and her news. We were traveling towards Ethan's apartment on Park Avenue.

"Oh, *Drake*," Kate said, her voice a whisper. "Maureen was pregnant when you broke up?"

I nodded, unable to speak.

"Does she want you to meet him?"

"She didn't say anything more than he was mine and we needed to talk."

Kate was silent for a moment. "I'm so sorry. You can drop me off at my father's."

I sighed as we came to a stoplight. "I don't know what she wants, but why else would she come back to Manhattan? You're my life, Kate." I was silent as I considered what to do. I had no idea what Maureen would want, but Kate was the most important thing in my life and I wanted her to come when I met with Maureen. "I want you with me all the time. If you're willing, I'd like you to come with me. She has to know you and I are together."

"Do you think she wants you back?"

I shrugged. "I have no *idea* what she wants. She married this guy Chris who she met before we broke up. She said she'd tell me when we met."

"Where?"

"The hospital in Washington Heights. A coffee shop we used to go to. It's familiar ground, I guess."

We drove towards NYP and I found a parking space close to the café where I was to meet Maureen. Kate and I walked hand in hand into the lobby of the building. I saw Maureen right away – her blonde hair and height distinguishing her from everyone else. She was silhouetted against the window, watching for me.

We walked up to her and she frowned when she saw Kate, looking her up and down, her grey eyes judging. "Is this your current *slave*?"

"This is Kate McDermott. Kate, this is Maureen Johnston, my ex-wife."

Kate nodded politely at Maureen. I couldn't believe Maureen was so rude as to suggest that Kate was my *slave* and that I would bring a mere submissive to a meeting with her but there was no way Maureen would ever understand the lifestyle.

"I need you to come with me," Maureen said, her voice clipped.

"Where?"

"To Morgan Stanley. The oncology ward."

"Your son—"

"*Our* son," she corrected. "He's got leukemia. He needs a bone marrow transplant and so I thought you'd agree to be tested. You could be a match."

Another wash of adrenaline went through me and for a moment, my sense of hearing dulled. Her son – *my* son had leukemia? I thought of the brother I never knew – the brother who died before I was born.

I'd passed the genetic curse along to my son. "Yes. Of *course*."

"Can we go somewhere and talk?" she said and sighed. "I suppose this has come as a shock."

I bit back a nasty reply, determined I'd remain in complete control. Maureen, and most of all Kate, didn't need to see me lose it. Maureen led us down the long hallway to a small coffee shop where we purchased some coffee. We went to an empty table surrounded by other visitors and patients.

"So, tell me," I said, my hands around my cup. "How is it I have a son and I never heard about him?"

Maureen took off her scarf, removed her coat. She sat down and stirred her coffee, taking her sweet time about it as if she wanted to gain the upper hand and ward off any kind of attack on my part. Finally, after taking a sip, she spoke, her voice low.

"I didn't think he was yours. I thought he was Chris's. It wasn't until we tested Chris as a donor that we found out he wasn't related. It was then I knew." She glanced up at me, her face red. "I must have miscalculated my dates. I probably didn't want to think he was yours."

I knew that Maureen was unhappy when we split up, but I had no idea that she had already started a relationship with someone else. When she left me, I thought it was truly because we failed, not because she had someone else waiting. She'd mentioned someone named Chris in passing before she left me, but I thought it was just a colleague. I'd been jealous at the mention of his name but too busy and self-absorbed to push her to find out more.

"So you *were* sleeping with Chris before we split..."

"Drake, I could have been sleeping with an entire college football team for all you'd have known. You were so busy in Africa and with lectures and surgery and your band to even notice that I was having an affair."

"And how do you know he's my son? I should be tested—"

"*Drake*," she said, her voice sounding frustrated. "It was either you or Chris. I wasn't seeing anyone else. Yes, you should be tested, but given it's the same leukemia as your brother, I assumed he's yours."

"Of *course*..." I stammered. "They'll find out when they test me for compatibility." I said nothing for a moment, reining myself in once more, holding my cup between my palms. I didn't meet Maureen's eyes, focusing instead on the table and my cup. "So you were fucking us both, obviously."

"I didn't mean to. You were pretty insistent when you were around. I tried to talk to you but you were always shushing me, trying to get me into bed. I finally gave up."

Kate stood up at that, obviously embarrassed to be listening to our private conversation. I grabbed her hand.

"Stay," I said. She sat back down, her cheeks red. I sighed heavily, feeling bad that she had to hear my dirty laundry, hoping that it didn't sour her on me – on us. "Tell me about my son."

"Liam," Maureen said. I glanced up at that. Maureen gave a half-smile, somewhat guilty-looking. "I always liked your father and that name, so I called him that when I found out he was a boy."

"Jesus *Christ*," I said, rubbing my eyes. "You never suspected that he was my son?"

"You and Chris look quite a lot alike. Dark hair, fair skin. He has hazel eyes, and yours are blue, but still. Liam could have been either of yours. I *assumed*," she said, her voice low. "I *wanted* to believe he was Chris's son. It wasn't until we needed a donor that I found out the truth."

"How long ago was this?"

"He's had leukemia for a year, but it wasn't until he didn't respond to chemo and had a relapse that we decided on stem cell transplantation. We tested everyone in the family and that's when we discovered Chris wasn't his father. As soon as I found out, I made an appointment with Krishnamurtha here at NYP Children's. I decided to come here, where I knew some of the nurses. NYP has one of the best pediatric oncology centers in the world. And of course, there's you. You're the same blood type. I thought you might be an HLA match."

"What's his diagnosis?"

"AML. M5. He has a rare 10:11 mutation and needs aggressive treatment. I should have known he was yours when I heard it, but I wasn't thinking about you."

"*Christ*," I said, rubbing my forehead. "How's he doing?"

"He's holding his own, but he needs a transplant. If you're a match, he'll be prepped for consolidation therapy. High dose chemo and radiation, followed by bone marrow or stem cell transplant. We looked for a donor but came up empty. If you're a match, will you agree to donate your marrow?"

I didn't hesitate. "Of course. *Anything.*"

"I know you're going to Africa, but I need you to do this."

"The semester doesn't start until March so I have some time. I was going to help with their surgical slate for a while, help with backlogged cases, but that can wait."

Maureen covered her face with her hands and cried in front of us, her sobs silent, her shoulders shaking.

Despite my anger and shock, I had loved her once and she was the mother of my son, so I reached out and squeezed her shoulder. Maureen seemed to snap out of it and reached into her bag. She fished through its contents and removed a tissue, wiping her eyes as she struggled to gain control over herself.

"Thank you," she whispered.

I shrugged. "How could I say no? He's my son."

"I knew you didn't want kids, Drake. That's why I never tried to find out if he was yours or Chris's. I knew you probably wouldn't want him anyway, but Chris *did* want him. He *wanted* a family."

I nodded. "I never wanted to have kids because of the chance of passing on the gene. I never imagined being a father."

"You are, but Chris is his *real* father, Drake. A father isn't just a sperm donor. A father is the man who reads you stories at night, who plays soccer with you in the summer and who takes you fishing. A father is the one who sits by your bed when you're sick."

I shook my head, filled with a sense of bitterness. "I guess I never had a father, then."

She glared at me, an exasperated expression on her face. "Look, Drake. If you do this, I don't want you trying to become involved in Liam's life. Leave things as they are," she said, her voice edged with warning. "It was hard enough telling Chris that Liam wasn't his. Liam doesn't have to know. It would break his heart to find out that Chris wasn't his biological father. Maybe some day when he's grown and able to handle it, but now? I don't want him to know."

I didn't say anything, biting back a nasty response about her morals but who was I to condemn her for being unhappy with me? I had been a self-absorbed bastard.

"Will you come up and see him now?" she said. "He's probably asleep, but you could look in on him." She turned to Kate. "You won't be able to go into the room. Only family is allowed inside."

Kate shook her head. "That's fine. I wouldn't presume to intrude on your private family business."

"Kate can come along if she wants, and wait outside his room." I turned to her and took her hand, squeezing it. I needed her with me for she was the light in my life, and I would need a lot of light now.

Kate nodded. Maureen didn't argue.

Maureen led the way to the elevator and down the hallways to the children's ward. I asked Maureen about Liam's diagnosis and treatment and she ran down the sessions of chemo he'd already gone through and how he responded initially, but went out of remission. When they exhausted all the meds open to them, Liam's oncologists decided on stem cell transplantation. I realized that Kate wasn't up on all the terminology so I turned to her.

"He has acute myelogenous leukemia. It's a cancer of the white blood cell at a certain stage of development. He has a rare mutation that makes it very aggressive and so they have to treat it equally aggressively."

"Like your brother's?" she asked.

I nodded. "Liam was diagnosed when he was four and died when he was five." We pushed through double doors and into the pediatric oncology ward. "I never knew Liam," I said, thinking of my mother's tiny shrine to him. "I was supposed to be the consolation baby, but apparently, I wasn't enough."

Kate took my hand and squeezed. I turned to her, and saw that her eyes were brimming. When I saw that, my heart warmed.

"Sweet sweet *Kate*," I whispered, leaning down to kiss her cheek.

We arrived at the pediatric oncology ward, walking past the playroom with brightly painted floors and walls in blues and yellows. I hadn't spent a lot of time on the ward, for I dealt with neurosurgery patients, but every now and then I had a pediatric patient with a brain tumor and so I had been there before to visit.

Kate sat in a small waiting room while Maureen and I spoke to the nurses at the nursing station.

"He's been stable, sleeping most of the time."

The nurses at the station didn't know the whole story and assumed I was just a consulting physician.

"Dr. Morgan is a friend and is going to check in on Liam."

The nurse nodded and we went back to Liam's isolation room. We entered the anteroom and suited up in gowns and masks. When we entered Liam's room, I got my first look at him. He lay on the bed, his tiny head bald from chemo, his face pale, his lips pallid. On oxygen, the nasal cannula circled his face, and an I.V. threaded into his arm.

I stood beside the bed and watched Liam as he slept, my emotions almost overwhelming me. I didn't know how to feel – incredibly shocked that I had a son, incredibly saddened that he was so sick and frail. A deep protective sense filled me, and I knew at that moment that I would do anything and everything in my power to save his life.

I reached out and took his tiny hand in mine, stroking my thumb over his skin, which was thin and pale. I had to bite back tears, and inhaled deeply in an attempt to gain control over my emotions. I glanced up at Maureen, whose own eyes were wet. Liam stirred briefly, and so I gently placed his hand back down on the covers.

"Let's go," I said, too close to tears to stay any longer.

We left the room and removed our gowns and masks before returning to the waiting room. I was surprised to see Chris there with Kate. She wasn't looking at him and her face was pale so I wondered if he'd said something to her.

Maureen turned to them. "I see you two have met," she said, her voice clipped.

"We did." Chris leaned over and kissed Maureen on the cheek.

I took Kate's hand and pulled her into my arms, needing at that moment to feel her warmth and her sympathy and love. I pressed my face into her neck and squeezed her. She ran her hands up my back, rubbing my shoulders to comfort me. I fought to regain control over myself.

"I'm so sorry," Kate whispered, and that made me even more emotional. I breathed in deeply, swallowing back my emotions. I pulled back and kissed her briefly.

"Thank you for being here." I ended the embrace and slid my hand down her arm, clasping her hand in mine, our fingers entwining. I wiped my eyes briefly and turned to Maureen.

"Call me when the arrangements are made," I said to her. "I'll come whenever his doctors need me."

Maureen nodded and I was so glad to leave the two of them, not wanting to break down in front of anyone. We went to the elevator and I pushed the button, waiting in silence because I was afraid my voice would falter if I spoke.

Once the elevator doors closed, I leaned against the wall and pulled Kate into my arms for the short ride down to the lobby.

"Christ, what a day..." I said and ran my hand over her hair as she leaned against me. "I'm so glad you were here with me. I don't know what I'd do if I were alone through this."

"What a shock for you," Kate said, squeezing me back. "To find out you have a son and that he's sick."

"At least he has a good father."

She glanced up at me. "I hope so. He was rather rude to me."

I frowned, anger welling up in me. "What do you mean?"

"He made comments that were suggestive. About you and about me."

I shook my head in disgust, wanting to go back up to the ward and give Chris a piece of my mind, but I knew that would be a waste of time. "I can't imagine what Maureen told him about me. Probably thinks I'm Hannibal Lecter."

"He only knows Maureen's side of the story, Drake."

I sighed and released Kate when the elevator reached the lobby and the doors opened. "I was a dick, Kate," I said, taking her hand as we left the elevator and walked through the lobby to the street. "I freely admit that. She had every right to divorce me. I was an absent husband."

"You did as well as you knew how at the time," she said softly, always sensitive and forgiving.

"I promise I won't be absent with you," I said and squeezed her hand. "I've learned about myself and about relationships since then. I don't want to be that man anymore."

"You aren't."

I smiled at her, touched by her generosity. "Sweet *sweet* Ms. Bennet," I said and brushed my fingers over her lips. "How lucky I am to have found you."

We embraced once more and went out into a cold Manhattan winter's night.

CHAPTER 11

WE DROVE down the snowy streets in silence. Kate took my hand and said nothing, as if she was waiting until I felt like talking. At that moment, I decided I didn't want to go back to my apartment in Chelsea. Instead, I wanted to go to 8th Avenue. My apartment in Chelsea was pre-Kate. It was sterile. It was nothing like the man I wanted to be.

"You want to go to 8th Avenue?" Kate said beside me when she noticed our route.

I nodded but didn't say anything for a moment, trying to sort through my emotions.

"I think of 8th Avenue as *our* place," I said finally. "My apartment is *me* as I was before you. I'm different now. Frankly, I'd like to sell it and for us to move into 8th Avenue or get our own place when we come back from Africa."

"Will you still be able to go? I mean, with the transplant..."

I shook my head. "I'll contact the head of the Neurosurgery program and let him know what's up. I may not be a match, but if I am, the procedures will take about four weeks. I'll have to cancel my slate, have someone else do my surgeries, but we can still go once I know Liam's OK, if I *am* a match. I wouldn't start teaching until March anyway." I pulled into a park and lock parking garage and found a spot. When I got out, I opened the door for Kate and took her arm and we walked down the stairs to the ground level.

"I hope to hell that I'm a match. He's so young and frail and this cancer is very aggressive."

"You'll have to stay for a while, see how he does."

I nodded. "I hope you don't mind. We just may have time to get your malaria meds all up to date before we go."

"Of *course* I don't mind." We entered the street, arm in arm, and we walked the block and a half to the building. "What's involved in the transplant?"

I opened the front entry door, holding it as Kate went through. "Testing to see if my HLA is a match for Liam's, and if I'm a match, they'll have two options. They can give me a drug called Filgrastim to increase my blood stem cells and harvest them from my blood using a machine that separates white from red blood cells, or they can go into my marrow surgically and take it out."

"Is it painful?"

"Filgrastim makes you really achy and tired for a few days before the donation because your marrow is producing more stem cells than normal. There's a recovery time after they harvest your cells. A week or so. Taking marrow directly out of the bone causes discomfort, but it's bearable with painkillers."

"How do they decide?" she asked as we climbed the stairs to the apartment.

"That's up to the oncologist but it's easier to do the peripheral collection."

Kate nodded, but said nothing more. I unlocked the door and we entered.

"How do they do the procedure?"

I took her coat and hung it in the closet while she

shucked off her boots. "They'll have me lie on a bed, cover me with warm blankets. They take blood out of one arm, run it through a machine that separates out the stem cells, and reinfuse it in the other arm."

"Is there any risk?"

I shook my head. "Not really. They're very skilled at this and have been doing it now for years successfully. It's amazing and has saved so many lives." I went to the kitchen, where I kept a bottle of Anisovaya. Yelena Kuznetsova's shot glasses were at Ethan's apartment, so instead, I sorted through the glasses in the kitchen cupboard and brought out two mismatched juice glasses.

"These will have to do," I said and poured two shots of vodka for us. I passed one to Kate and held up my own. "*Za vas,*" I said, unable to muster much enthusiasm.

"*Za vas,*" Kate replied, and I could tell she was forcing a smile, trying to get me out of my bad mood. The only thing that could do that was to lose myself in her body and so I took her glass put them both on the side table.

I pulled her into my arms. "What a night," I said, thinking back at how I felt when I first learned I had a son and that he was very sick, perhaps dying. "I feel like I've been hit by a truck."

Kate squeezed me tightly. "You've had a shock. Shock after shock. To learn you have a son, and that he has leukemia, and that you might be a match for a bone marrow transplant… It's a lot to take in at once."

I nodded, my hand stroking her hair. I knew what I needed. I needed to wash away the pain and shock and sadness. I kissed the top of her head. "I need you," I said softly. "I need to get lost in you."

She looked up in my eyes, her expression so warm and accepting.

"I'm yours," she said, her voice choking up a bit. "Whatever you want. Whatever you need."

I kissed her, amazed that I found her, that she was actually mine. I kissed her softly at first, but soon, I felt as if I couldn't get enough of her, that I wanted to devour her, my hands stroking down her back to her ass, squeezing it with both hands.

"I need you naked, *now*," I said and began stripping away her clothes, impatient to see her naked before me.

"So *beautiful...*" I said, admiring her clear skin and heavy breasts, her tiny waist and curvy hips.

I pulled her to the bedroom, and without any preliminaries, pressed her face down over the edge of the bed, one hand on her shoulder.

"Clasp your hands together," I said. "Spread your legs farther apart."

She complied without a word or hesitation, her hands sliding up so they were above her on the bed. I unfastened my belt, unzipped my pants and shoved my cock deep inside of her. She gasped as I filled her up.

I fucked her. *Hard.*

Fast.

I gripped her hip with one hand and with the other, I twisted her hair into my fist, holding her down.

Like a rutting stag, I said nothing, just thrust hard and fast, my body ramming into her, my pace increasing, my heart racing.

Kate did and said nothing. She let me do as I wanted, what I needed. I thrust blindly and without concern for Kate's needs. I leaned over her and bit down on her shoulder, kissing the spot afterwards, my mouth next to her ear.

"I'm just going to *fuck* you," I said, my voice harsh. "I'm just going to *fuck* you. Do you understand?"

"Yes," she whispered.

My orgasm started, my balls tightening, a sweetness

spreading out from them as I began to ejaculate.

"Oh, *fuck*, Oh, *fuck…*"

I collapsed on top of her when I was finished, my cock still deep inside of her. Finally, I rose up and pulled out of her slowly, careful not to miss watching my semen seep out of her.

I left her on the bed and went to the bathroom to get a wet washcloth so I could clean her off. When I returned, I stroked it over her gently. When I was finished, I lay on my back beside her on the bed, and watched her.

"Thank you."

She smiled and reached out to touch my cheek. "Thank *you*."

I nodded, knowing that we both got what we needed. I rolled over and threw my arm and leg over her body, pulling her closer.

"I like that I can fuck you with no preliminaries. That you want me to when I need you that badly. It makes me happy."

She smiled without responding. I knew it made her happy, too.

"I'm exhausted," I said, pulling away, rising from the bed to undress.

After we both brushed our teeth, we crawled into bed and I pulled her into my arms, thankful that I had her with me, that she was mine. I don't know what I would have done if I had been alone, if I had no one who I loved or who loved me when I heard the news about my son.

My son…

I lay awake with thoughts of my frail son lying on the hospital bed, IVs threading into his arm, his skin pale, and his face gaunt. I knew that he was in for the fight of his life. A battle for survival.

I was determined to do whatever I could to help him win.

CHAPTER 12

I WOKE EARLY, while the sky was still dark and the streets outside the window silent. Sleep eluded me most of the night, after I learned that I had a son and that he was dying from leukemia—likely because of the genes I unknowingly passed on to him. Filled with nervous energy mixed with dread, I wanted to start the testing process and any preparations for treatment as soon as possible. I could only hope and pray that I was a match for Liam and could help to save his life.

Kate was fast asleep beside me, her hand tucked beneath her chin, the covers almost over her head. I felt such warmth for her while I watched her sleep. She'd been there for me from the moment I learned about Liam and had stood up to Chris when he was rude to her and said bad things about me. I really wanted to go and punch the bastard out but that would do no one any good.

What was needed was calm patience. I'd have to work really hard for both.

I slipped out of bed without waking Kate and went to the bathroom to get ready. While I passed my chest of drawers, I checked my cell for messages and sure enough, there was a text from Liam's oncologist who wanted me to come in as soon as possible for the test. I felt relieved that things were in place and would move quickly. Being a doctor really helped grease the wheels when you had a medical issue.

I went to the bathroom and began my morning routine with a shower. Then, as I brushed my teeth, I heard Kate yawning in the bedroom and I peeked at her. She looked ravishing with her messy hair and sleepy eyes. As much as I would have liked to climb back under the covers with her and snuggle down onto the bed for some morning sex, I had to keep moving. If I thought too much, I knew I could become upset very easily.

"You're up early," she called from the bed.

I rinsed my mouth and went to the side of the bed.

"You were sleeping like a baby. You tossed and turned until pretty late, so I figured I'd let you sleep in."

I leaned down and kissed her as she lay under the thick coverlet.

"Are you coming back to bed?" she asked as she brushed a strand of damp hair from my eyes.

"No can do. The oncologist called and left me a message. I have to get my test today. What are your plans?" I said as I started to dress after I selected a shirt and tie from the closet.

"I have absolutely nothing to do." She stretched her arms out and smiled.

"Don't forget to take your meds," I said. "Even though we might not be going for a while, you should build up your levels. Text me so I know you're okay. Malarone can have side effects, especially for people who've had previous periods of clinical depression."

She nodded and smiled. "Always the doctor."

"You know it." I leaned down and kissed her once more.

"I'll miss you."

"I'll miss you." I smiled at her and pulled on my pants. "I'm not used to having a woman in my bed. I think I should have woken you for a quickie. You look very delicious, lying there all warm and naked under my covers, Ms. Bennet."

"You should have. I might just have to look at dirty pictures on the web and do myself." She grinned mischievously.

"You'll do no such thing, you *tease*," I said as I fastened my belt. "You are *not* allowed to masturbate unless I'm watching."

"What you don't know will please me," she said, biting her lip.

I frowned and leaned back down again, bending over her. "No, Kate. I'm serious. When you're mine, I own *all* your orgasms. No masturbation unless I'm watching. Do you understand?"

She frowned. "I can't masturbate unless I'm with you?"

I nodded, because I needed her to understand how possessive I was about her pleasure. "I thought you understood. You're *mine* sexually. Would you like it if I was to masturbate when we're apart or would you prefer that I save it all up for you?"

She shook her head. "No. I understand. I was kidding."

I exhaled. "I don't want to be overly possessive, Kate. But this is important. I'm very jealous and want every orgasm you have to be mine."

"I understand. I was making a joke, teasing."

I nodded and buttoned my cuffs. "In a D/s relationship, there can be no hiding things from your Dom. Anything to do with sex, with our relationship, you have to be completely honest and open with me. You have to trust me and I have to trust you or this won't work. That means, as hard as it may be at times, complete honesty."

She exhaled. "I'm sorry. I'll try to be as honest and open as I can."

I leaned down closer. "I love you, Kate." I kissed her once more but was unable to get back into a playful mood.

"I love *you*," she said, and I thought I could finally see her take what I said seriously. "I wish you could stay."

"You know I want you," I said, truly regretting that I had to leave, "but we'll have to hold that thought."

She slipped her arms around my neck. "I understand."

"This won't take long. They'll take some blood and then we'll meet in his office. I expect he'll run through the procedures in case I'm a match."

"I hope you *are* a match."

I nodded, but the chance was slim. Often, parents weren't a good match. "Liam has a very rare mutation. I probably passed it to him. If we're a good-enough match, he'll have the best chance at survival without as many problems with rejection."

"How long before you know?"

I sighed, thinking of the usual time it took to process the tests. "We'll try to speed up the process. I know a technician and can probably pay him to stay late and run the test. I wouldn't bump anyone out of line. Physicians have these ins with technicians that we can sometimes use when we need fast results."

"If it was me, I'd do the same thing."

"Money talks."

She nodded and slipped her arms around my shoulders as she stroked me affectionately. "A parent will do anything for their child."

I harrumphed at that. "Not all of them."

"*You* will."

"I *will*." I would. I was determined to be the opposite of my father. "It may be the only thing I *can* do for him." I pulled her more tightly against me. "I'm sorry to be dragging you into all this. I'm sure you didn't expect a lot of drama when you signed the agreement, but that's what you've got."

"I signed up to be with *you*—because I wanted you. I love you, remember? *This*," she said and kissed me. "This *drama* comes with the territory."

"I love *you*." I lifted her up and out of the bed, pressing my face in her neck as my emotions overwhelmed me. I knew how lucky I was to have her. I kissed her once more, passionately, and then let her slide down my body so that her feet were on the floor. "Sweet *sweet* Ms. Bennet with the overly-big heart."

"Sweet sweet Drake who can't keep his potatoes from mixing with the gravy." She smiled up at me and brushed a hank of my too-long hair from my face. "I wish you didn't have to leave." She ran her hands up my chest and down to my waist.

I turned and went to the kitchen, took my coffee cup in hand and drank down the last drops. Kate followed me and threaded her arms around my waist from behind. "I look forward to our morning surprises."

"Here at Morgan Enterprises, we aim to please, Ms. Bennet," I said and chuckled as I pressed my ass into her. "But I just can't offer my services this morning."

"So you *did* you read those books," she said with mock surprise.

"What books?" I feigned innocence and turned to face her again. "You mean, Dale Carnegie on how to win friends and influence people?"

"You know very well what books."

"The first one," I said. I was curious as hell about the books and how they portrayed BDSM. "I think pretty much every Dom I know read some, to see what the public might learn about the lifestyle."

"And?"

"I claim the Fifth," I said, for I didn't want to insult her, but I was more of a thriller reader. "Romance isn't my thing. But I will say I have several things in common with the hero."

"Such as?"

"Well, for starters," I said and put down my coffee cup before pulling her into my arms once more. "One *very* inquisitive sub who asks a lot of questions and who makes him lose control of scenes because of her impertinence..."

"*Impertinence*," she said and kissed my shoulder.

"But I'm an old man compared to him, and not a self-made boy genius billionaire so you must be disappointed."

"Oh, *terribly*," she said and kissed me, but I knew she was joking. We kissed once more, unable to get enough of each other. My body responded to the feel of her warmth against me, her breasts pressing against my chest, the soft swell of her buttocks under my hands. I stroked up her back under her baggy t-shirt and only then did I realize that she wasn't naked as I demanded.

"What's with the shirt? I thought I made it clear that I wanted you to always be naked when we were alone here."

She laughed. "In case you didn't notice, what with your incredible hotness and all, it's cold in your apartment. But you'll keep me warm," she said and pulled me against her firmly, grinding herself against my semi-erect cock.

"You'll make me late if you keep that up," I said playfully.

"That's the idea..."

"If I had time, I'd say yes," I said. "Making you all hot and bothered is my greatest desire, but I can't this morning."

"How long will you be?"

I rocked her in my arms for a moment, trying to think about what I still had on my business agenda. "It should take about an hour. Then I have to go to the Foundation and do some paperwork, and *then* I have to drop in at the business office to sign some papers. If the meeting this morning doesn't take too long, I should be back for dinner. Then I want us to meet back here." She was still standing in the kitchen as I got my coat and boots and left the apartment.

I DROVE to the hospital and parked in my usual spot, although I'd soon lose it when my contract expired. I walked to the medical offices wing and went in to see Jim Kerrigan, Liam's oncologist. A portly man with a shock of white hair and southern charm, Kerrigan stood up and shook my hand when his receptionist escorted me into his office.

We sat down and discussed Liam's case, how he had gone through every chemo protocol and after an initial response, had come out of remission due to a particularly aggressive form of leukemia.

"Bone marrow transplantation is his last hope at this point. We're really hoping you're a match, but if not, we can still look at our national databases. Liam's young and very sick and so he'll be on the priority list."

I nodded, a sick feeling in my gut at the prospect I wouldn't be a match, for I knew how hard it was to find tissue matches in time, especially with such an aggressive form of leukemia.

I shook Jim's hand once more and then went to the lab where my blood samples would be taken in preparation for the test. I went back to my office once the technician was finished and got a fresh coffee. Then I sat down and sorted through my contacts in the hospital to call in some markers and get the test done as quickly as possible. Finally, I found a tech with whom I had a good relationship and offered to pay him to stay after hours to run the tests.

He agreed and I relaxed a bit. If it was going to be bad news, I wanted it fast.

ONCE I FINISHED a last check on my remaining patients for the day, I headed to the Foundation. As I drove down the streets of Manhattan, I wondered if I'd be able to go to Nairobi after all. If Liam was going to die, I couldn't imagine leaving and not being around for the funeral. It was a terrible position to be in—to only recently discover I was a father to a dying son, and I might only see him a few times before watching as he was lowered into the ground.

In my career as a surgeon, I'd seen a lot of death. Losing patients was hard, but you had to mourn briefly and then shut it off. How could I shut off the loss of a son?

Even if I never had a relationship with him, knowing he was alive and then dead all too soon was something I just couldn't turn off the way I could with my own patients.

I was once again so glad that I had Kate. What would I do without her? How would I get through this?

I pushed that thought out of my mind, for it was far too unpleasant to even consider.

AFTER GOING over some paperwork at the Foundation, Dave Mills and I had lunch at one of our favorite delis a few blocks away from the office.

We sat at the table in the window, and dove into heaping piles of pastrami on rye.

"So, you're taking Kate with you? That's a shock. I never see you with women. What happened to you?"

I laughed and chewed my sandwich for a while, thinking. What did happen? Kate was different. She was... the kind of woman I had always wanted.

Intelligent, well-bred, beautiful, sensitive, submissive...

"She's the one," I said, but didn't want to be any more specific, considering Dave had designs on her at one point.

"She must be," Dave said, and made a face of surprise.

"You're a lucky man, Drake. You know I had a thing for her a few years ago but she was pretty immune to my masculine attractions."

"Go figure," I said and laughed.

"Yeah, who can understand women?"

He said nothing more, obviously getting a clue for once.

We spoke about Liam and the tests and how I would donate my stem cells in the hopes his new bone marrow would cure his leukemia. He asked about any change in plans for the trip to Nairobi because he had lined up a few hospital visits for me. I reviewed them and asked him to put everything on hold until I learned more about Liam.

"Makes sense," he said, although I knew he'd put a lot of work into the trip and those involved in the hospitals would be disappointed. My family, such as it was, came first.

I wouldn't make the same mistakes my father did and put career above everything else.

AFTER A FINAL TRIP to the corporate office, where I signed a few papers authorizing a temporary replacement for me, I went to my club and worked out. I needed to build up a sweat and get rid of some of my nervous energy. I showered once more and dressed, before I drove back to the apartment. I called Kate on my way back and asked her about supper. We agreed that I'd stop on the way home and pick up some Thai food, pho and spring rolls as well as a rice dish.

I wasn't up to a scene. Instead, Kate and I sat on the couch and ate our takeout, talked about my day and what I'd done.

I felt quite down, so I lay on the couch with my head on Kate's lap, and watched the news while she ran her fingers through my hair. I turned onto my back at about ten o'clock and looked up into her eyes, touching her cheek affectionately.

"I'm sorry I'm not up to too much," I said. "I'm a bit exhausted for some reason."

She leaned down and kissed me. "You've had a huge shock. It's understandable."

"Do you mind if we just go to bed to sleep tonight?"

She shook her head. "Of course not." She forced a smile, but I knew she was disappointed that we wouldn't have sex. I couldn't even think of it for some reason, so as much as I wanted her happy, I couldn't get past my thoughts of Liam and of my test results.

We went to bed and lay in each other's arms. I was exhausted, but couldn't sleep. I tossed and turned with Kate awake beside me.

I'd get the results in the morning, and my gut was knotted as I wondered if the news would be good or if we'd have to start looking for other matches.

Sleep was a long time in coming.

CHAPTER 13

I WOKE to find that Kate was up already, which was unusual, since it was me who had business that required me to leave the apartment. I saw she was sitting at the dining room table so I decided to have a quick shower and get ready, just in case I got a call with the results of the compatibility test.

As I washed, I wondered what would happen if I wasn't a match and how long it would take to find a suitable tissue donor for Liam. He wasn't doing well and had one of the most aggressive forms of leukemia, which no longer responded to chemotherapy. Sadly for Liam, it was stem cells or death.

I finished up and wrapped a towel around my waist, then glanced through the bathroom door and saw Kate standing there, watching me.

She smiled slowly and there was a definite expression of desire and lust in her eyes. I left the bathroom and went to her.

"There you are," I said, pulling her into my arms. "I have a meeting with the oncologist about my test results. My tech promised me he'd work on the test last night so he should have finished the tissue study and sent the results over by now."

"How certain is it? As his father, are you more likely to be a tissue match?"

I shook my head. "Not necessarily. Sometimes yes, sometimes no. It depends on the roll of the genetic dice. Identical twins are the best source, and then siblings, but sometimes a perfect stranger can be the best match."

Kate put her cup of coffee on the windowsill and leaned against me. "If you are a match, how soon before they start the procedure?"

"Hopefully, right away. Depends on how the oncologist wants to proceed. I won't be feeling too well for a week or so while they stimulate my bone marrow, so I hope we can do our scene tonight when I'm done with all my meetings."

She looked up at me and I could tell she liked that idea.

"I think you're ready," I said and stroked her cheek. I imagined what she would look like as she knelt by the bed, blindfolded, wearing only her hose and garters. "If I tried it too soon, you would've been overwhelmed. Now, you're more familiar with submission so you'll be able to enjoy every element."

She sighed and slipped her arms around my waist. Then, the landline rang and I let go of her, pulling out of the embrace to answer the phone.

"Drake Morgan," I said.

"Hey, Dr. Morgan, it's Jake at the lab. We got your test back."

My heart rate increased immediately. "Oh, hello. Thanks for calling. What have you got for me?"

"Good news. You're a match."

Adrenaline surged through me. "Are you certain?" I said, my voice choking a bit. I turned away, one hand on my forehead, overwhelmed.

"Absolutely. Test came back and you're the best possible match."

I couldn't keep a huge smile off my face. "Best possible match?"

"Yes. On all markers you were almost perfect."

"OK, thank you so much for calling."

I hung up, clasped my hands behind my head and just stood there. I looked out of the living room window but didn't really see anything, my mind consumed with the news. Kate came up behind me but didn't say anything at first.

"I'm so happy, Drake."

I nodded, but didn't turn around. Then, I exhaled. "*Christ.* I was so worried. There was a chance I wouldn't be a match, so I didn't want to get my hopes up..."

She stood closer then slipped her arms around my waist, laying her head against my back. We stood there for a while, the apartment silent except for the noise from the street that filtered up through the windows.

Finally, I turned around and embraced her. My arms slipped around her waist and pulled her against my body tightly. I had to fight off tears, so I held my breath as I tried to gain control over myself.

The positive test results meant I could save my son's life —the son I never knew I had and would probably never get to know until he was an adult—if he survived.

Finally, I released Kate because I had to let Michael know I'd be late coming to Africa and wouldn't be able to take over a slate at the hospital.

"I'll be right back," I said. "I'm going to send an email to Michael in Nairobi that I'm a match and will have to give up my OR time."

She followed me to the desk in the dining room where I had an old computer.

"That's too bad, Drake. I know you wanted to help out."

She stood in the doorway and watched as I opened the laptop on the desk.

I shook my head. "What's a surgical slate compared to a son's life?"

Then, my cell phone rang back in the living room, the trill urgent.

"Can you get that?" I asked as I checked my email.

"Yes, sure," Kate said and went back to the living room to my cell phone.

In a moment, she walked back to where I sat and handed me the cell. "It's Maureen."

I took the phone. "Hey," I said and ran a hand through my hair.

"Did you hear?" she said, her voice a bit breathless.

"Yeah, I just got the news. I'm so pleased."

"Thanks so much for agreeing to do this. Chris and I really want you to know we appreciate it. I know you have to change your plans in Kenya…"

"No, it's no problem. I'm glad to help. Anything to help."

"Listen, Drake," Maureen said her voice lowering. "This doesn't change anything. Don't think this means you can get involved, get to know him or anything. There's enough turmoil in his life without learning Chris isn't his biological father. It broke Chris's heart to learn Liam wasn't his and that I was still sleeping with you. You have to understand. This could have broken us up. Please don't push. Please keep this limited to making the donation."

"I *will*," I said, irritated that she was reminding me something I had already agreed to. "I understand."

"Seriously, Drake. No sneaking in to see him or anything."

"No, I said I *understand*. You don't have to worry. Chris is his father. I'm a total stranger." Emotion built in me and I exhaled in an attempt to regain control. "I'm meeting with the oncology team and will make the arrangements. Thanks for calling."

I hung up and stood there, shaking my head.

"What's the matter?"

"She wanted to remind me," I said and my voice broke for a moment. I took in a deep breath to calm myself. "She wanted to *remind* me that this didn't change anything. I'm still not going to be part of Liam's life. As if I don't already know that. *Jesus*, she must think I'm a real idiot."

I turned away and leaned against the windowsill once more, watching the cars on the street below as I tried to pull my thoughts together. Kate came over to me and touched my shoulder gently. "That wasn't very nice of her, especially considering how cooperative you are."

I sighed. "She doesn't want to screw things up with Chris. He was shocked to learn Liam wasn't his. It meant she was still fucking me when she was fucking him. That must have hurt," I said and sighed. "They almost broke up about it, so you can imagine how hard this has been for her as well. And for Chris."

"Hard for all of you."

I sighed and said nothing. She stood quietly behind me. I didn't feel guilty but I felt I needed to clarify the situation for Kate. Finally, I turned back to her.

"Kate, she'd like to think I forced her to have sex, absolve her of responsibility for fucking me even after our marriage had failed, but I *didn't*. I remember the last time we had sex vividly. She had sex with me, willingly. She was maybe a bit reluctant at first, claiming she wasn't feeling very romantic, so I," I said, shrugging. "I seduced her. I didn't force her. I want you to know that. We hadn't been having sex very much. I'd been away a lot. I would never force her."

"Of course you didn't, Drake. I know. You wouldn't force her or anyone."

I looked deeply in her eyes to see if she believed me.

"Listen, let's forget about this," she said. "You have such good news to be happy about. Can I get you a cup of coffee? Something to eat?"

"Sure," I said and sighed, brushing my fingers against her cheek. "Thanks. I've got to call Michael, explain things. It's early evening in Africa, so I'll call him at home. He'll under-stand. He said that if the match was good enough, and I stayed to donate, he could find someone to take over my cases."

"Are we still going to go to Kenya?"

"Not for a while. I'm sorry, it's not only the transplant, but Liam…" I said, taking in a deep breath. "While I'm a perfect match, there are still risks. I want to stay around for a few weeks, see how he handles the transplant. They'll put him on anti-rejection drugs but still, there's always a chance he could reject the transplant—or it could reject him. Maybe not until March, right before class starts depending on how Liam does."

She leaned in closer and hugged me. I bent down and kissed her then buried my face once more in her neck and rocked her for a moment.

"I better get dressed," I said and pulled out of the embrace. "I have a meeting with the hematologist and later, one with a colleague about a paper we were collaborating on. We'll have to rebook our flights for next month at the earliest, depending on how long I take to recover and how Liam does."

She forced a smile and I knew she was disappointed that we weren't going to spend much time together. I went to the bedroom while she went to the kitchen to fix us breakfast.

Kate had been so excited to go to Africa and now I was asking her to hold off her plans. She would be upset, espe-cially after I asked her to take a semester off to come with me. Still, I could tell she understood how important this was and squelched any disappointment, putting on a happy face for me.

I appreciated it deeply.

I DRESSED QUICKLY and had a quick meal of toast and fruit. Then I kissed her after I put my coat on by the front door.

"How long will you be?"

I sighed. "I should be pretty busy all morning. What are your plans for the day?"

"I think I'm going to make a canvas for a painting I'm planning. If we're going to stay for a while until you give the donation and see how it takes, I think I'd like to work on a new piece."

"Oh? You're painting again?" I said, my interest piqued. I felt bad that she had been planning on painting again but hadn't said anything yet. I had been too busy focused on my own issues.

"Yes, and the painting's going to be pretty big, so I'm going to a friend's studio to start work on it."

"What painting?" I asked, curious about her plans.

"It's a secret," she said, smiling coyly.

"I don't like secrets, Ms. Bennet," I said and grinned. "I hope you know I'll do everything in my power to find out what it is."

"It's a gift," she said and pouted. "I don't want you to know until it's done."

"Whose studio is it?" I tried not to sound jealous of her time away from me, although I was definitely jealous.

"This young artist from Texas who's here taking his Masters of Fine Art at Columbia. He comes from a very rich family in the oil business and so he has this great studio. I can make the canvas there using his materials, and then work on it, too, if I need space."

"You two close?" I asked, kicking myself that I couldn't just accept that she had friends outside of our relationship that didn't involve me. Still, it alarmed me that she had been planning all this but hadn't spoken to me about it yet. I'd been neglecting her and would have to try harder.

"He's a good friend from college, but he's a real artist," she said. "Unlike me, who's just a weekend variety."

"Don't put yourself down like that," I said and frowned, noting a tendency in Kate to diminish her own abilities. "You're talented. You've just chosen a different path. Which you could always change, if that made you happier."

She sighed. "I might deviate from that path for a while, now that I'm on leave from grad school. I want to get back into art, since I have the time."

"So, who is this rich kid from Texas and talented artist friend of yours? I need to know if I should be jealous..."

"Drake!" she said and stepped closer to me as I wrapped a warm scarf around my neck. "He's two years younger than me, is a pothead, has tattoos and piercings. The last time I saw him, he had a bright blue streak in his long blond hair. At first I thought it was paint, but no. It was blue hair color."

I laughed at the image she painted of her friend. "Still, artists are pretty sensual people," I said, wagging my eyebrows, fighting the jealous part of me but losing spectacularly.

She wrapped her arms around my neck. "You have no cause for jealousy. He's one of those free spirits who flits from lover to lover like a butterfly from flower to flower."

That made me think immediately of him tasting Kate of course and I felt an intense possessiveness towards her that I hadn't felt for a very long time—if ever. "Has he sampled any of your nectar?"

"*No*," she said and gave my shoulder a playful tap.

"Maybe I should come with you, take a look at this *studio*," I said, wanting to see this guy and the space she would be sharing with him.

She nodded. "If you want. I'd love to show it to you, but you are *not* allowed to see my painting until I feel it's ready. I've just done a few sketches at this point, so it will be a while before it's finished."

"When do you want to go?" I kept my voice light, not wanting to make her feel smothered.

"I thought you'd be busy all morning so I asked him if I could come by…"

"I could make some time after I speak with the hematologist." I stood still for a moment and just looked at her.

"Call me and let me know when you're done," she replied and nodded. "I'll text Nathaniel and let him know we'll be by."

"Sounds like a plan."

I kissed her, deeply, wanting to ensure she knew I wanted her, that I was her Dominant and her lover. I wanted to leave her breathless so she couldn't wait for me to return. I told myself I didn't have to worry about potboy, but I'd still do everything I could to make sure of it.

I SPENT my morning at the hospital. After meeting with the hematologist on Liam's case to discuss the procedure through which they would extract my stem cells, I spent time on the wards checking with the nurses about Liam. I made sure not to run into Maureen but I did sneak by Liam's room when Maureen was out getting coffee. Just a quick peek through the window. He was there with Chris, and looked so frail and small that it made my gut clench.

I went back to my office and sat quietly, reading over the

latest research for a paper I was writing. Then I met a fellow neurosurgeon to go over the research we were collaborating on. I kept busy, which I needed so I wouldn't dwell on the worst case scenarios that I knew could happen. Even with me being a perfect match, there were still a lot of potential problems that could arise. Liam wasn't out of the woods by a long shot.

He wouldn't ever be out of the woods completely. Children who survive leukemia often have other cancers later in life due to the effects of the chemotherapy on their bodies and the radiation used to destroy their bone marrow.

I knew it would be a difficult few months for Liam, Maureen and Chris. I would do everything I could to help and to keep out of their lives. I knew I was the interloper—the outsider. I'd do my part and not expect anything in return except news on how Liam was doing.

IT WAS while I was in my office after my meeting that I received a text from Kate.

DRAKE, I spoke with Nathaniel and he's agreed to let me use the studio to work on a canvas. I can go before lunch. Also, my father called and wanted to meet us at Katz's Deli for lunch. I'd like to go if you're able.

I TEXTED her back right away:

KATZ'S SOUNDS GOOD. Haven't been for a while. I can pick you up at around eleven to go to the studio. Will you be ready?

SHE AGREED and so I picked her up at about 10:45, texting her that I was on the street waiting. She emerged with her sketchbook and backpack, sliding into the passenger seat and leaning over to kiss me.

"So, where is this artist's hideaway?" I said while she buckled her seatbelt. "Where do young artist-type pot-smoking hipsters hang out now? When I was in college, it was in Soho, but it's really expensive there now."

"In an old commercial building on West 36th and 7th Avenue. It's not too far from your place in Chelsea."

"That's some pretty expensive real estate."

"His dad is like Rockefeller-rich in the oil business and could probably afford to buy a whole city block in Chelsea," Kate said.

I parked the car in a park & lock that was near the building. There was no security system, so we went right in and up the elevator to the top floor. Before we even reached the floor, I could hear music blaring from the studio. As we went into the studio, I stopped and took it in. Large tables, full-length windows, sinks splashed with multicolored paint, the walls splattered with bright colors, canvases lined up against the walls. Power tools, easels, work benches. Art work hung on the walls.

The studio was a totally different environment than any I had been in. It was crazy, mayhem, chaos, and I wondered if Kate liked this kind of life. It was such a sharp contrast to my own studious past, the labs, the science, the precision required in surgery.

For a moment, I felt like such a stranger.

Some guy with long blond hair was bent over a table. Kate went up behind him and I followed her, eager to meet the man she'd be spending time with. Alone. She tapped him on the shoulder and he turned around, made a face of recognition. Thankfully, he turned the music down so we could hear ourselves think.

"Hey, *sug*," Nathaniel said. Then he checked me out, and gave Kate a hug.

I didn't like him touching her, although I couldn't imagine that she could prefer a man like him over me. The toque he wore had a marijuana plant emblazoned on it, and a row of tiny silver hoops pierced his eyebrow. He wore Jamaican colors and sported a Bob Marley t-shirt. Sleeve tattoos covered each arm, and his faded jeans were torn. To top it all off, he was tall and skinny.

"This is Drake," Kate said and pointed to me. I did my best to smile, but I felt like an alien in this world.

"*Dude*," Nathaniel said and waved his hand. "Come in, I don't bite unless I'm asked."

I went over to where they stood.

Nathaniel turned to Kate, his eyes moving over her. "You look as sweet as ever, Katie. I heard you won the thesis prize. Way to go."

Kate smiled and glanced at me quickly. "I'm taking some time off to go live in Africa for a while in March."

"Africa? *Cool*," Nathaniel said, eyeing Kate up and down. "So you're going to get back into art? I've got lots of wood for frames, and tons of canvas. There's gesso and all the tools. If you need any help, let me know. We'll whip up a couple of canvases in no time."

"Sounds great. When can I come by?"

"If you want, you can stay now and we can get started. I need a break. The schedule's over on the counter by the sink," he said and pointed to the kitchen. Kate smiled and went over to the schedule on the wall. I followed her, wanting to see for myself when he would be working.

Kate turned to me and smiled. "I can't wait."

I returned her smile and ran my fingers over her cheek.

"I'm glad you'll be able to work on your art." I bent down and kissed her, wanting pot-head-boy to know she was mine and to lay off.

"Who are the other two guys?" I asked, when I saw names on the schedule, trying to sound nonchalant.

"I don't know—a couple of Nathaniel's friends.

"So you'll all work together here?"

"We'll each have our own rooms."

I sniffed the air. "Smells like he smokes pot here, too. Are you okay with that?"

Kate shrugged. "He's a big boy. I'm not interested in getting high on anything but human endorphins. I'll be here to paint. I might get high off the paint thinner, but that'll be accidental." She grinned up at me. "Drake Morgan, are you jealous?"

I laughed and took her by the arms. "Always. Totally. Completely. I may have to come by and see these other characters before I approve."

"*Drake...*" she said, frowning. "You don't get to approve."

"Just kidding," I said, although I wasn't. "Of course, you're free to do what you want outside of our agreement. I'm just curious to know the competition."

"There's no competition so don't even go there."

"I'm a man, Kate. I go there without even thinking."

"I love you," she whispered and pulled me down for a kiss. I kissed her back, the kiss deep, my hand cupping her face.

"I love you," I whispered back, wanting her to know it without any doubt. I didn't want to ever give her any reason to turn to another man.

"Do you have something to do for an hour? I'd like to start making a canvas while I'm here. You could pick me up at 12:15 so we can get to Katz's by 12:30."

"Sure," I said, although I was hoping to take her home for a quickie before going to Katz's for lunch, but I didn't want to deny her the chance to start working on her art. "I can pop by the Foundation. I'll text you when I'm back."

She walked me to the door and kissed me once more. I held onto the door for a moment and watched her walk back to Nathaniel. She waved at me and finally I closed the door and left. It wasn't that I thought Kate would cheat on me. She would only turn to someone else if I gave her good reason. I was determined not to do that.

I wouldn't be my father.

I WENT to the Foundation and sat in my office, at a loss for something to do. My admin, Nancy, had nothing pressing on her desk for me to look over and Dave was at an outside meeting so I sat and surfed the internet on the laptop in my office.

When my hour of killing time was up, I drove back to the studio in Chelsea and sat outside in the car.

I took out my cell and texted Kate to let her know I was there.

Your carriage awaits, my Lady...

She texted me back.

I'll be right down.

I GOT out of the car and stood beside it, waiting for her. When she came out of the building, I bent down to kiss her before she could open the car door.

"Hey," I said. "You've got sawdust in your hair."

Kate ran her hand through her hair, shaking out the bits of wood.

"We cut wood for the frame and then we had to miter the corners and make dados."

"Sounds complicated," I said and opened the passenger door.

"No, it's pretty straight forward once you have your dimensions. My canvas is pretty big so we had to do a lot of bracing so the canvas would be strong enough. I didn't even get a chance to stretch the canvas yet. I'll do that tomorrow."

She smiled at me and got in. I closed the door and came around the other side.

"You didn't have any time on the sheet tomorrow."

She nodded. "Nathaniel said I could come in and work in the main studio."

"How nice of him," I said, deadpan, as we drove off. I couldn't be jealous of him, but I was. I was jealous that he was a part of Kate's life that I could never really share.

If Kate caught the jealousy in my voice she didn't say anything in rebuke. Finally, she reached out and took my hand.

"You know the first time we met outside of class, Nathaniel was stoned and called me '*dude*.'"

I laughed at that, glancing at her. "Well, he must have been really stoned because there is no way any man in his right mind would call you *dude*."

"He's *harmless*, Drake."

I shook my head. That was incredibly naïve of Kate but I relished it in her. "No man is harmless, unless you're going to tell me he's really gay, and even then, they've been known to change teams."

She laughed. "No, he's just a manslut. He'll gladly sleep

125

with any pretty thing that will have him. No steady girl-friends. He's not my type in the least. *You* are."

"I am, Ms. Bennet," I said and touched the collar around her neck to remind her of its existence. "And you're mine."

WE DROVE up to the deli and I dropped Kate off outside while I went in search of parking. The streets were busy and the parking a bitch, so I wanted Kate to go in and find her parents, and get her order.

I drove a several block radius around Katz's Deli until a spot came open and then I walked back to the restaurant. I searched in the window and saw Kate and her parents, then I wound my way through the line until I was able to make it inside the restaurant. I smiled when I saw Ethan and Elaine, and we shook hands as per our usual routine.

"Congratulations, young man," Ethan said to me, pumping my hand. "Katherine's told us the news. You must be so relieved."

"Ethan, you don't know how relieved."

"We're so happy for you, Drake." Elaine kissed me on the cheek when I bent down to her.

I decided to go right to the counter to place my order, not wanting to delay any longer since they had already been waited on. I stood at the counter and ordered a pastrami Reuben with fries. As I waited, I glanced around at the room with its crowed rows of tables filled with hungry customers. Once I had my order, I put my tray down on our table and everyone admired the food while I removed my coat, hanging it on the back of my chair.

I handed them my plate of fries to sample.

The restaurant was packed with diners, the atmosphere busy and loud. I looked around, smiling as I remembered going with my father.

"This was one of my dad's favorite places when he visited me at Columbia. We always came here for a pastrami sandwich and the fries."

Ethan laughed. "We came here as well a few times. I knew it would probably be one of your favorites."

I took Kate's hand and squeezed it on top of the table. "Yes, it is."

Then I told Ethan and Elaine about Liam and the donation. Finally, the talk turned to Africa and our impending trip that would be delayed.

"I'm sorry Kate has to wait, but once we get there, I'll keep her busy visiting my favorite places. I can't wait to introduce her to some good Kenyan food."

"I know something about African food," Kate said, smiling at me, real excitement in her eyes. "Rice and millet, spicy meats and vegetable stews."

"Wait till you taste *ugali* and *nyama choma*—a paste made from cornmeal that you eat with vegetables and grilled meat. Very simple food, but very tasty."

The waitress brought the rest of the order and we all began to eat, enjoying the great deli food.

"You must have been worried that you weren't a match," Elaine said during a break in the conversation.

"I thought I'd be a good match since we have the same blood type," I said. "Sometimes totally unrelated people can be a better match than your closest relatives."

Ethan cleared his throat, and when he spoke, his voice was low. "I told Kate if you wanted to push paternal rights, I could help you with that."

I took in a deep breath. "Thanks, Ethan. I don't think I'll be pursuing any rights at this point." I shrugged, for I truly was torn. On the one hand, I had done nothing other than have an orgasm to produce Liam. On the other, he was my son. My *only* son. "Maureen wants to keep the fact I'm Liam's biological father quiet until he's old enough to understand. I can't blame her. Chris has been a good father so far. I don't want to intrude."

"That's very noble of you, Drake, but if you change your mind and want to push access, you have every legal right. You were married to her when he was conceived and he is your biological son."

I shook my head. "No, it wouldn't be fair at this point to tell Liam his father isn't his biological father. It would be too traumatic. If I thought for a *minute* that Chris wasn't a good father I might feel differently, but from everything I can see, he's been good for both Maureen and Liam. I can't interfere."

Ethan nodded. "Well, if you ever change your mind, I know some pretty good attorneys who would be able to help with that."

"Thanks for the offer," I said, wanting Ethan to know I appreciated his offer of help even though I fully intended to decline it.

Luckily, Kate changed the topic to Africa once more and then Ethan expounded on the upcoming nomination process for the open seat in the district, and we spoke of everything but Liam.

I finished up quickly, checking my watch. I had a meeting scheduled with one of the physicians who was taking over my caseload and I wanted to be there early to make sure I had everything ready.

"I have to run," I said, putting on my coat once more. "I have another meeting so can you get a ride with your dad?"

Kate nodded and I leaned down and kissed her cheek softly.

"I'll let you know when I'm finished. We can discuss our plans for tonight. I have something special planned to celebrate."

I caught her eye, hoping she understood what I meant. I wanted to do a full scene with her.

"You two have plans tonight? Going somewhere?" Ethan said, his face bright.

"We have something special planned," I said, smiling.

"Understandable," Ethan said, nodding his head in agreement. "You two take it easy. Will you be staying at Drake's place?" he said to Kate.

She glanced up at me, looking for my decision.

"Maybe 8th Avenue tonight," I said. I wanted to spend the night there and go through my father's boxes. "There are a few boxes I want to go through."

"Of course." Kate smiled up at me while I bent down and kissed her once more, this time on the mouth.

I left the restaurant, threading through the tables and lines of eager patrons.

CHAPTER 14

I MET with Ben Stanford who would be taking over my caseload at NYP and we discussed each case and the plans for treatment. Then I sat alone in my office and thought about my son.

My brother Liam died before I was born. In fact, I was conceived as a way to help my mother overcome her depression following Liam's death. After Liam's long battle with the same kind of leukemia that my son now had, my mother wasn't able to recover. She was probably still in a full-fledged depression when I was born, for I was told that she never did bond with me. Instead, she would often sit and let me cry while she smoked cigarettes and watched soap operas all alone in their apartment while my father pursued his busy career.

My father either didn't recognize her deepening depression and neglect of me or didn't know how to deal with it. As a trauma surgeon, he was used to fixing broken bodies, but not broken minds. I felt as if I never really had a father—not in the same way Kate did. I knew that Chris was a good parent but there was still a part of me that wanted Liam to know who I was. Who his grandfather was. I wanted to look through my father's boxes for a picture of him receiving his medal. That would be something my son could appreciate one day when he was a grown man.

I sat and tried to close out some patient files and finish some other hospital related business, but as I did, my gut was in turmoil and a darkness descended over me. I felt a need to get drunk and not give a fuck for a while.

I picked up my cell and sent Kate a text.

I KNOW you were probably hoping we'd do our scene tonight, but frankly, I'm not really up to it. I thought a quiet evening at 8th Avenue would be in order. I want to go through my father's things. There's something I want to get for Liam, just in case... Maureen might not agree to it, but I'll try anyway. I think Liam should at least have something from his namesake.

SHE TEXTED ME BACK, agreeing without protest.

I LEFT the hospital and drove to the 8th Avenue apartment, eager to get home and relax after a long day in meetings. As often seemed to be the case, I was there before Kate so I changed out of my suit into jeans and a white linen shirt, ready to be comfortable. I put on a selection of old music that my father used to play when I was growing up and poured two shots of Anisovaya.

Kate arrived some time later, while I was in the kitchen.

"There you are," I said and met her at the door. I took her coat and hung it up in the closet. I hugged her once she had her boots off, and we swayed a bit in each other's arms.

"This is an oldie," she said, tilting her head as she listened to my selection of music for the evening. "One of your dad's?"

I nodded and let her out of my arms to go search through the albums that were lined up in a shelf on the wall. I pulled out the original cover from my father's vinyl collection. The Mammas and the Pappas, with the artists sitting together fully dressed in a bathtub.

"Appropriate, given we're in the middle of a storm in New York," I said as "California Dreaming" played over the sound system. "John Philips wrote the song in 1962 during a New York snow storm. I love New York, but wait until you see Kenya. It's so beautiful in places and the weather is always warm."

"You sure you still want to go in March?"

I shook my head, uncertain what would happen. "We'll stay here for a few weeks until I can see if the transplant takes. Maureen doesn't want me involved, so I'd have nothing to do but sit around moping, waiting for news. If we go to Kenya, I'll be busy teaching and doing surgery. There's nothing I can do here anyway and I could always fly back if anything happened with Liam."

I put the album down and went to the sideboard where I had a couple of shots of Anisovaya waiting.

"Here," I said, handing one to Kate. "I need this. I think I want to get drunk tonight. What do you say?"

She smiled. "Sounds perfect. We can be hung over tomorrow. I have nothing planned besides working on my canvas. I can do that hung over."

"Me neither. *Za vas!*" I held up my shot.

"*Za vas,*" she replied.

Together, we shot back the vodka. Then I pulled her back into my arms and kissed her, wanting to catch the taste of the Anisovaya on her tongue. She responded, wrapping her arms around my neck and her legs around my waist as I lifted her up. We remained like that for a moment and then I let her slide down my body.

"First," I said, brushing hair off her cheek. "I thought we'd make a nice light dinner after that mountainous sandwich at lunch. Then, we can talk about our plans and get sloshed."

"Sloshed?"

I grinned. "My father's term for floor-licking pissed."

"I like it," she said and leaned against me. "I don't know if I intend to lick any floors though…"

I laughed at that and embraced her more tightly, breathing in her perfumed hair.

"Sweet Ms. Bennet. What would I do without you?"

"I don't even want to think about us not being together," she said softly.

The song ended and one of my favorite Lennon and McCartney songs came on.

"What's this?" she asked, slipping out of my arms to check the playlist. The song was from *Rubber Soul,* which had been released in 1965.

"In My Life," I said, coming up behind her, slipping my arms around her waist. "Another appropriate song, because I *do* love you more," I said, kissing her neck. She put the cell phone down and held my arms.

"I love you, Kate," I said softly.

"I love *you*," she said, her voice nearly a whisper. We stood in an embrace for a while, enjoying each other. Then I let go of her and led her to the kitchen.

"Come to the kitchen," I said. "I've got some vegetables for a salad. I thought we'd have some chicken."

She followed and while Kate took responsibility for the salad, I grilled the chicken breasts, dredging them in flour and sautéing them in the pan. Kate sipped some wine I poured for her while I acted as chef. I even tied a white apron around my waist.

"It won't take long," I said and turned to her. "I have a nice baguette that we could have as the starch."

"When did you get so domestic?"

I laughed and reached into a bag on the counter, removing the long thin loaf.

"I lived by myself for five years after the divorce. It was either learn to cook decent food or live out of restaurants."

We sat at the table, set with some linens and cutlery I found in my father's things. Before we ate, I took Kate's hand.

"I'm not really religious," I said, squeezing her hand. "But I want to say how thankful I am about the tissue match."

She nodded, her eyes wide. "Me, too."

I smiled and let go of her hand. "I'm also thankful that I found you. Such a delicious morsel of prime womanhood."

"You're hungry," she said, grinning back. "You need to eat."

"I *do* need to eat," I replied and wagged my eyebrows suggestively. "But dinner first."

We discussed details of our trip. Even though it would be delayed for some time, there were still plans to be made and while I'd have to alter dates, for now at least we could still enjoy planning it together.

"We'll be staying at the Hilton for a while until I can find a nice home," I said. "A colleague has suggested Kitusuru Village as a place to rent where there are a lot of expats living. Most of them are families with children, but there may be an area where singles and younger couples live. We'll see once we get there." I looked at her. "Do you have a preference for where to live? I mean, apartment or house?"

She shrugged. "I don't really care. I have no idea what to expect because I spent all my time in the relief camp in Mangaize or in hotels."

"I have a contact in Nairobi who's already looking for a

nice house. I think it would be great to actually live in a house for a change, instead of an apartment."

"I've always lived in an apartment," Kate said, "except for our cottage in the Hamptons. It would be nice. Whatever you think, Drake."

"From what people who have lived there say, once you're inside the compounds, you won't know the difference between Nairobi and Los Angeles. They're gated communities where most of the expats live. Very safe. Large estates with parks and shopping."

I was busy describing things, eating my meal, not noticing that Kate was pretty silent. I glanced at her, catching her eye.

"What's going on in that mind of yours, Ms. Bennet? Something good, I hope, from that wistful smile."

She smiled more broadly. "Was it wistful?"

I nodded and reached out to take her hand. "Yes, very."

She shook her head. "I've never done this kind of thing before."

I frowned. "What kind of thing?"

"Lived with a man," she said softly. "Planned to move somewhere with him. Planned to pull up roots and move to another continent."

"You went to Africa with Nigel," I offered.

"Not quite the same thing…"

I chuckled at that. "Not quite." Then I put down my fork and inhaled deeply. "I know this is a huge commitment, withdrawing from your semester, letting your apartment go, coming with me to Nairobi, living with me. Now with the delay, I know it seems like I haven't given you what I promised."

She reached out and took my hand. "You don't have to feel bad about that at all. Of course, we'll stay here – as long as you want and need. I just want to be with you, wherever that is and whatever we're doing."

I leaned over and kissed her. "I don't know what will happen between us, Kate, but I can't imagine doing anything without you."

She smiled. "Me either."

WE CLEANED up quickly and then I brought out a bottle of vodka and the two shot glasses. Kate followed me to the living room, where we sat by the fireplace. I poked the logs into renewed life and we sat in front of it, the bottle of vodka on the coffee table.

I turned to her, quirking my eyebrow. "Now, Ms. Bennet, I intend to get you *drunk*."

She laughed, and snuggled in closer to me. "Are you sure you want to? You have no idea what kind of drunk I might be. And besides," she said, poking my arm. "As a physician, shouldn't you be advocating for moderation?"

"Moderation in most things, yes," I said and poured two shots. "But in love and when it comes to vodka, there's a time for indulgence."

Then I proceeded to get her drunk, downing shot after shot.

"I'm not much of a drinker," she said after the third shot. "I can't do anything more or I'll throw up. How romantic would that be?"

I laughed and put the bottle of vodka down. "Okay, *okay*," I said. "I'll let you off the hook for now. I really need to relax and forget everything for a while. Doing a scene requires my total concentration and I have to be sober. I felt like getting drunk tonight. I hope you don't mind too much."

"Whatever you need or want, Drake." She laid her head on my chest, and I pulled her into my arms, pleased that she was so willing to let me take the lead.

IN THE END, Kate and I weren't very drunk, despite my plan. I did jumble up the words while I sang "House of the Rising Sun" on my karaoke machine, and we laughed so hard, Kate and I both had ears running down our faces.

Kate was reluctant to sing but I encouraged her.

"No, no, *no*," I said, taking hold of her arms and pulling her up. "You have to sing something. What's your favorite oldie?"

She tried to wrestle out of my arms, but I grabbed her from behind and wrapped my arms around her, laughing.

"No escape, Ms. Bennet. You must sing or I'll have to go all Dom on you."

"*All Dom*," she said, giggling when I tickled her. "Oh, all right!" She tilted her head to the side. "How about something by ABBA?"

"*ABBA?*" I said, making a face of mock disgust. "The 1970s? *Sacrilege...*" I searched through my songs and found "Take A Chance On Me."

"Here," I said, handing the phone to her. "This is perfect."

"Oh, *God*," she said when the music started and she had to stand in front of me.

I sat back on the couch, and nodded, getting comfortable for her performance. It was good to make Kate let loose now and then. She really was very uptight, which was why submission appealed to her so much.

"Sing."

She did, her voice soft at first, hesitant, self-conscious about performing, but soon she started to dance a bit, swaying to the music as she sang. I wolf-whistled and clapped when she was done and she enjoyed it so much, she sang the next song on the ABBA karaoke playlist. "Fernando."

I took another turn and chose "Born to be Wild" by Steppenwolf, acting as silly and theatrical as I could muster and when I was done, we were laughing so hard, we collapsed onto the couch together.

After we calmed down, we listened to one of my 60's playlists. I kept pounding back the shots, and didn't even remember falling asleep the first time, but I was warm and comfortable on the couch with Kate lying beside me, her head resting on my chest, my arms around her.

I woke up when she shook my shoulder.

"Maybe you should have some coffee," she said.

I shook my head. "Water." I got up from the couch, pulling her along with me. "And aspirin."

I searched through the cupboard for a glass and almost dropped it in the sink. Kate took over, pushing me gently out of the way.

"Let me do this," she said and poured a glass of water for me, which I drank down while she watched.

"Nurse Bennet, are you taking care of me?" I said, quirking my eyebrow.

"You're lucky it's not Nurse Ratched."

I laughed at that and when I was done, I pulled her into my arms.

"Let's go to bed," I said. "I'm not up to much good so I hope you're OK with us just sleeping."

She slipped her arms around me. "Whatever you want, Drake."

I led her to the bathroom, where we went through our nightly routine. When it came time to undress, Kate helped me after I fumbled with my buttons.

"I'm sorry if you're disappointed that we didn't do our scene," I said, watching her undress me with some amusement.

"Shh," she said, pulling my shirt off and unfastening the button on my jeans. "We have all the time in the world for that. You needed this tonight."

"I did," I said. "But seeing you undress me makes me a bit hard." It was true, but I knew I'd be worth next to nothing in the bedroom department.

"If you ignore it, it will go away," Kate said, a naughty expression on her face. "I seem to recall you telling me that on a fateful night in November…"

"That it will." I closed my eyes when a wave of dizziness struck. "Oh, Katie, I am so *drunk*…"

"You *are*." She led me to the bed and I fell onto it, laughing at my own lack of balance, my eyes closed. I snuggled under the blankets and soon, I felt Kate slide in beside me. I turned and she crawled into my arms and then we lay there in the dark and listened to the sounds from the street.

WHEN I WOKE the next morning, I felt only half-hung-over. I checked the clock radio and saw that it was about six in the morning. I slipped out of bed and had a quick shower before I went to the kitchen and put on some coffee. Kate loved fresh squeezed orange juice, so I took out a few oranges from the refrigerator and made some, leaving it in a glass pitcher on the counter beside a bottle of aspirin. It was hard for me not to follow my usual routine of getting up early and getting ready for work, even if I had a very light workload.

I checked my email and then saw my guitar sitting there, neglected, and decided to play for a while. I went through a few of my favorite songs, playing softly so I didn't wake Kate. I was completely absorbed in the music and didn't hear her get up but I caught sight of her out of the corner of my eye and turned to where she stood listening in the entry to the living room.

She came over and bent down to kiss me.

"Good morning," she said. "You seem no worse for wear after last night."

"Drink plenty of water and take two aspirin," I replied and smiled. "Works every time."

"What are you playing?" She sat down on the couch and watched over the back while I strummed a few chords.

"Playing an old Beatles song I like. Do you want to hear?"

She nodded, an expression of pleasure on her face, her eyes soft.

"I'd love to hear you sing and play. You have a really nice voice."

"I get by," I said, pleased that she thought so. I played around for a moment, tuning the strings, and finding the chords. "It's called, *And I Love Her*."

A classic, I was certain that this song would live on for centuries. It was epic and beautiful, showcasing McCartney's songwriting skills, although Lennon argued that he wrote part of the song. Written and produced in 1964 at the Abbey Road studio, it was only performed once outside of the studio yet it remained a favorite of Beatles aficionados.

When I finished, I turned to Kate, who had tears in her eyes.

What could I say about that moment? It made me love her even more than ever, if possible. Her tears at the concert showed me that she was deeper than she appeared on the surface, moved by music, preferring classical to contemporary, willing to be different from the rest of her peers. Her tears for my playing was like gravy.

"I *do* love her," I said, choking up. "I love you, Kate. Thank you for being here for me."

She came over to me, blinking back her tears. "I love *you*." She bent down, her hands on either side of my face and kissed me. "Thank you for letting me be here with you."

She left me sitting with my guitar in hand and went back to the couch, her back to me. I knew she was trying to gain control over herself so I strummed the guitar for a few moments, letting her have her moment of privacy. Normally, I'd want to go to her and force her to show me her tears, enjoy them, but at that moment, I felt a need to protect her instead. To give her a moment to recover. Finally, I put my guitar down and brought my coffee with me to sit on the couch beside her.

"What's on the agenda for today?" I said, and then I frowned, remembering she was going to go to the studio. "Oh, yeah. I remember," I said, a bit sourly. I didn't want to be jealous of her old friend. I knew I shouldn't feel threatened by him especially because he seemed like the opposite to the kind of man Kate needed. But still... "You're going to spend time with Mr. 'Hey, *Dude*.'"

Kate nodded. "I want to go work on my canvas for a while this morning, but after that, nothing."

"I can do some work at the Foundation if you're going to be at the studio," I said and swallowed back my jealousy, "but we should plan on spending the afternoon together."

"Sounds great."

I put my arm around her and we finished our coffee, enjoying a few quiet moments together before our days began.

I STOOD and watched Kate while she got dressed and fixed her hair in front of the mirror in the bathroom.

"You still look good enough to eat, Ms. Bennet," I said. "I don't know if I like you spending the morning alone with a bunch of artist-dudes."

"They have nothing on you, Drake. They're still at that flaky stage of manhood. You know, not wanting to settle down. Looking to hookup with as many women as they can, sow their wild oats. I'm not interested so you don't have to be the least bit concerned."

"I know," I said and sighed. "Just want to defend my prized territory."

"You and Sun Tzu..." She turned to me and frowned. "Or was it Machiavelli?"

"Both. There's a reason they say all's fair in love and war. Both involve conquering and surrender."

"I already surrendered, remember? The agreement?"

I grinned, my arms folded as I leaned against the bathroom doorjamb and watched her.

"You did. I enjoyed it immensely, even though I'm not so sure you're all that submissive in the end and that's just the way I like you."

She frowned. "What do you mean?"

I shrugged. "I don't want a submissive woman. I want a woman who submits in the bedroom. There's a difference."

She nodded slowly. "I like that." She came to me and put her arms around my waist. "I want to submit to you in the bedroom. Outside of it, I want to be strong. Competent. Capable of looking after myself."

"You are. But let me take care of you as well. Everyone needs someone to fall back on when things get too heavy. Just so you know you have me."

"And you have me."

I kissed her, pulling her against my body, doing my best to dampen down my jealousy. It wasn't so much that I felt Kate would want to have sex with any of them. They were flakes, as she noted. I remembered that age – twenty four or five, insatiable hunger for pussy. It was that they shared something with her that I never could. I had no talent in art and couldn't draw a stickman so this was something apart and separate from our life together.

I wanted to share everything with Kate but art was one thing I would have to merely appreciate from a distance.

WE MADE a plan that I'd come and pick Kate up when she texted me. She said she'd probably be a couple of hours, no more and maybe we'd do a late lunch.

After I dropped her off, I went to the Foundation and sat with Dave, shooting the shit as men are wont to do at times, especially when I wanted to kill time waiting for Kate to be finished at the studio.

"So where is the lovely Ms. Bennet?" Dave asked as we sat in his office, a cup of coffee in hand. "Finishing up stuff at Columbia? She withdrew from her semester for you. That's huge."

"I know," I said. "I asked her to."

He shook his head, examining me carefully. "That is so not the Drake I know. You really must be addicted if you're asking her to come with you."

"A very pleasant addiction," I said, giving him a half-grin. The other half of my wanted to give him a punch, but I held back.

"I tried to win her heart," Dave said, leaning back, propping his feet on the desk, his hands behind his head. "I was persistent but she turned me down each time."

"She's not the sleep around kind of woman. You're the sleep around kind of man. She knew that."

"She's spoken to you about me?"

"Not really, but she did corroborate your story of persistence." I grinned at him, enjoying the expression on his face. "She said you were a pleasant lothario."

"She said that?" He frowned. "Pleasant was not what I was going for." He grinned and then laughed at himself. "I was trying to be seductive, but obviously she was immune to my masculine charms."

"Totally immune."

"Obviously she wasn't immune to yours. Tell me, what's

your secret? Is it the money? The MD after your name? The guitar?"

I studied him, unable to tell him the truth—that she was attracted to the Dominant in me and that is why she would choose me over him. He had no real idea about my involvement in the lifestyle and I wanted to keep it that way.

When an hour had passed, and we had discussed Africa and what the Foundation would do in my absence, he shuffled his papers around and seemed a bit uncomfortable.

"As much as I'd like to shoot the shit with you all morning, Drake, I do have a conference call in half an hour and need to go over my notes."

"Oh, sorry," I said and stood up abruptly. "Of course. I'll pop into my office and see what's on my desk."

We said our goodbyes and I left him in his office, flipping through files. I felt at a loss for I wasn't used to not having business to attend to. I went into my own office down the hall and sat behind the desk. Then, I stared out the window and wondered how long Kate would be, trying my best not to get jealous.

When she still hadn't texted me after two hours had passed, I decided to drive over and pop in. She may have lost track of time. Part of me felt a bit guilty doing so, for I should have waited until she contacted me but I was so damn curious to see what they did while I wasn't there.

I PARKED close to the building and walked down the street to the entrance, annoyed once more by the fact that it was open to the public and anyone could just walk inside. I took the old creaky elevator to the top floor and could hear the music blasting even before I arrived. I went to the studio, opened the door and stood inside.

Some kind of industrial music played on the sound

system, grinding, like metal. I glanced around and saw Kate standing between two men dressed in jeans and hoodies, the air blue over their heads, the stench of weed strong.

The two men passed a joint between them. On her part, Kate stood with her back facing me, washing items in the sink.

I caught Nathaniel's eye. He turned to Kate and gestured to me with his head, saying something that I couldn't hear over the music.

Kate turned and saw me, our eyes meeting. I raised my eyebrows suggestively, not all that pleased to see her standing so close with the two men.

She glanced around and said something else to Nathaniel and then turned back to the door.

"*Drake*," she shouted, drying her hands off on her apron. She went to the sound system and stopped the music. Then she came over to where I stood and put her arms around my neck. "I didn't hear you come in."

"How could you hear anything?" I said, smiling at her, trying to put on a good front despite finding her sandwiched between two artists who were much younger than me. I slipped my arms around her waist, pulling her against my body.

"What time is it?"

I smiled. "It's 1:30."

She inhaled sharply. "I forgot to check. Have you been waiting long?"

I shook my head. "I decided to come by and see what was going on. I figured you were otherwise occupied and just forgot about the time."

"I did. I was so busy putting on the gesso I lost track of time. Forgive me?"

I kissed her quickly. "Nothing to forgive. Let's go. Unless you want to stay…"

She shook her head. "No, let's go. I can't do anything until the coat dries. I have to finish cleaning up first."

I released her and she went back to the sink to finish drying off the brushes. I moved a bit closer and glanced at Nathaniel and then the other man, trying not to laugh out loud at the two of them.

The other man with long hair to his waist held the roach out to me. "Have a toke, man," he said.

I shook my head and held my hand up, palm out. "Thanks, but no."

He shrugged and sauntered back to his studio.

Kate said goodbye to Nathaniel, thanking him for helping her with the canvases and we left. She asked me how my morning went and I described trying to find something to do while she was busy. When we arrived at the car, I opened the door for her and then went around to the driver's side.

"Did you smoke pot with them?" I asked, trying to keep my voice light.

She glanced at me. "No," she said. "I'm not really much of a pot smoker. Never did like it. Besides, with the hanging judge for a father? No *way*..."

I smiled in relief. I didn't like the thought she was getting stoned with anyone else but me, my jealousy rearing its ugly head once more.

"You looked right in your element at the studio with that paint on your apron and cheek," I said and reached over to touch her skin. "You looked really happy."

"I was. I am," she said and took my hand. "I haven't even started on the work but it feels so good to be doing art again."

I squeezed her hand, knowing I had to swallow my petty jealousies over Kate being alone with men who were more her age. This made her happy and a happy Kate was my goal in life, even if it meant I had to let her outside my immediate control. It was hard, but I fought my Dom tendencies as much as possible outside the bedroom.

After we returned to the apartment, we sat on the couch and watched the news, cups of tea in our hands.

LATER IN THE AFTERNOON, Maureen called, asking me to come by to talk about Liam's case.

"She wants me to come by to talk about Liam," I said to Kate. She was in the kitchen trying to decide what to cook for our supper.

"Do you have the memento you wanted to give to him?"

I nodded. "Yes, I'll bring it along. I hope she lets him have it. I don't know what cover story she can give him, but it should be his."

"What is it, if you don't mind me asking?" she said, trying to sound casual but I knew she was curious.

"A picture of Liam outside a field hospital in Vietnam receiving the Medal of Honor for saving the lives of two soldiers who were in a burning helicopter that crashed." I thought about the picture I had always treasured. "I hope that, one day, Maureen will show it to him and let him know who his real father and family were."

Kate said nothing but I could see doubt in her eyes. "Speaking of later tonight, I was thinking about supper," she said, as if trying to change the subject. "The fridge is pretty empty. Should we have supper with my father and Elaine? Or would you rather stay here?"

I shrugged. "Up to you. I am entirely at your command."

Kate hesitated. "Let's go to my father's for dinner. Once we go, I won't see them for six months, so it would be nice to see them as much as possible."

"Fine with me."

Kate left the kitchen and called her father to make

arrangements. Then, she and I spent the afternoon listening to news of an earthquake in China, lounging around, reading the paper and talking about the trip. Doing ordinary things that couples did.

I hadn't done them with a woman for years, and it felt perfect.

CHAPTER 15

THE AFTERNOON PASSED QUICKLY and soon it was time for us to get ready for dinner at Ethan's. While I dressed in the bedroom, Kate was doing her makeup in the bathroom. I watched her from where I stood by my chest of drawers and was amazed that she was mine. She had no real idea how delicious she was with her curves and milky skin and breathless desire for submission. Although I felt an incredible need for her body, it was her mind that captivated me. She wanted to be taken places sexually she was too afraid to go on her own. She needed a dominant man for that.

I was perfect for her and she for me.

I went into the bathroom while she was bending over, pulling up her stockings, and the sight of her bare ass was far too tempting to merely watch. I wanted to feel her body against mine and run my hands over her skin so I grabbed hold of her hips and pulled her against my body.

"Ms. Bennet, when you stand like that, with just your garter belt and your bra, I'm unable to resist you." She tried to stand up, but I stopped her, wanting her to remain in that position while I enjoyed the view. "No, stay like this for a moment. I like this position. I'm getting *ideas...*"

Kate glanced up into the mirror and our eyes met. She smiled as I ran my hands over her back to her buttocks, pulling her against my groin and my growing erection. I wasn't planning on fucking her at that moment, but I wanted to enjoy her luscious body and most of all, my complete freedom to touch it and arouse it and play with it whenever I chose.

I released her and she stood facing the mirror with me behind her. Our eyes met once more in the mirror and she watched as I stroked her belly with one hand and cupped a full breast with the other. She was mine – all mine. I exhaled and bent down to kiss her shoulder then slid my hands down her arms to clasped her hands in mine, our fingers entwining. We stood like that for a few moments, my cheek resting on her shoulder. I wanted her every moment of the day, but what I first took as sexual need was now trans-forming into a need just for her presence. To touch her and have her close.

"Well, as much as I'd love to fuck you right now, I guess we better get going," I said and released her hands. "Don't want to keep your father waiting."

Kate nodded without a word, although I was pretty sure I had aroused her with my touch. Still, she didn't protest or push for sex. Instead, she resumed dressing, my good little sexual submissive.

Exactly what I needed.

Exactly what I most wanted.

I felt a tiny bit selfish, but I knew that for Kate, I was what she needed and wanted as well.

WHEN WE ARRIVED at Ethan's, he and Elaine were sitting in

the living room, drinking cocktails and listening to some music on the sound system.

"Come in you two," Ethan said in his gravelly voice. "What can I get for you?"

I held up my hand. "Let me bartend," I said and went behind the bar. I opened the small bar fridge and removed Yelena Kuznetsova's shot glasses and poured two shots of Anisovaya, then brought them over to the couches by the fireplace. I handed one to Kate and then held up my glass.

"To us," I said.

"To us," Ethan replied. We toasted each other and then Kate and I shot back the vodka.

Kate sat on the couch beside Elaine and I sat beside Kate, my arm possessively around her back.

"We've been so looking forward to dinner tonight," Elaine said. "We thought you two would be gone in a few days. We're glad we'll have you here for a few more weeks, even though the circumstances aren't happy."

"I'm happy to stay for as long as Drake wants," Kate replied. "Everything's packed and repacked and repacked again. We have our passports and Drake has his papers and offers of employment so as soon as Drake's ready, we can go."

"So Drake," Ethan said, turning his attention to me. "You're still going to be able to teach?"

"Luckily yes," I said. "The third semester starts in March. I'm going to teach two courses in the Masters of Medicine Neurosurgery program. One is intro to neurosurgery and the other is for 6th year students and was the final neurosurgery course in the program. It's called *HMS 1001:Principles and Practices of Neurosurgery* and focuses on the kind of surgery I do at Columbia. Stereotactic surgery for epilepsy and deep brain stimulation for Parkinson's and other movement disorders."

"Are they lectures or is there actual surgery involved?"

"Both," I replied, eager to teach the classes. "Lectures, demonstrations, and surgical rotations with me. It's really hands-on at this point. The final course is taught in the last year of their neurosurgery program so they're almost finished."

"You must be pleased."

"Very. I've wanted to go and teach there for a while. Ever since I did some volunteer work a couple of years ago."

"Sad that you have to cancel the surgery you've got lined up."

I shrugged, although I felt bad for Michael. He had such need for support, especially when it was mainly wealthy doctors like me who could afford to put a practice on hold and volunteer our services. "It'll be hard for them to find someone qualified to take over on such short notice, but it's my son."

"Do you like to teach?" Elaine said, as if trying to change the subject.

"*Love* it," I said, as I took Kate's hand in mine and gave it a squeeze. "I love teaching *almost* as much as doing. I love to watch students develop their skills, discover new knowledge, improve. And Kenya has a severe shortage of neurosurgeons, so this is important work getting more students to graduate. I'll get privileges and will be on call in the ER and scheduled surgeries. I'll be really busy, but hopefully not too busy or Kate will get really bored." I turned to her. "But she's started painting again, so maybe we'll get her some studio space and she can work on a collection while we're there."

Kate smiled back at me. "Thank you," she said and kissed me on the cheek.

Ethan turned to her, smiling broadly. "Well, that's just great," he said. "I'd love to see some new work from you, sweetie. What are you working on?"

"It's a secret," Kate said. "A gift."

"For Drake?"

She shook her head "No, for me."

"Be mysterious," Ethan said, shaking his head. "I can't wait to see it, whatever it is."

Elaine and Ethan seemed pleased that we were together, that we were going to Africa, and that Kate would start painting again. It was almost enough to wash away the darkness inside of me as I worried about Liam and whether the treatment would work. I pulled Kate a bit closer, and she responded by snuggling into my embrace. If it wasn't for Liam's illness, I didn't think I could be any happier.

THE MEAL WAS CATERED and was delicious. Kate and Elaine discussed the food while Ethan and I caught up on how his campaign plans were progressing. I related how I was wrapping things up at the hospital, the Foundation and the Corporation.

Beside me, Kate seemed especially happy to be with her father and Elaine. I watched her drink a bit more than usual, amused that she was getting a nice buzz from the wine.

When we were alone for a few minutes, while Ethan left for his office and Elaine went to the kitchen to fix us tea, I leaned over to Kate.

"You're flushing from the wine. You look very alluring. I wish I could take you home right now instead of going to meet Maureen. Later," I said. "We'll do something special."

AFTER TEA and some more discussion of life in general, we said goodbye to Ethan and Elaine and I led a slightly tipsy Kate down to the parking garage. Kate tripped and laughed when I caught her, steadying her against my body.

"You and high heels," I said. "I'll have to make sure you

always wear them when we go out so you'll remind me of our first meeting in the bar."

I helped her into the car and buckled her seatbelt while she sat with her eyes closed, smiling. She actually giggled when I adjusted the shoulder belt, and my hand brushed her breast. She opened her eyes and stared into mine.

"You're *drunk*, Ms. Bennet. I'll have to find a way to take advantage of you tonight."

"Mmm," she said, closing her eyes again. "I like it when you take advantage of me."

"You'll be an even easier lay, with all that wine in you."

"An easy lay?" she said with mock-affront. "May I remind you that you went to a lot of effort to finally succeed in ravishing me?"

I laughed and went around to the driver's side. "I *did* go to a lot of effort. You're worth every ounce."

ONCE BACK AT the apartment in Chelsea, I helped Kate with her coat and heels, and carried her to the living room. I lowered her to the couch, and went to the kitchen to pour her some water and get her two aspirin.

"Take these," I said, handing them to her. "Drink up. I'm going to fuck you when I get back from seeing Maureen. I want you wide-awake and responsive. No falling asleep or I might have to spank your cute little round ass."

She leaned her head back against the couch. "I didn't like it when you spanked me at the dungeon party," she said. "I thought I might like it, but I didn't."

"That was a punishment spanking," I said. "It's not supposed to feel good. I'm glad you *don't* like it. We would likely never have clicked if you had enjoyed it."

She nodded, and took the aspirin, then drank down the rest of the water.

"I'll make you a cup of coffee before I go. I want you to sober up a bit." I went to the kitchen and prepared her a cup and then kissed her goodbye. "Wait up for me. I probably won't be too long."

"I will."

I LEFT Kate alone on the couch and took my car to NYP to see Maureen. In my pocket was the picture of my father receiving the medal of honor in Vietnam and a news clipping telling the story. I would give it to Maureen and ask that she show it to Liam and make up some story about how the man in the photo was a relative without directly naming him or his relationship to Liam. I wanted him to know who his forefathers were. If I couldn't know Liam, I wanted him to know about me and especially about his grandfather. Neither of us were inconsequential men. I thought we were both men of which he could be proud.

As I arrived at NYP, I felt certain that Maureen would grudgingly take the picture and news clipping, show them to Liam and just keep the details sketchy. After all, I was undergoing a medical procedure that was meant to save her son's life. I felt it was the least she could do.

Sadly, I was wrong.

I MET them on the ward and went in to see Liam.

"You can see him now, when he's sleeping," Maureen said, "but after this, I don't want you to come back. I'm only letting you see him now in case he dies before you leave for Africa."

I nodded without really thinking about it, so glad to have the chance to see him without having to sneak around. The three of us gowned up and went into Liam's room. He was as pale and fragile as before, his skin so thin it seemed almost translucent, and he had so little body fat that I could see veins in his scalp and the outline of his skull.

I stood by the bed and watched him breathe, filled with a profound sense of loss. Here was my father's grandson—the grandson he never knew about or met. Here was the son conceived with the woman I though I'd spend the rest of my life with.

I'd blown it so badly.

I took Liam's hand and mercifully, he didn't wake up, for Maureen stepped closer when she saw me, and I knew she didn't approve of me touching him. For God's sake—did she think I was contagious or something?

We finally left the ward and went down to the café. We each got a coffee and then sat at a table by the window.

"What's that?" Maureen said when I reached into my pocket and withdrew the envelope.

"It's a photograph of my father," I said and handed it to her, "receiving the Medal of Honor for saving the lives of two soldiers in a helicopter crash. I want Liam to have it. I'd like you to show it to him so he knows what kind of man his grandfather was."

She took the envelope but didn't even bother to open it, staring at it like it contained a contract for her soul directly from Satan. She glanced up at me and then at Chris, who frowned. She shook her head, shoving the envelope back at me.

"I can't take this. Drake, I told you. Chris is his father, not you. All you contributed was a single cell. Chris has been there right from the beginning."

"How can you say that? That single cell is why Liam is alive today," I said, anger welling up inside of me.

"It's also because of you that he has cancer in the first place," Chris said from across the table.

I fisted my hands, biting back an angry retort. "Life's like that. The good comes with the bad."

"Drake, why are you doing this? I though you agreed to say out of Liam's life."

"Until he's old enough to understand—"

"Which won't be until he's eighteen," Chris said, interrupting me. "Thirteen years from now."

"I won't try to contact him until then but you could always tell him about his family—"

"He's already met his family," Maureen said, her voice shaking. "Chris's family. *My* family. You're no part of it. You haven't been and you won't be. This donation changes nothing. You agreed to be an anonymous donor."

"Maureen, he'll figure it out eventually. If he learns his blood type, he'll figure out that he's not Chris's son. I'm A positive, you're A positive, and Chris is B. That alone will prove that he's not Chris's."

"Why would he ever have to learn his blood type?"

I shrugged. "I don't know but they learn about blood type in science class in school."

"We'll deal with it when we have to. Right now, I want you to just let this go. Don't try to see him again, okay? He's too sick for anything too disrupting. Surely you can understand that."

I nodded, angered but not wanting to be insensitive.

"I'll take this, Drake," she said and took the envelope. "Maybe I'll consider giving it to him when he's eighteen but if you try to push things, I'll go to court to get a restraining order to stop you, so don't push me."

We parted company and when they went to get dinner at the hospital cafeteria, I went to my office, needing to calm down a bit before I went back to Kate. On my way to the office wing, I saw a man pushing a small boy in a wheelchair and thought about Liam. In that moment, I made a decision that I knew I'd probably regret but I couldn't stop myself. I couldn't imagine not seeing Liam again so I went back to the children's ward and popped back into Liam's room after suiting up in a gown and mask. He was still asleep, as the oxygen hissed and the monitors hummed behind his bed. The light was low, and he looked so pale. So fragile.

It was my brother all over again, except this time, I'd get to witness it.

He woke briefly and sat up, looking a little bit better.

"Are you a doctor?"

I nodded and took his wrist to feel his pulse. "I'm Doctor Morgan. How are you doing, young man?"

"Okay I guess. Where's my mom?"

"She and your father are down at the cafeteria for supper. They'll be back soon."

He said nothing and looked up at me.

"Are you happy about finding a donor?" I asked, wanting to keep him talking.

He nodded, his face grim. "We were lucky. My mom said that the man was our only hope. I'm going to get radiation to kill all my bone marrow and then they'll give me new cells. Then I won't have cancer."

I nodded and we discussed the procedure for a few moments.

He was very brave, talking so matter of fact about the whole procedure, but children with cancer had to grow up so fast.

He yawned and I checked the clock on the wall. I'd already been in for ten minutes and didn't want to stay any longer.

"I'm sure glad you're getting your transplant," I said and squeezed his hand briefly. "You'll be feeling better in no time."

"Me, too," he said and nodded.

I left the room, my throat choked about not seeing him again. I went into the soiled linens room and removed my scrubs, and was just on my way out when I saw Chris coming down the hall toward me. I thought he and Maureen would be gone for a good half an hour but he must have come back for something.

"What the *fuck*..." Chris said when he saw me. "What were you doing in there?"

"I just wanted to see him one last time. Let it go."

I went out the door and down the stairs to the rotunda, hoping to escape a confrontation but no luck. Chris followed me, obviously not willing to let it go. He stopped me, grabbing onto my shoulder.

"Do we have to get a restraining order?"

I pulled away. "You're being unreasonable."

"Liam has enough to worry about without learning that the father he loves is not his biological father."

"It's the truth."

"The truth is," Chris said and stepped closer to me, "you're not the kind of father he should know about until he's old enough to handle the truth."

"What the fuck does that mean? I'm a neurosurgeon, a member of the faculty at the Columbia College of Medicine. I'm the head of the Liam Morgan Memorial Foundation. I'm Chairman—"

"We all know what you are," Chris said, his voice raised. "We also know about your involvement in less savory pursuits. I'm sure your employer would be interested to know it, too."

"Is that a threat?" I said, my face hot.

He moved even closer to me as if to intimidate me. "If you dare go back and see him again, it's a promise."

"Back off," I said and stepped away.

"No," he said and stepped closer. "*You* have to realize you won't ever be part of Liam's life. If we have to go to a lawyer to extinguish any parental rights, we will. We won't hesitate to bring up your S&M practices."

"I'm not into S&M," I said and clenched my fists.

"There are pictures," he said. "We won't hesitate to use them."

"What?" I frowned in disbelief. They had pictures?

"Yeah, that's right. We have pictures of your handiwork so stay the fuck away."

I pulled away, but he must have taken that as aggression and he swung at me, his fist connecting with my cheek.

I lost it. When I recovered, I swung at him, connected with his jaw, but my punch wasn't enough to knock him down.

Maureen came running up and stepped in between the two of us.

"Grow up, the two of you!" She kept us apart, and we both nursed our wounds and stared each other down. "Leave, Drake, or I'll call hospital security."

"I'm leaving," I said and held up my hands, turning away. With that, the two of them walked off, leaving me to rub my cheek where a nice abrasion was growing.

I went to my car and sat in it for a few moments, trying to get hold of myself.

Then I called up Dave Mills.

"Dave, I need to get drunk. Fast."

He didn't hesitate. "I'm your man."

WE MET at a pub in Chelsea, and downed shot after shot while I told him about my encounter with Chris.

"You should have broken a chair over his head," Dave said. "Knocked the bastard out."

"I probably would have caused a brain injury and then Liam would have an even bigger imbecile as a father."

"Then you should've kicked him in the balls," Dave suggested.

"If I could find them."

The evening went on more or less like that, until I was so drunk that I could barely stand up. We took a taxi home and I stumbled up into the apartment after midnight only to find that Kate was fast asleep.

Even in my drunken state, I didn't want to wake her up and have her see me like that—inebriated, pitiful. Instead, I took two aspirin and drank down a big glass of water and lay down as gingerly as possible on the bed beside her and promptly fell asleep.

MORNING CAME ALL TOO SOON. Kate woke me up when the sun was up, the light way too bright for me.

"Drake," she said. I turned over onto my back, a hand covering my eyes, and peered at her through my fingers. She leaned on her elbow, looking at me with an expression of concern on her pretty face, her green eyes wide.

"Ms. Bennet, what's going on in that mind of yours so early in the morning?"

I pulled my hand away and knew she'd see the bruise on my face from Chris's punch.

"Drake, what *happened*?" She examined me closely. "You're hurt."

"I got into an," I said and hesitated. "An altercation."

"What?"

"I don't want to talk about it."

Mercifully, Kate didn't push. I opened my eyes fully, blinking against the brightness of the morning light.

"Why didn't you wake me up when you got home?" she

asked, as she examined my bruise. "If I had known you were injured…"

"If you had known, you wouldn't have slept."

"What happened?"

I exhaled heavily. "Maureen and I had it out and I kind of lost it. Chris and I had a pushing match and I came out worse for the wear. Luckily, neither of us pressed charges. Then, I kind of lost myself for a few hours. When I came home, I was too drunk to even get undressed."

She frowned. "What do you mean, 'lost myself'?"

"I drank with Dave Mills. I believe he drank me under the proverbial table and had to bring me home in a taxi. I'm surprised I didn't wake you up."

"What happened to make you and Chris fight?"

I sighed. "I don't want to get into it. Suffice to say Maureen pretty much rejected my request to give Liam the photo of my dad."

"Oh, *Drake*…" She kissed me briefly. I said nothing, too tired to talk anymore. I turned over and she let me be.

WHILE I REMAINED on the bed, Kate had a shower. I fell back asleep for a while and when I did wake, Kate was elsewhere in the apartment, so I got up and had a quick shower myself. When I was finished, I went to the kitchen and poured myself a cup of fresh squeezed orange juice and sat at the island, looking out the window at the blue sky.

Kate handed me a cup of coffee without a word and I smiled at her, thankful that she was giving me space to recover but I knew I would have to tell her what happened in more detail.

I sighed heavily, thinking about the incident.

"Drake, tell me what happened."

I made a face and turned away, back to the window and the Manhattan skyline.

"Maureen didn't promise me anything except that she'd give the picture to Liam when he was eighteen."

"Why did she want you to come to the hospital?"

I said nothing for a moment, trying to gain control over myself for the thought of my time on the ward with Liam and what happened afterward was making me upset once more.

"She wanted me to see him," I said, my voice breaking. "In case he died before we left for Africa." I rubbed my forehead. "She also wanted it to be the last time I made contact with her or him until he was eighteen. She wants me to give the donation and fade into the background. I asked her if I could meet him, talk to him after, but she said no. She told me not to bother making contact with her or him and if I did," I said, my voice really low. "She said she'd get another restraining order."

"That's *horrible*," Kate said, her voice mortified, "especially since it wasn't you who made contact in the first place."

"I guess I shouldn't have expected anything more from her." I sat and stared out the window. "When they left for supper, I went back to Liam's room. I know the nurses and they looked the other way because they know I'm his biological father. I spoke with Liam. Told him I was a doctor and wanted to check in on him. He talked to me for a while about the whole procedure. He's such a strong little boy." I said nothing for a moment, overcome with emotion. "I was leaving when Chris came back for something and saw me. He confronted me, followed me out of the hospital and we had a scuffle outside in the parking lot."

"Oh Drake, I'm so *sorry...*"

I shook my head. "I was good enough when I might be a potential tissue match for Liam, but once I agreed to donate,

I'm back to being the evil ex-husband with perverted proclivities."

"Hardly perverted. You're mild compared to the Doms whose profiles I read on FetLife."

I rubbed my forehead. "You know that and I know that, but to Maureen, I'm the Devil's spawn. I *was* a jerk, Kate, not really knowing what I was doing, clumsy, demanding, but I wasn't nearly as kinked out as many Doms are. And I would never say anything to Liam about who and what I am to him. I just wanted to speak to him, hear his voice…"

Kate reached out and took my hand, squeezing it.

"I never thought she'd be so nasty to me, despite the divorce," I said, still hurting. "I was generous with her. I didn't fight her demands when we split. I was too devastated. She made me feel like a perverted monster. How she must hate me…"

"Your split with Maureen sounds like my split with Kurt, except it must have hurt much more since you two were actually married. Kurt and I were only together for a few months."

"It was hard." I turned back to her. "To be married for five years, to get that close, to become so used to having someone there all the time, and to have it go sour and fall apart." I shook my head. "I was so blind back then. So focused on my career, on my place in the world, I failed to work on my marriage. She had every right to fall out of love with me. Even hate me. It's a mistake I'll never make again."

"What mistake?" she asked softly. "Not pay attention to your relationship?"

I nodded. "I won't neglect you, Kate. If you ever feel the least neglected, let me know, for it won't be intentional. I want you to feel completely loved and cared for, the focus of my attention when I'm with you."

She smiled and leaned over to kiss me and I was overwhelmed with feelings of warmth for her.

"I want you to feel the same," she said. "I've never lived with a man before, so I don't really know what to expect, but if I ever fail to please you, if I ever neglect you, I want to know."

"Living with a man?" I said and grinned. "Let me give you some advice. Expect a *lot* of sex. Expect him to fall dead asleep soon afterwards. Expect him to watch you greedily all the time, like you're dessert and he can't wait to get to eat you. Or, at least, that's the way I feel when you're with me."

She smiled back, a gleam in her eye. "You can eat dessert whenever you want." She crawled onto my lap and wrapped her arms around my neck.

"*Mmm*, Ms. Bennet," I murmured against the skin on her neck. "I think you might seduce me with that coy look of yours, but I'm not in any shape for anything this morning."

"Of course not," she said. "Let's take it really easy today. I have to go back to the studio and apply the next coat of gesso, but otherwise, we should just stay home and recover."

I shook my head. "I have some work to do and will be busy all day."

"I can't talk you into taking the afternoon off? Even you deserve a vacation…"

"I don't think I can," I said. "Since I'm staying longer, I have finish up some work for our next shareholder meeting. Then I have to go in and get my first shot. The oncologist wants to do a peripheral blood stem cell harvest. I have to take growth factors that will increase the number of stem cells in my blood."

"The Filgrastim?" she said, her expression thoughtful.

I nodded. "I'll be taking it for four days before they do the harvest."

"I did some reading," she said, her brow furrowed with concern. "You won't be feeling well for a while?"

"Just mild bone pain. Nothing I won't be able to handle. Nothing worse than how you feel the day after a really hard workout at the gym." I smiled softly. "We'll have a nice quiet night together."

She hugged me more closely, and we remained in each other's embrace for a nice, long time. It was just what I needed at that moment and it felt wonderful.

CHAPTER 16

I DROPPED Kate off at the studio and went to the Corporation to deal with some business matters involving temporary transfer of management to my replacement on the board.

My next stop was at NYP to see Liam's oncologist and get my first shot of Filgrastim. After I was finished, I spent some time reviewing case files that I would consult on during my extended stay, and spoke on the phone with the physicians who were taking over my cases.

I received a text from Kate late in the afternoon, and texted her back that I'd be home by dinnertime. I hoped to spend a quiet evening with her on the couch, trying to recover from my fistfight and drunken stupor of the previous night.

I ARRIVED at the apartment to find Kate had dinner ready and we sat together at the dining room table and ate, talking about her day at the studio and my day at the hospital.

After we washed up, we made our way to the living room and stretched out together, warm in each other's arms, a selection of old music on the sound system. She ran a hand over my stomach, touching the bandage from my first injection.

"Will they give you another needle in your gut tomorrow?"

I nodded. "I'll be a real pin cushion when they're finished. But what I'm going through is nothing compared to what Liam's experiencing."

"What's happening to him?"

I sighed thinking of the whole procedure and how dangerous and at the same time life saving it was. "They have to give him drugs to destroy his bone marrow. Chemo-therapy and radiation."

"For how long?"

"Four to seven days, depending. By the time my donation is ready, he'll be ready to take it."

"When will you know if the transplant takes?"

"A couple of weeks. Maureen said she'd keep me updated and I have my own contacts in the hospital, so I should know by the end of the month if his body is tolerating the new stem cells and the transplant has been successful." I hesitated, wanting to gauge her feelings about delaying our trip. "Do you mind waiting? I know you withdrew from the graduate program, thinking that we'd be in Africa by now."

"I don't mind waiting at all," she replied, her voice earnest. "I want to be with you, wherever that is."

"Thank you," I said and kissed the top of her head. It was a lot to ask of someone who barely knew me. Considering my secret life as a Dominant in the BDSM lifestyle, I was surprised she was so willing to give it all up for me.

"Life's too short to worry about a few months when something as important as this comes up," she said, staring into my eyes, her expression serious. "Columbia will still be here when I get back. My scholarship's safe as long as I start up again at the end of my leave. Besides, I'm so happy to be painting again."

I pulled her even closer. "I don't want you regretting being with me. When we come back, I'll make sure not to distract you from finishing your Masters. Or focusing on your art. Whatever makes you happy."

"I won't regret this," she said, her voice firm. "I'm *so* looking forward to Africa and that surprises me, considering my history. I *want* to go to Kenya, go on safari, see the positive things you've described. I want to wash away the bad memories from Mangaize."

"I want you to see it," I said and stroked her cheek. "I want the ghosts of the camps to be chased away by good things."

She snuggled more closely in my arms.

"I think I'll sneak in before Liam gets the transplant. Maybe when he's sleeping, so I can check on him. As his biological father, I think I have the right."

Kate didn't say anything in reply as if she didn't approve. Then she took in a deep breath.

"Drake, there's something I have to tell you."

I frowned. "What?"

"Maureen called. She told me that she was informing the staff at the hospital not to allow you to visit Liam and if you did, they were instructed to call the police."

A shock went through me and I sat up, pulling her up with me.

"Fucking Christ," I said, adrenaline making my heart pound. "She actually said staff would call the *police* if I went to the ward again?"

I raked my fingers through my hair, unable to believe how much Maureen must hate me. I held my head in my hands, trying to calm down.

"I'm sorry," she said and stroked my back. "She said you punched Chris."

I glanced at her and shook my head. "Yeah I *punched* the *sonofabitch* after he punched me. He said he didn't want a pervert anywhere near his son as long as Liam was a minor. As if I'd be some bad influence on Liam. *Christ*," I said and got up, going to look out the window. "All I wanted was to see him and speak with him, give him the photograph of his grandfather. I don't care *what* they told Liam—say it's some distant uncle on someone's side. Let him know he had a relative who was heroic and maybe one day tell him the truth about me. But no. So, yeah, when he punched me, I *popped* the bastard a good one in return."

Kate stood and said nothing and I knew she was shocked to see me so angry. I had always kept my emotions in check when around her. It was my thing—control. I didn't want to change that perception in her mind so I took in a deep breath and pulled her into my arms.

"I'm fine," I said and exhaled heavily. "I got the message. I won't go in again to see Liam."

She squeezed me hard at that, her expression so serious, so much empathy for me in her eyes.

We went to bed soon after that, and I tossed and turned, unable to sleep, thoughts of Liam and Chris and Maureen dogging me.

WE BOTH KEPT busy over the next few days.

Kate went to her studio each morning while I went to the hospital for my shots and I kept busy so she could stay at the studio as long as her heart desired.

I wasn't up for much because of the effects of the Filgrastim, my bones aching as they pumped out more stem cells into my bloodstream.

By the fourth day of my shots, I felt like an old man and spent the afternoon and evening lying on the couch with a blanket covering me, drinking hot tea and eating Kate's homemade scones with jam. She mothered me, which was something I wasn't very used to given my childhood.

I ate it up like it was candy.

THE DAY of my procedure came and I woke up with a nasty headache.

Kate snuggled against my back. "How are you?" she whispered, her arms slipping gingerly around me.

"As much as I'm glad I'm able to do this," I said with a moan. "I'll be really happy to get rid of this headache."

She stroked my back. "How long before you start feeling back to normal?"

I rolled over and faced her. "A few days. It's really nothing. Just a few aches and a headache. Nothing more than what I'd get after a really intense workout or a flu."

I leaned down and kissed her and then rolled slowly out of the bed, sitting on the edge for a moment, rubbing my head. I went to the bathroom and had a pee and then started the shower.

"You not going to join me?" I said from the bathroom.

"No, you go ahead without me," she said. "I'll have one later."

The hot spray woke me up, taking away the fuzz in my brain and I hummed to myself as I washed, glad that the day had come and soon I'd be feeling better.

I finished and wrapped a towel around my waist, then stood in front of my closet, sorting through my shirts and suits.

Kate lay on the bed and watched me dress. I felt her eyes on me, and looked forward to reestablishing our sexual relationship, which had been on hold for the past week.

"What is going on in that mind of yours, Ms. Bennet? You're being far too quiet."

She smiled. "I was thinking how nice your ass is and how I intend to touch it and run my hands all over your body when you're feeling up to sex."

I pulled on my shirt and fastened the cuffs and buttons, watching her while I did.

When I was done, I went to the bed and leaned over her. "I'm sorry we've been so chaste the last few days. I'll make it up to you."

"You don't have to make anything up," she said, pushing a hank of wet hair behind my ear. "I understand. Besides, I'm under the weather, too."

"I didn't let you get away with that excuse, so technically, you shouldn't have let me, but I tell you what," I said stroked her cheek. "When I feel better, you can give me a nice massage and pretend you're my favorite harem girl."

"Sounds perfect," she said. "Except, maybe your *only* harem girl, because you've given up all the others, sending them away because they can't satisfy you any longer. Only me."

I smiled and then kissed her. "Only you."

Then I stood up and finished dressing.

"How long will the procedure take?" she asked from the bed.

"About six hours, depending on how fast they can process my blood. I should be home later in the afternoon."

"You're wonderful for doing this."

"He's my son," I said, shaking my head. "How could I say no?"

She didn't say anything but when I glanced at her, I saw her eyes were brimming. I went back and leaned over her once more. "I love you."

"I love you," she whispered, cupping my cheek. "You sure

you don't want me to come with you? I'd be more than happy to if you want company."

I shook my head. "No. I'll have lots of company. There are nurses who stay with you the whole time. Besides, it's really early and you need to sleep some more. I know this is your heavy day. You stay in bed and take some Advil. Don't even bother to go into the studio. Later, we'll have a nice dinner delivered here and drink some wine for your cramps."

"Will you be okay driving?"

"I'll take a taxi there and back."

I bent down one last time and kissed her, unable to ever get enough of her. Then, I left her on the bed with a promise to return as soon as the procedure was over.

I WENT TO NYP, to the Weill Cornell Medical College, which ran New York Presbyterian's stem cell and bone marrow transplant program and met with the apheresis team of nurses who would do the transplant.

The nurses were all very sweet and doted over me, knowing that I was doing the donation for my son, so I was treated extremely well the entire time. They found a separate space for me so I would be alone, hooked me up to the apheresis machine via an intravenous catheter, and ran my blood through the machine to harvest the peripheral stem cells. The whole process took only four hours and because Liam was so young and small, they were pretty sure I wouldn't have to do another donation and so I was discharged home once the procedure was complete.

I arrived mid-afternoon and by the time I got in the door, I was exhausted.

"How are you feeling? You look tired," Kate said as she came to help me, hanging up my coat while I removed my boots.

"I feel like total and complete crap. I need to lie down for a while."

After she hung up my coat, she took my jacket and hung it up, then followed me into the bedroom to watch while I undressed.

"Can you bring me some tea?" I asked once I was in my sweats and a t-shirt.

"Sure. Do you need some food?"

"I ate after the donation, but I feel pretty weak so I'm done for the day."

I went to the living room and crashed on the couch, pulling the soft wool blanket over me, my head on the pillow.

She bent down and kissed me, stroking hair from my face. "What kind of tea?"

"Whatever you want. And some of those scones, too, now that you mention it."

She smiled and went to the kitchen. I decided I wanted to watch some news and switched on the television, turning to CNN.

When Kate returned, she set the tray on the coffee table and sat on the couch beside me. She babied me, fixing a scone and pouring sugar in my tea the way I liked. When she handed me the plate with the scone on it, I sat up a little and bit into it hungrily.

"Mmm," I said. "These are so good."

We ate our scones and drank our tea in silence, watching the news. When I was finished my scone, I took a big slurp of tea, sighing in contentment.

"I'm sorry I'm not much good today. I know I promised you a scene and that it never happened. It will."

"No worries," she said, shrugging. "We have time for that. Considering your noble deed, you deserve to be waited on. I'm happy to do it."

I put my cup down and nestled back into the pillows and

under the cover. "I'm exhausted. I hope you don't mind if I sleep for a while."

"Of course not."

I closed my eyes and drifted off to sleep.

I SLEPT through the evening and Kate didn't even wake me for supper, letting me rest until I woke up on my own around nine at night. She brought me some supper of fish and salad, and I lay on the couch with her for a while, and together we watched a show on the National Geographic channel.

Then it was to bed for another eight hours of sleep. I had never slept so long before, outside of having the flu and sleeping for almost sixteen hours straight once. The sleep was revitalizing and the next day I was eager to call the hospital and see whether Liam had his transplant procedure yet.

I spoke with the nurse heading up his care team and was pleased that he received the transplant almost immediately. They coordinated the donation and transplant so they could do the two procedures as close as possible. All that was left was the wait to see whether the transplant took.

I gradually recovered over the next few days and kept busy at the Foundation or Corporation. After so many years in medical school and in specialist training and then in practice, I was used to being extra busy. I couldn't stand to lie around too much with nothing to do, so I hung around a bit at the hospital, feeling like I was at least useful.

Kate spent her time at the studio working on her canvas. In this way, the two of us kept to as normal a schedule as possible while we waited for news of Liam's transplant.

In truth, I felt completely distracted by the whole business of discovering I had a son and that he was sick. My run in with Maureen and Chris only served to remind me of how poorly I had managed my marriage and relationship with Maureen. I had no idea she was having an affair, busy as I had been running between the hospital, Mersey and my work with Doctors Without Borders.

ONE MORNING, Kate woke up earlier than usual and crept back into bed with me, slipping her arms around me. She kissed my shoulder and lay there, her hand resting on my abdomen. I knew Kate was feeling deprived for we hadn't had sex since before the transplant.

I didn't know why I felt no desire, but I didn't. It was as if the sexual part of me shut off during that time. I read up on the side effects of the medication, but there was nothing about any decline in sexual desire.

Whatever the case, I felt too distracted, too sad, to think about sex. I didn't feel like talking about my lack of desire either, even though I had the sense that Kate was frustrated.

I gently moved her arm from around my waist and slipped out of bed, hoping that she wouldn't push because I couldn't face it. Not then. Most men would probably look to sex to distract themselves from their problems, but for me, sex had never been a distraction.

I went to the bathroom and started a shower, glad to feel the hot sting of the stream of water on my face. I stood and luxuriated in the steamy enclosure, when I realized that Kate and entered and was standing beside me.

I smiled, but I felt wary and hoped she wouldn't try to initiate anything.

"Ms. Bennet, why are you up so early?"

"I'm all bright-eyed and bushy-tailed this morning for some reason," she said and stepped a bit closer to me, letting the water wash over her. She had to know how much I loved shower sex, and seeing her deliciously ripe body all wet and sudsy.

"Excuse me," she said and leaned in front of me to get to the soap dispenser. She lathered her hair, the suds slipping down over her body, her breasts and between her thighs. Then she began to wash herself, and of course, I couldn't help but watch.

When she bent down to wash her feet, her ass on display for me, I groaned.

"*Kate...*" I said. "What are you up to? Are you trying to seduce me?"

"I'm *trying* to have a shower."

When she started to rinse off her hair, I leaned over her, my hands on the wall on either side of her, so that she was confined against the shower wall.

"*Katherine...*"

She said nothing but glanced down at my throbbing erection.

"What are you *doing*?" I said again, wanting her to admit she was trying to seduce me.

She blinked several times, all innocent. She knew the rules. I decided when we would have sex and how.

She finally closed her eyes. "I'm sorry. It's just that," she said and shrugged her shoulder, looking away guiltily.

"It's just that *what*?"

She said nothing, merely looked back at me, searching my face as if looking for a sign of sympathy or tolerance on my part.

"I'm... *horny*."

I smiled at that. "Why Ms. *Bennet*, I do believe you've been trying to seduce me with your nice wet body and soapy hands lathering your nether regions."

"My *nether* regions?" she smiled up at me, acting deliberately coy.

"May I remind you that we have an agreement?"

"I *know* we do but we agreed to be spontaneous some-times, and you're obviously hard and, well. I *thought*..."

"When it comes to sex," I said, my tone pedantic, "it's not your place to think, *Katherine*. That's my job. But I'm glad you finally told me why you're being deliberately disobedient, trying to seduce me."

"You are?" she said, and I knew from her expression that she was hoping she'd seduce me and I'd be unable to resist.

"Yes," I said and moved a bit closer. "That way I'll know why I'm spanking you."

She frowned and closed her eyes. "Drake, I *need* you." She opened her eyes and stared into mine, unashamed. "Either that, or let me masturbate."

I shook my head. "No," I said. "We'll do something later this afternoon. I haven't decided what just yet, but I want you nice and wet and desperate when the time comes."

"I'm nice and wet and desperate right *now*," she said in frustration.

"I know it's been a while, but I've been under the weather. You can wait."

Then she turned and ducked under my arm, leaving the shower, wrapping a towel around herself. I followed and pulled a towel around my hips and my still-erect cock.

"No one said it would be easy, Kate."

She glared at me. "It doesn't make sense. I'm horny and you're hard. We should just ... *fuck*. It's been almost a week."

"I don't want to *just fuck*. That's an end to it, *Katherine*," I said, wanting to stop this before it got too meaningful. I just couldn't do it at that moment but Kate couldn't seem to understand that I wasn't a stud service.

She sighed and turned away, heading to her dresser drawers to pick out some clothes for the day. I followed her and stood behind her.

"How does it feel?"

She pulled a drawer open a bit too roughly and it almost fell out. "You know very well how it feels."

"No, I *don't*," I said. "I don't have a delicious little woman's body like you. Tell me. Close your eyes and describe how your body feels."

She stopped what she was doing and closed her eyes. I went around to watch her, wanting to know how she felt.

"Butterflies in my stomach," she said. "My body aches, everything feels swollen. It's throbbing a bit, like a heartbeat. I feel a little breathless. I'm wet and I feel like I want to squeeze my thighs together. Rub my clit." She opened her eyes. "I want your cock inside of me."

I leaned against the dresser, and watched her.

"If I was to fuck you now," I said, aroused in spite of everything, but wanting to assert control, "it would be over in about two minutes. You'd orgasm and then two minutes later, I would and it would be finished."

She nodded. "*That* would be a relief. I could get on with my day."

"You make sex sound like a simple bodily function," I said, grinning briefly. "Sex between us is more than that, Kate. It should be special."

She sighed. "You're trying to keep the potatoes and gravy separate on the plate, Drake."

When she turned away, I grabbed her arm and stopped her, pulling her back to face me once more.

"*Kate*," I said. "You're here with me all the time now, pretty much every hour of the day when we're both free. What more do you need?"

"I'm not with you very long. You keep extremely busy, even now when you aren't working as a surgeon. Even when you don't *have* to be away. I'm afraid that you're trying to avoid me."

She pulled her arm out of my grip and grabbed her clothes, dressing quickly while I stood by helpless.

"I'm not the only one who's busy," I said. "You spend every day at the studio and do I complain? *Why* would I try to avoid you?"

She shook her head as she dressed. "I don't know. You're the one with an undergraduate degree in psychology. Your life's getting too messy and out of control? You're afraid of being hurt again?"

"You're not afraid of being hurt?"

She shook her head. "I'm more afraid of feeling *nothing*. No love. No pain. *Nothing* feels like," she said. "Like death. Like the people I saw in the camps, skeletons, barely alive but living despite everything, their eyes huge, blank. Even pain is better." She came to me and stared up into my eyes. "I want to *feel*, Drake. Everything, good and bad. It was like I couldn't feel when I was depressed. *Nothing*. That's what *I'm* afraid of."

She sighed and pulled her sweater over her head. "You're here with me but you still need to keep it all separate. Now, you do it all with me present. But none of it really mixes. It's like you're keeping that part of yourself separate, not emotionally involved in sex, so that it's pure. You can control it. Protect yourself. It means you can never get really close to me."

I frowned and rubbed my forehead. "I don't understand. What more do you want from me? We sleep together. We eat together. We fuck. A *lot*."

"Not lately."

"I have a good reason," I said, hurt that she wasn't giving me the space I needed, considering everything that had happened.

She shook her head as if she realized she was being insensitive. "I'm sorry, that was wrong of me. Of course you have a good reason. But I can't be the one who initiates. Why? Does it threaten you that I have desire outside of your actions?"

"No, of course not. I *know* you do. But submission requires that you turn over your desires and choices to me. It frees you so that you no longer feel responsible for your desire or when we have sex. That's what submissives crave."

"I want it spontaneous sometimes," she said, her voice frustrated. "Whenever either of us feels a need, we fuck. I also want bondage and dominance. I love it. But can't we mix it up a bit? What's wrong with that?"

"I'm a Dominant," I said firmly. "You knew that when we started this." I stood there, hands on hips. "For God's sake, Kate. That's what you were looking for when you found Lara. Now, it seems as though you don't really want it. You want a vanilla relationship with me, with a bit of bondage and kink thrown in when *you* decide you want it. Submission doesn't work like that."

"You were a lot more spontaneous when we were first together at 8th Avenue. What happened?" She put her hands on my chest and stared up into my eyes. "Things have changed since Maureen came here and you learned about Liam."

"Kate, I'm a *Dominant*," I said again. "I need control. We've been over this." I studied her face. "Are you unhappy with me?"

She sighed heavily. "I *love* you, Drake but you told me to tell you if I felt neglected. Well, I feel neglected."

I stared at her. "I understand, but I'm not fucking you now," I said, forcing myself to be calm. "You'll have to wait."

"Fine," she said and pulled on her socks. She went to the closet and grabbed her things. Then she picked up her bag and went to the door.

"Where are you going?" I asked, standing in the entryway, watching her, feeling completely helpless and out of control.

"Outside to work off some of this unresolved sexual tension. Outside of sex, I'm a free agent, Drake. I'm not submissive. I can do whatever I please. I'm going to the studio. Then, I might go to my parents. I might go to an art gallery. Who knows?"

"Don't do this, Kate. Don't leave angry."

"See you *later*," she said, slamming the door behind her.

I was left alone in my apartment, the way I had been for five years since Maureen left me.

Was I already blowing it with Kate?

CHAPTER 17

WHEN KATE SLAMMED the door and left me alone, it really threw a damper over my morning. As soon as Kate left, I thought of Lara. I needed someone to talk to and Lara was the only person I knew who understood me. There really was no one I could talk to about Kate except for Lara so once more I found myself calling her up to ask for advice.

"Problems in paradise?" she said in her droll way. "Shouldn't you be on your way to Africa?"

"We haven't even left yet," I said. "We won't be at least until the end of February. Maybe later, depending."

"Depending on what?" she asked, and I could tell she finally was giving me her undivided attention. Until then, she sounded a bit distracted, probably clearing cases off her desk.

I sighed. "You won't believe what's happened in the last few days."

"Try me."

I took in a breath. "I have a son."

There was a moment of silence. "What?" she said, her voice rising.

"Maureen was pregnant with my child when she moved

185

to California. She thought it was her new boyfriend's. She hoped it was his, but the boy is mine."

"A boy? How do you know he's yours? Jesus, Drake…"

"I know. Total shock. I know he's mine because she had her husband tested and he wasn't related to the boy. Whose name is Liam, by the way. He's five years old and dying of leukemia. I just went through a round of treatment so I could give him a stem cell donation."

"Wait, *what?*" she said. "Whoa, Drake. Slow down. He's got leukemia? The same as your brother? The one who died before you were born?"

"The same. I passed it to him."

"Christ. And Maureen never bothered to tell you he was yours all these years?"

"She honestly didn't know or didn't want to know. It wasn't until they tested Chris as a possible stem cell donor that they learned the truth. You can imagine their shock."

"So the slut was fucking the two of you."

"*Lara…*"

"Drake, she was a total bitch to you, and was having an affair," Lara said, her voice hard. "Out of the blue she tells you she's leaving and when you dare to try to talk to her, stop her from leaving, she gets a temporary restraining order. Don't tell me she isn't a fucking bitch."

I smiled at the vehemence of Lara's hatred of Maureen. Lara had never liked Maureen when they met before we married. Then Lara and I lost touch. When Maureen left, we reconnected when I reached out to her for help.

"Okay. She's a bitch. Compared with Kate, she's the Wicked Witch of the West."

"Speaking of Kate, how's she taking all this?"

I shook my head, so glad that Kate was there for me, even if she wasn't there for me at that precise moment.

"She's fantastic. Like a rock about it."

"That's great. I knew she'd be good for you. So tell me about Liam?"

I described him to her, talked about meeting him and seeing how frail he was. I even told her about the fistfight with Chris.

"Holy crap, Drake. You should have called me sooner. I can do something to help you get access to Liam if you want."

"No, that's all right. I don't want to intrude. Chris looks like a good father and I don't want to confuse Liam. They have enough to worry about without me barging in on their lives."

"They didn't think twice about barging in on yours..."

"Lara, it was to save Liam's life," I said, surprised that she couldn't understand. "Of course, they had to contact me."

"So, why did you call me? What's up, beside having a son, who has leukemia, doing a stem cell donation and delaying your trip to Africa? Oh, and getting into a fight with your ex's husband..."

I could imagine her smile as she sat at her huge mahogany desk in her office.

"I called you because of Kate."

There was a pause. "I thought you said everything was good with her..."

I sighed. "Things are wonderful, except she became quite upset this morning after I wouldn't have sex with her. She likes sex in the morning, but I wanted to wait until this evening when we could do a full scene. She actually slammed the door when she left the apartment."

I heard her chuckle.

"It's not funny, Lara. Seriously. I'm having problems maintaining the proper Dom / sub relationship with her when it comes to sex."

"Why?"

I thought about our relationship. I was ecstatic with Kate,

but felt out of control. "We're really sexually compatible, but she doesn't quite understand that she doesn't get to make decisions when it comes to sex."

"Have you *shown* her this? I mean, in your behavior with her? You have to be firm. If you give in, she'll learn she can push you. Twist you around her finger. That won't make a sub happy and soon she'll be looking for someone who will be strong with her."

I nodded to myself at that. "She's pretty good overall. But this morning didn't go well."

"What are you afraid of?" she said. "I mean, what's keeping you from enforcing things with her?"

I shrugged. "I don't want to scare her off…"

"Drake's in love…" she said and I could hear the tease in her voice. "Drake, I shouldn't have to tell you this, but not showing your dominance with her is more likely to drive her away than if you do. She wants you to take control or she wouldn't be interested in D/s. Period. End of story. Show her you love her and indulge her outside of sex. Be firm when it comes to sex."

"You're right, of course." I would have given myself the same advice. I guess I just wanted to hear it from Lara, to reinforce what I already knew to be true.

"Thanks, Lara. I know you're right."

"I am. You already knew this. Now, go and take what you want. That's how you'll give Kate what she needs."

ALTHOUGH I FELT BETTER after speaking with Lara, I went through the motions of my morning with very little enthusiasm. It wasn't just that Kate expressed her dissatisfaction with me. It was everything. Maureen's return, Liam's existence and illness, Dawn's meddling, Chris's disrespectful treatment of Kate, my fight with him…

All of it conspired to make me feel particularly down.

I dragged myself to the hospital to read over patient files and check in on a few stragglers who were still recovering on the main surgical ward. I even called up Ken to see how he was doing. All of it meant to keep busy until Kate calmed down and contacted me. I probably should have contacted her first, but I wanted to give her the space to decide for herself to text or call me.

Later that afternoon, while I was sitting in my office reading a paper I was working on with a colleague, my cell chimed.

A message from Kate:

I'M SORRY, Drake. Please don't be mad at me. I was being a spoiled child. Forgive me? It's just that sometimes, I have so much desire for you, I forget how to submit.

I SAT and tried to compose a response that would both satisfy her and yet didn't give in or apologize. As Lara said, Kate wanted me to be a Dom, but that wasn't something that I could turn off and on at will like a light switch.

Sexually, I was a Dom all the time. Even when I tried to yield power, I topped from the bottom.

Finally satisfied with my message, I pressed send.

OF COURSE I'm not mad at you. There's nothing to forgive. I always want you to be completely honest with me, even when it might be something painful for me to hear. I know submission isn't easy. If it were too easy, you'd grow bored.

I LOVE YOU.

I DIDN'T RECEIVE a response so I got in the car and drove to the Foundation. I hung around and talked with Dave about Liam and the delay in my plans for Africa. Finally, I received a response from Kate

I LOVE YOU.

THAT MADE ME HAPPY, a sensation of warmth spreading through my chest. When Dave and I were finished discussing project plans, I sent Kate another message.

I'M COMING home in an hour, Katherine. I want you naked, wearing your garters and stockings, kneeling by my bed. Use the blindfold in my closet. I want you to think of all the things I'm going to do to you. I want you wet and ready, waiting for me. I'll call and let the phone ring twice before hanging up. That will be the signal that I'm almost there. You should be ready for me, nice and wet and submissive when I arrive.

I KNEW that Kate wanted to do a full scene like the one in my letters to my subs. I had delayed giving it to her because I wanted her to be ready to experience submission fully and completely with as little hesitation as possible. I had to push her boundaries and still have her yield power to me voluntarily. She had to try things she might not think she'd like, so I could show her that they could be enjoyable.

I had about an hour left before I could leave as I was

meeting with the accountant to go over the funding for various campaigns in Africa before I left. Waiting an hour to be with Kate was going to be very difficult, especially with a semi straining against my pants. I had to focus extremely carefully on the numbers so that I was able to listen to him talk funding and actually hear what he had to say instead of thinking of the creamy soft curves of one naked and submissive Katherine McDermott.

Finally, I was able to leave the Foundation and take the car to my apartment in Chelsea to pick up a few items I'd need for our scene. Then, I drove to the apartment on 8th Avenue and to Kate.

I HAD everything planned out including how I'd approach her. I was going to ply her with vodka to loosen her up enough so that she'd relax. She was usually wound up tight, and always needed something to loosen her up, which was why bondage worked so well with her. She needed to lose total control in order to relax.

I turned the key in the lock and listened when I stepped into the apartment. There was no music, just the soft sounds of traffic coming in from under an open window.

I removed my boots and coat and went to the bedroom to check and see if she was in proper position. There she was, kneeling on a pillow beside the bed as I commanded, a scarf around her eyes, naked except for her garters and hose. Her full breasts jutted forward because her hands were clasped behind her back, her nipples erect in the cool air.

My cock thickened at the sight of her, a delicious ache building in my groin, and I couldn't wait to enjoy her body and mind as I took her in our scene.

I went to the refrigerator for the chilled bottle of Anisovaya and brought two glasses with me to the bedroom. I placed them on the dresser and then began to undress, stripping off my clothes and watching Kate while I did, enjoying her naked beauty.

I went to stand beside her and stroked her head and when I touched her, she parted her lips.

"Now remember your safewords, Katherine," I said. "Yellow is for when you need me to slow down and red stops everything. Do you understand?"

"Yes," she said. "I won't need either one, Master."

"I don't expect you will, but just in case, I want you to feel completely safe. Now, open your mouth wider," I said. "I've got some Anisovaya for you."

She took the glass from my hands and drank it down. I kissed her as quickly as I could, wanting to taste it on her tongue. When I sucking her tongue into my mouth, she murmured in response, her tiny whimper sending a jolt of lust through me. I pulled away and stroked her cheek with my fingers.

"Have some more," I said and poured another shot, then placed it in her hands. She frowned, but didn't argue, drinking down the liquor.

Then I slipped a finger into her mouth. She sucked on it, her tongue rolling around the tip the way it would around the head of my cock.

"Good *girl*," I said and took the shot glass out of her hand. "Open wider."

When she complied, I placed the tip of my cock against her lips. She licked, tasting my fluid, then opening wider to accept the entire head. She sucked and licked and I groaned in response.

"Take as much as you can," I said, my voice low.

When I pressed a bit too hard she gagged, so I withdrew a bit before beginning a slow gentle thrust in and out, fucking her mouth, one hand holding the back of her head to guide her and take more control.

Finally, I withdrew slowly and she waited for what would happen next.

"Have more," I said, handing her another shot of Aniso-vaya. She drank that down and licked her lips when a bit spilled down her chin.

"You're getting me drunk, Master?" she said, smiling.

"Shh," I said and put a finger against her lips. "A good submissive just submits, Katherine. She doesn't question."

She nodded without speaking.

I took the shot glass and lifted her up, pulling her into my arms and kissing her deeply. I ground my erection hard against her belly and tweaked a nipple between my finger and thumb, eliciting a groan from her.

She stumbled against me, so I pulled her over to the bed and sat on the edge. I directed her between my spread thighs and squeezed and stroked her lush breasts while I sucked her nipples to hardness. In return, she gasped and writhed when I ran my teeth over each one, biting down just hard enough to almost hurt but not quite, then I sucked each one softly.

"Are you nice and wet for me, Katherine?"

"Yes, Master," she said, her voice wavering.

I slid my fingers between her labia, slipping them into her body, my thumb pressing against her clit. She was nice and wet, her silky warm folds inviting. I could barely wait to push myself inside of her, but I would. I had much planned for her and wanted to prolong each step.

I left her standing by the bed and retrieved a collection of leather strips that I used to bind my submissives. When I returned, I began to wrap them around her, under her arms and around her breasts and soon, each breast was bound, squeezed, her nipples hard points. I sucked each nipple while my hands caressed each plump breast. Then, I wound the strips of leather around her waist and down over her hips and belly, lacing them between her thighs on either side of her labia.

"Lie on the bed with your hands above your head." I helped her onto the bed and cuffed each wrist to the bed frame. "Spread your legs, wide, and rest them on the edge of the bed."

When she complied, I wove leather strips around her thighs and cuffed each ankle to a spreader bar. I had never used one on her before, so it would be a night of firsts.

She was completely immobile, bound, blindfolded and totally under my control. Her body and mind went into subspace. I could actually see the change in her when it happened, her body totally relaxing.

I bent down between her thighs and covered her pussy with my mouth, stroking her clit with my tongue. She groaned and arched her back.

"Oh, God, *Master*…"

"You're so wet and so ready, Katherine," I said when I pulled away. "But you're going to have to wait." Then I bent her knees and took a tube of lubricant. I dripped it on her and as soon as she felt it, she tensed, inhaling loudly.

"*Relax*, Katherine," I said. "Do you trust me?"

She said nothing for a moment, and I knew she was fighting with herself. She wanted to resist out of fear of anal play, but she also wanted to please me.

"I said, do you *trust* me, Katherine?"

"Yes. But I'm afraid—"

"Shh," I said and lay on top of her, my body between her spread thighs, my erection jutting against her belly. I kissed her, warmly, deeply, my hand cupping her cheek. "You only need four words. Yes, Master, yellow and red. Do you understand?"

"Yes, Master."

"Do you believe that I love you?"

"Yes, Master," she said immediately.

"Do you trust me to know how far and how fast to go?"

At that, she hesitated. "When I did it before, it felt like I had a knife inside of me."

I embraced her, kissing her tenderly. "My poor sweet Katherine," I whispered. "I promise you when I do, you'll feel pleasure. Do you trust me to know how and when?"

She nodded. "It's just that I'm still so scared..."

"I know. That's why you have to trust me to know when you're ready."

I kissed her once more, touching her tenderly until she relaxed a bit. I then aroused her, stimulating her with my fingers and mouth until she was breathing fast, her body trembling. I knew that now was the time to introduce the dildo, get her used to it so that it wouldn't distract her later.

I drizzled more lubricant on her and then slipped the dildo inside of her an inch or so while I continued to stroke her clit with my thumb. She groaned and wriggled under my touch.

I slid the dildo in a bit farther, stroking in and out slowly while rubbing her clit until she moaned once more.

"Master, I *think*..."

"Good girl," I said in reply, withdrawing the dildo. Then, I pushed her knees up even higher and began to stimulate her, my finger circling her anus, the tip slipping inside to open her, get her to relax. When I felt she was ready, I pressed the lubricated plug against her and immediately, she tensed.

"*Relax*, Katherine."

In response, she took in a deep breath and blew it out as I had instructed before. Finally, I slipped in the dildo once more so that she had both the plug and dildo inside while I stroked her clit with my fingers. In this way, I built her up to the point of orgasm, watching her body and breathing carefully to judge when to pull back. I wanted to have her so ready that she couldn't resist. When I had built her up several times, I withdrew the dildo and plug, and flipped her quickly over onto her knees, removing the cuffs from her ankles to allow her to spread her legs wide.

I stroked her clit and then slipped a lubed finger inside her and once more she tensed.

"Shh, Katherine," I whispered, my finger still inside her. When I tried to insert two fingers, she gasped.

"*Master*, I—" but I leaned down and kissed her shoulder, both my fingers inside of her, slipping easily past her resistance, moving slowly in a circle to loosen her even more. I didn't stop stimulating her clit, hoping to overwhelm her senses with pleasure so she'd focus on that instead.

When I thought she was ready, when I heard her breathing hard once more, felt her tremble, I withdrew my fingers and replaced them with my erection, slipping the tip easily past her entrance.

"*Relax*, Katherine," I said. I added more lubricant and pushed slowly inside her a bit deeper, meeting more resistance. "Exhale. Blow out your breath."

She did without protest, and I was almost all the way inside.

"It's *too much*..." she said with a gasp.

I pulled back but didn't withdraw completely. Instead, I added more lube and pushed more slowly until I was all the way inside.

"Drake, *please*, I don't want this," she said, her voice pleading. "I don't know if I can do this,"

"You already *have*," I replied, and she was so tight, it felt incredible.

She sucked in a breath. "You're inside of me?"

"Yes," I said. "*All* of me."

I didn't move for a moment, wanting her to adjust. She

relaxed a little beneath me, and so I began once more to stroke my fingers over her clit without moving. When she pressed against my fingers, I knew she was ready.

"Good *girl*," I whispered. "So *good…*"

I began to move very slowly while I stroked her, and each inch of her tightness made me ache with need. I had to use every ounce of my control not to thrust harder, faster for she was so tight. The thought I had penetrated her completely aroused me even more.

"Oh, *God*, you feel so good, so *tight*," I said and groaned, my lips at her shoulder. "Tell me when you're going to come.

I held back as much as possible, slowly withdrawing and gently thrusting, my fingers on her clit. Soon, I felt her body tense, her breathing hitch.

"Oh, *God…*" she gasped, *"Oh, ohhh, ohhh."* Her body spasmed around my cock, clenching around it. I stopped and enjoyed the sensation.

When I felt her orgasm had waned, I kissed her shoulder and then turned her face to the side and kissed her mouth. When our kiss ended, I began thrusting again and I was so close, so aroused, that I came within moments, my body shuddering as I ejaculated.

"Fuck, fuck, *fuck…. Kate…*"

Kate collapsed onto the bed with me on top of her, still deep inside, still shuddering with pleasure. When I was finished, I lay still and gasped for breath, my orgasm so powerful that I needed a moment to recover. I kissed her neck and her shoulder, my pleasure intense, my love for her overwhelming.

I rose up and withdrew slowly, watching with my hands on her ass, spreading her cheeks so I could watch my semen seep out of her body.

I caught her smile before she could turn her head away.

She was amused at my kink. I sighed in mock frustration and lay back on top of her, kissing her cheek.

"*Katherine*, how can I be expected to stay in proper Dom headspace when my sub is so easily given to mirth?"

"Sorry," she said. "It's just that—"

I bent down once more, turning her face to me and kissed her to silence her, but I could barely stop from grinning myself.

"You make me so happy," I whispered. Then I kissed her neck, her shoulder, her cheek. "Stay here, my love."

I pulled away finally, kissing her shoulder and went to the bathroom. After I washed myself off, I ran a clean washcloth under the hot tap so I could provide her with aftercare. I returned to the bed and unfastened the cuffs around her wrists, then removed all traces of lube and semen from her body because I knew she'd be squeamish.

"I would have liked to have had a photographer here, you looked so delicious lying there all bound and wet."

When I was satisfied that she was clean, I stood her up and removed the blindfold and turned her around, untying the leather bindings, one by one. They left faint red lines crisscrossing her flesh, around her breasts and between her thighs.

"You look absolutely well-fucked, Katherine," I said as I took her in, enjoying the signs of my bondage on her body.

I led her to the bathroom and we showered together. I took care to wash her tenderly. When we finished, I dried her off, and took her back to the bed. I sat on the edge and pulled her onto my lap.

"So," I said, running my fingers down her neck to her breasts. "How was that?"

"Can't you tell?" she asked, her cheeks pink from the shower, her hair wet.

"I want to hear your assessment. You were anxious."

She inhaled. "I was afraid. I knew it was supposed to be painless when done properly, but those were just words I've read or assurances from people. I was afraid you were too big for me. You *are* larger than average."

"I am," I said, grinning. "But that meant I had to take extra care to prepare you, make sure you were completely ready and relaxed. I would never do anything that hurt you, Kate. As long as we communicate freely and you trust me enough to relax, it won't hurt."

She nodded, not meeting my eyes. I tilted her chin up so she couldn't avoid me.

"So, you enjoyed it? It didn't hurt?"

"It *almost* hurt," she said. "It did burn and there was intense pressure..."

"You were right to tell me when it was starting to be too intense. I pulled back, took more time, used more lubricant. At the first sign of discomfort of any kind, you have to tell me. I'll adjust what I'm doing."

"You *really* enjoy this?"

I nodded. "I do. We won't do it a lot, because it's like a fine caviar, to be enjoyed only occasionally."

"I didn't think that I could come," she said, her voice sounding surprised. "I didn't think I could come the first time we tried. I thought it would take a lot of practice."

"It can be very powerful for a woman, if done properly. For me, while the tightness adds to my pleasure, it's really the trust factor—the submission factor—that gives me pleasure. You trusted me enough to do it, despite your fear. You almost asked me to stop, but I pushed a bit and you gave in, letting me have my way. This was something you were reluctant to do. Doing it anyway to please me, aside from the pleasure we both got from it—that's what I enjoyed the most. It meant you submitted completely."

I kissed her, pulling her against me tightly. This was the

last barrier I had to break down. She'd submitted despite being afraid. She hadn't used her safe word, and that trust and willingness to let me have my way with her filled me with so much pleasure.

When I pulled back, I held her face between my hands, my gaze moving over her face.

"Now you're mine – every part of you. *Completely.*"

CHAPTER 18

As any nurse will tell you, physicians make the worst patients. Surgeons are probably the worst because we're used to taking action when faced with illness, opening up a body to find the source of disease and usually cutting out an offending tissue or organ.

With a virus like influenza, there was nothing to do but suffer until it ran its course.

Whether it was the stress of the whole business with Liam or the effects of my donation on my immune system, I woke up the next morning at the Chelsea apartment with a cold and sore throat.

"I think I've come down with the flu," I said, pulling the covers around me even more tightly.

Kate felt my forehead, her brow furrowed. "You're hot. You have a fever. I'll get you some Tylenol." She left the bed and while she was gone, I drifted in and out of sleep. I woke once more when she returned to the bedroom with a glass of water and pills.

"I have to go to a fundraiser tonight for my dad," she said, watching while I swallowed the pills. "Both he and Elaine are sick, too, and can't go. He was going to present a check and so he wants me to go on his behalf. Do you mind? It'll only be for an hour."

"No," I said, and grimaced because my throat was sore. I shook my head, feeling so bad that all I really cared about was the meds kicking in. "By all means, go. I feel like total crap. I'll watch those funny home videos or something."

"Nigel will be there so I won't be totally alone," Kate said, looking somewhat skeptical about the evening. "My dad said I could stay for the wine and cheese portion of the night, and skip the dinner."

"Stay with Nigel for the dinner if you want." I didn't want to deprive Kate of an evening with Nigel. Hopefully, we'd be leaving for Africa in a month or so and she'd miss him. "But if you're bored, skip it by all means. Don't come back just because of me."

"I don't want to stay without you there," she said and stroked my forehead tenderly. "I want to come home and make dinner for you and then lie here and watch some old movie."

I smiled, warmed by her thoughtfulness. "Sounds like a date to me."

KATE LEFT me alone and took a cab to the studio. In her absence, I slept, altering between shivering with fever and a deep sleep brought on when my fever was reduced from the aspirin.

She returned from the studio later in the afternoon and made sure I was well-supplied with tissues and hot tea with honey, then changed into something suitable for her event. She looked spectacular, as usual and wore pretty dress with a modest neckline but which hugged her curves and made me regret I wasn't well enough take her. As I lay on the sofa, I watched her put on her boots and coat in the entry. I hated being sick, and cursed my luck. After the previous night when Kate submitted totally to me, allowing me to have my way with her even though she was afraid, I had planned on taking her out to celebrate.

Instead, I lay aching on the couch, my nose running.

She kissed my forehead one last time and left me alone with the business news playing on the flatscreen. I felt so bad, I couldn't even focus on the news. Eventually I gave up and fell asleep, hoping I'd feel better when she returned.

KATE WOKE ME HOURS LATER.

"There you are," I said and sat up. "What time is it?" I checked my watch and frowned. "Have I been asleep all this time? When did you get back?"

"I was back pretty early, but you were sleeping so soundly, I didn't want to wake you."

I yawned and stretched, admiring how lovely she was and regretting that I was unable to go to the event with her. "I missed you."

"I missed *you*, more than you can know," she said and sat on the side of the couch. She leaned over and kissed me, cupping my cheek.

"*Why* did you miss me, Ms. Bennet?" I said. "What was it that you missed?"

"I wish you'd been there with me," she said, making a face. "I couldn't wait to get out of there."

"Was Nigel there at least?"

She nodded. "Yes," she said. "We had a nice visit, such as it was."

"Anyone else I'd know?"

She pursed her lips. "Captain Donnelly was there. You'd

know him from Doctors. Dave Mills was, but I didn't speak with him. I'm sure the regular crew was there."

I sighed. "Sorry I wasn't up to it, but I'm sure your dad appreciates that you went in his place. It's good PR for his campaign to be seen giving away his money to a non-political social cause."

"I suppose," she said. "What do you want for supper? Should I order in from *Clair*? Something light – maybe some fish and vegetables? A salad?"

"Sounds great." I sat up a bit more. "I needed that nap. I feel like an old man falling asleep in front of the television."

"You're hardly an old man," she said. "You're in your prime, Drake. Prime Grade A Manflesh."

"My manflesh is still a bit sick tonight, I'm afraid," I said and groaned.

"Just as well." She tucked a hank of my hair behind my ear. "I'm under the weather anyway."

"A bit hung over from the Anisovaya?"

She nodded.

"You should have taken some aspirin and drunk copious amounts of water."

She smiled and pecked my cheek. "Always the doctor."

After Kate called *Clair*, I moved over on the couch and pulled back the blanket.

"Come and snuggle with me," I said. "I need some affection. And more Tylenol."

Kate brought me more Tylenol and snuggled into my arms and we spent the next few hours like an old married couple.

Which was perfectly fine by me.

I SLEPT in the next morning and felt much better. Although I still had a cold, my aches were gone and my fever down. Kate had been up for some time, had already showered and was making coffee when I finally stood in the doorway and watched her pour herself a cup.

"Good morning," I said and went to her, tilting her chin up so I could kiss her on the cheek. "Why didn't you wake me up?"

"You needed more sleep," she said, matter of fact. "I didn't want to bother you."

"I do feel a lot better this morning than last night," I said, glad that the worst part of the virus was over. "I was exhausted even lying on the couch all evening."

"How's your cold? Are you almost back to normal?"

I shrugged and breathed in through my nose. "It's better. I don't think I have a secondary infection. Luckily, we have nothing to do except enjoy each other's company."

She smiled and slipped her arms around my waist, resting her head against my chest. "Luckily."

OVER THE NEXT FEW DAYS, I gradually recovered, and it was the first time off I had since our trip to the Bahamas. While Kate spent time at the studio working on her canvas, I read over my notes for the paper I was working on and did some writing on my laptop while laying on the couch. Gradually, my cough lessened and my nose stopped running. My fever cleared completely and by the third day, I was up early and had showered and was standing at the closet, selecting a tie to wear before Kate even woke.

I heard her yawning and turned to see her still snuggled under the covers, watching me.

"What's going on in that mind of yours, Ms. Bennet?" I asked, enjoying the feel of her gaze on me.

"Just admiring the view."

"Oh, you were, were you?" I said and smiled at her. "See something you like?"

"Something I like very much."

I turned back to the closet, selected a tie and then turned to face the bed, watching her while I tied it. "You can have it later this afternoon if you want. I've deprived you for the past few days. I don't want you unsatisfied."

"I've been very busy the past few days working on a project," she said, smiling coyly.

"How's your painting going? Can I see it?"

She shook her head. "Not until it's finished. It's a gift for you."

I smiled. "I'm glad you're painting again. I was worried that you'd be really bored with nothing to do, now that you've withdrawn from courses and took a leave from the paper."

She yawned and stretched her arms. "I'm glad to be painting again."

I finished dressing, and was busy fastening my belt when her expression changed.

"There's something we have to talk about, Drake," she said. From the tone of her voice, I knew it was something important but I didn't have time to give it my full attention.

I bent down and kissed her, regret filling me that I had to leave. "Sure," I said. "I'm a bit rushed, but later, when I get home."

Kate ran to the bathroom and before I finished dressing, she returned, slipping under the covers quickly. I sat on the edge of the bed and leaned over her, kissing her, unable to get enough of her with her mussed hair and sleepy eyes.

"You look so delicious Ms. Bennet," I said, admiring the curve of her breast peeking out from under the sheets. "I think I'm crazy to leave you here all warm and snuggly under the covers."

"You have things to do," she said and nestled into the pillow. "I'm glad you're feeling so much better. Can you join us for lunch at my parent's today?"

I nodded and ran my fingers down her cheek. "Should I pick you up or will you get a ride over to you father's?"

"I think I'll walk. I've been locked inside the studio for a couple of days. I need the exercise. I'll meet you there at 12:30?"

"Sounds like a plan." I kissed her again and smiled. "Then, after lunch, I want dessert. In other words, I want *you*," I said and slipped my hand down under the covers to her breast. "I have to make up for lost time. I hope you're ready for me, because I'll be *more* than ready for you."

Her eyes widened. "I'll have a hard time eating my lunch when you talk that way."

"Good. I'm feeling *very* deprived. I'm sure you feel that way as well."

She shrugged. "You were sick. But now..." She bit her lip and raised her eyebrows.

I smiled and squeezed her breast. "Now I feel almost my old self. I think I want that massage you promised."

"Your wish is my command, oh *Sultan*." She fluttered her eyelashes.

"I wish that you'll give me a very long and very sensuous massage when we get back from your father's," I said. "Use some nice scented oil, have some soft music in the background, light some candles..."

She smiled. "Sounds heavenly."

I checked my watch and sighed, wishing I could stay home with her, take off my clothes and slip back under the covers. She was nice and warm and now her eyes were bright. I knew she loved sex first thing in the morning and regretted that I had to leave.

"Now I *do* have to go." I leaned down and kissed her deeply. "Hold that thought."

I reluctantly left the apartment and while I was glad to be up and around again, I would have preferred to spend a leisurely morning with Kate, fucking her slowly, relishing the intimacy of our naked skin against each other.

I WENT to the hospital and headed directly to the pediatric oncology ward to speak with the nurses and see how Liam had been doing. I'd been in contact with Liam's doctors via email but hadn't been well enough to visit the hospital. I was infectious as long as I had a fever so I had to wait until it broke, and my cough had subsided enough, so I wouldn't put the sick children at risk. They were especially vulnerable when fighting cancer, taking chemo drugs. Liam had a barely functioning immune system.

It would take weeks before we knew for sure whether my donation was successful but I had real hope for the first time that it would.

Once I was satisfied that Liam was doing as well as could be expected, I went back to my office and went over my paper once more, looking at the revised tables my colleague had submitted for my review. I approved the changes and made a few edits and then sent it off to him in an email, apologizing for my delay but explaining that I had been ill.

It felt so good to be working again. By the time I checked my watch, a couple of hours had passed and so I decided to pop by the studio and see how Kate was doing and if she was ready for lunch with her parents. I decided to surprise her. I wanted to see her in her natural state, and maybe peek at her canvas. I hated secrets, and hoped I might catch a glimpse of what she was working on.

I parked the car and walked up to the building. When I

arrived at the studio, I opened the door quietly so I wouldn't bother anyone. Kate sat at a table in front of a canvas that looked much darker than her art. Behind her stood a young man I hadn't seen before. He leaned over her and was talking to her, pointing to whatever it was she was examining. I couldn't help but feel jealous that some other man was sharing her art and had seen her paintings but tried my best to tamp it down.

They must have heard me for they both looked up at the same time and immediately, our eyes met. He said something to Kate that I couldn't hear. Kate stood up, a bit of a guilty look on her face when she realized I had caught her in a rather intimate moment with a strange man. She came right over to me and took hold of my coat by the lapels and pulled me down for a kiss.

I let her, glancing away from the young man. I kissed her finally, pulling her against my body possessively.

"I thought I'd pop by and see how you're doing," I said, raising an eyebrow suggestively.

"Almost done," she replied. "Just finishing up the last touches."

"Can I see?" I went to the canvas, which was over by the far window, facing the other direction. Kate ran to the painting and tried to block me from seeing it.

"I don't want you to see it just yet, Drake." She stood with her body blocking my access to the canvas. When I tried to sneak by, taking her shoulders and pushing her gently out of the way, she resisted, so I tickled her. She couldn't help but squirm in my arms, giggling.

"No, Drake!" she said, fighting to appear angry, but I could see her grin.

Then the other guy came over and tried to block me from seeing the canvas.

"The lady said no," he said firmly.

I stopped and put my hands on my hips. "Take it easy," I said, my voice tight. "I was just playing around."

The guy glanced at Kate, a frown on his face.

"It's OK," she said. "He was just having fun. He knows I don't want him to see it yet."

The guy held up his hands and backed away. "Sorry."

Kate took my hand, trying to diffuse the situation. "This is Keith," she said. "He's one of the artists who uses Nathaniel's studio. Keith, this is Drake, my..." she hesitated as if she didn't know how to describe our relationship.

"I'm her *boyfriend*," I said as authoritatively as I could.

Keith eyed me up and down, as if measuring whether I was good enough for Kate, and then he backed down and went back to his table. While I didn't really feel much of a threat from the two potheads I saw Kate with previously, this Keith guy was much more like the kind of man Kate could be with. He was good looking enough and seemed protective of her—the way I would be if I had found her in the same situation. I had to admit to myself that I could get very jealous if Kate was going to be spending any length of time with him—especially alone.

I tried to swallow my jealousy but it wasn't easy. To be honest, *not* being jealous where Kate was concerned might not even be possible.

I TOOK Kate back to my apartment in Chelsea, where she showered and dressed in something pretty for our meal with Ethan and Elaine.

As usual, Kate was breathtaking in her cashmere sweater, the soft fabric hugging her lush curves, accentuating her ample breasts and curvy hips. When I saw her, and thought about her eager willingness to submit to me, I felt incredibly lucky that we stumbled together on the way to the bathroom that first night at the pub. If it hadn't been for Kate's interest in D/s, I probably would have been matched with some new submissive and would be going through my same old routine of work, the band, and a very sterile session of B&D with someone I cared nothing about.

We drove to Ethan's but instead of going up with Kate, I dropped her off because I received a text from my answering service. I needed to stop by the hospital for a moment to check on a patient who had experienced a few complications post-surgery. I didn't bother Kate with the details but told her I need to run an errand and would only be a few minutes.

I drove to the hospital and popped onto the ward, meeting with the nurse who was providing care for my patient. We discussed his case and then I met with my fellow neurosurgeon to discuss treatment options.

After I was finished, I stopped at a little market to buy some roses for Elaine, in thanks for her generosity towards me. As I walked through the narrow aisles crammed with groceries to the rack of flower bouquets, I thought about how lucky I was that she intervened that day. Elaine was one of the main reasons Kate and I were now together and I wanted her to feel appreciated.

I selected some beautiful yellow roses and had them wrapped. When I checked my watch, I realized I had taken longer than I expected. Kate would be wondering where I was and why I was taking so long.

I rushed back to Ethan's apartment and parked in the guest parking in the basement. I took the elevator to the penthouse, eager to see them all. I'd been gone over an hour and hoped I hadn't delayed lunch for too long.

I entered the apartment and was greeted by the three of them seated in the living room.

"There you are, young man," Ethan said, smiling broadly. "We were beginning to worry about you."

Kate followed her, smoothing her skirt and sweater. I caught her eye and tried to look apologetic.

"Sorry I'm late," I said, and showed the flowers to Elaine, who rose to meet me at the door. "I wanted to stop and get you something on my way. Here," I said, handing the bouquet of roses to her. "Something to brighten up the table." In my other hand was the bottle of champagne I picked up at the liquor store on the way.

Elaine took the bouquet and kissed me on the cheek.

"Why, thank you so much, Drake. Fresh flowers are always nice." She turned and pointed to the kitchen. "I'll go put them in some water."

I handed an eager Ethan the bottle of chilled champagne. "I'll get some glasses," he said, smiling. "We have lots to celebrate."

Kate came up to me and after I hung up my coat and removed my boots, I leaned down to kiss her, pulling her briefly into my arms, rocking her gently for a moment. Ethan returned all too soon with champagne glasses and the bottle in a chiller. We took our seats while he opened the bottle and then poured champagne into the crystal flutes. He seemed his jovial self so he was obviously recovered from his own bout with the virus.

"Ethan," I said, looking him over, checking his color. "Good to see you're feeling better."

"You as well, young man," Ethan replied, smiling. "You're a hero with all that's happened this past week."

I shook my head and put my arm around Kate, leaning back. "I'm no hero. Liam's my son. It was the least I could do."

Elaine returned with the flowers in a vase. "Katie, do you want to help me in the kitchen?"

Kate stood up to leave, but when she got to the door, Ethan's cell phone rang and he looked at the call display.

"Oh, *damn*," Ethan said, shaking his head. "Gotta take this,

Drake. You relax for a bit, read the paper, watch some headlines."

He handed me the channel changer.

"No problem, Ethan. I had a busy morning so I'm glad to take it easy for a moment."

I leaned back on the couch and put my feet up on the coffee table. Kate stood in the doorway as if unable to decide what to do. I caught her eye. "Were you going to help Elaine?"

She seemed startled but finally nodded. "Of course." Then she left me alone.

While she and Elaine fixed lunch, I scanned the television channels for news headlines and then I searched for the paper. I found it and flipped through the pages, searching for sports highlights, eager for some lunch.

In about ten minutes, Kate returned and startled when she saw me.

"Is lunch ready?" I said, wondering about the expression on her face.

"Yes," she said. "Come to the table. I'll get my father."

I nodded and folded the paper, placed it on the coffee table and then made my way down the hall. Kate went to her father's study to let him know lunch was ready so I went to the dining room. Elaine was there, putting a bowl of salad on the table.

"How is Liam doing?" Elaine asked, an expression of sympathy and concern on her face.

"He's doing as well as can be expected," I said. "He's had his bone marrow destroyed and my stem cells transfused. He'll be a very sick boy for a few weeks."

Kate returned and stood in the doorway, looking strangely anxious. I smiled, and she smiled back and then entered the living room. I pulled out a chair for her and seated her, bending down when she was settled to kiss her neck in a moment of affection, hoping to calm her down about whatever it was that was making her anxious. Ethan arrived just as Elaine came in with a big plate of pasta.

"Sorry I'm late," he said. "Miniature crisis at the campaign office. Some mix up about my record as a judge, rulings on controversial issues. Had to clear it up. Don't want false data circulating. Someone from the office gave out inaccurate information and we got a call from a reporter hoping to drum up a scandal."

"Was the information good or bad?" Elaine asked, as she passed the salad.

"Bad for me, unfortunately," Ethan replied. "Some people don't like my rulings on certain cases, but my record is my record. Don't want anyone to think I'm being deliberately misleading."

"Honesty is the best policy," I said. "In politics and life, it's better to clear up any misunderstandings as soon as possible, to avoid looking like you're being deceptive."

"Absolutely," Ethan replied, smiling at Elaine when she handed him a plate of pasta. "Get the facts out there so there's no misinterpretation."

I let go of Kate's hand and then passed her the salad.

"You all right dear?" Ethan asked Kate. "Your cheeks are red."

"Just the heat from the stove, I guess," Kate said, forcing a smile. She turned to her father. "Did the person who released the wrong data do it deliberately to make your record look better than it is?"

"No," Ethan said, shaking his head. "He used data that was preliminary instead of the final data. It wasn't deceptive, just incorrect. Unfortunately, it makes my staffers look either like liars or bumbling incompetents, so either way it's not a good news day for me."

"That's too bad, Ethan," I said, hoping that the screw up didn't hurt Ethan's campaign. I knew he'd make an excellent

Congressman if elected. I intended to do what I could to help him get there. "What will happen to the staffer?"

"He'll have to be reprimanded of course," Ethan replied. "He shouldn't have released the data until he cleared it with Greg, but I'll have to have a little talk with him, make sure he wasn't doing it to hurt the campaign. You know, sabotage it. Can't ever know what's going on in someone else's heart, can you?"

I nodded, for it was true. You never knew what someone else was thinking or feeling. I glanced at Kate and thought how well I usually read her and right then, she looked extremely nervous about something.

Ethan didn't seem too worried about the mix-up, and dug into his pasta with gusto.

"Darling," he said and turned to Elaine. "I do believe this is the best you've ever made."

Elaine smiled and I turned back to my meal and wondered what was up with Kate. Was she coming down with the virus and not feeling well? I couldn't figure out what was wrong with her, but I knew something was bothering her.

"Drake, is it not to your liking?" Ethan asked.

"Hmm?" I glanced up to see Ethan eagerly eating his meal. "Oh, sorry," I said. "No, I was just thinking about what you said." I lifted a fork to my mouth and then smiled at Elaine. "The pasta is delicious. Worthy of a restaurant. Bravo."

Elaine looked pleased at the compliment and gave me a smile.

Beside me, Kate seemed preoccupied and barely ate her own food. Ethan, ever watchful, noted it.

"Sweetheart," he said and pointed to Kate's plate. "You're not eating your pasta."

Kate put her fork down. "I'm not feeling all that well," she said, wiping her mouth with a napkin. "A bit tired, I guess. It's been a stressful week."

Ethan seemed satisfied and then turned back to his food.

"Excuse me," Kate said suddenly. She stood, knocking her chair back and left the table.

"Are you all right, sweetie?" Ethan called out to her. Kate didn't reply and so I got up and put my napkin on the table. I was on edge because of Kate's behavior and wanted to be alone with her so I could find out what was wrong.

"I'll go see what's the matter," I said and turned to Ethan and Elaine. "She may be coming down with this virus."

Elaine forced a smile. "Thank you, Drake. You may be right."

I went down the hall to Kate's old bedroom and saw that she was in the en suite bathroom. I knocked at the door.

"Kate?"

"I'm okay," she said. "Just feeling a bit queasy."

"Let me in," I said softly.

"I'm *okay*, Drake," she said. "I'll be out in a minute."

I didn't believe her for a moment. Something was wrong. "Are you sure?"

"Yes. I'm fine."

"If you say so, but I *am* a doctor."

"I know you are," she said through the closed door. "I'm fine."

When she opened the door, I was waiting at the end of the bed. I was going to force her to tell me what was wrong.

"Why are you in here?" she said, her voice shaky. "You haven't finished lunch yet."

"I was concerned about you," I replied. "You don't look well."

"I'm fine." She tried to leave the room without saying anything more, but I grabbed her hand and stopped her, maneuvering her between my legs. I wasn't going to let her escape without an explanation. If I knew anything about BDSM relationships, it was that a Dom had to insist on openness and honesty from his sub. The submissive couldn't keep anything from the dominant or else the relationship was doomed to fail. There could be no secrets between partners in the lifestyle. Secrets were like a slow poison that crept in between the couple and ruined the bond.

"What is it, Katie?" I said, keeping my voice soft and unthreatening. "Tell me what's wrong."

"*Nothing*," she said, forcing a smile. "I'm just tired and stressed out over everything."

"As long as you're okay," I said, but I knew she was being untruthful. I didn't want to punish her for being deceptive. Instead, I wanted her to feel safe enough with me so that she'd open up. I brushed her hair back from her face, touched her cheek tenderly.

"Drake, we really need to talk," she said, but at that moment, I wanted to diffuse her anxiety completely.

"Shh," I said and kissed her, wanting her to feel safe, rather than assuring her with words. "We'll talk later. I love you, Kate."

"I love *you*," she said and slipped her arms around my neck, kissing me. I kissed her back passionately, my arms around her, pulling her into my embrace.

Then Ethan popped his head into the room.

"Hey, you two lovebirds. Your food's getting cold." Ethan smiled and then left us alone.

I looked up at Kate. "What do you say we go back and have lunch now that it's settled?"

"What's settled?" she asked, frowning.

"That we love each other," I said and smiled.

Kate nodded. "Sounds like a plan."

I took her hand and pulled her down the hall, following Ethan back to the dining room where Elaine sat alone, her face expectant. When she saw us return, she went to the kitchen and brought our plates back after heating the pasta up in the microwave.

"Feeling better?" she said to Kate when she sat back down.

Kate nodded and I took her hand under the table and squeezed. She turned to look at me, and I could see that there was something seriously wrong. Kate looked like she was afraid, and I felt a knot in my gut at the expression on her face.

What was wrong?

I couldn't figure it out and she wasn't going to say anything – not now. We'd have to wait until we were alone. I turned back to my meal, but made sure to keep her hand in mine under the table so that whatever was bothering her, at least she knew I cared.

The rest of the meal went well, and we talked about Liam, our trip, about Ethan's campaign and the usual political developments in the nation.

I held Kate's hand as we drove back to the Chelsea apartment, hoping she knew that whatever was bothering her, I was there. In the elevator, I pressed her against the wall. "How are you feeling, Ms. Bennet? I'm a bit sleepy after that heavy meal. What do you say to a bit of a nap? You said you were tired."

She nodded. "Sounds good to me, but we really should talk first." She unbuttoned my coat, pulling my scarf away from my neck.

"We'll talk after we fuck," I said, wanting to reassure her. Whatever she had to say would be better said once both of us were in that pleasant state after a good orgasm. "I have it all planned out."

"You do?" she said, smiling coyly in the way I loved. "I have nothing else to do and so I'm all yours."

"All mine?" I said, grinning, my mind already going to

where I wanted to take her – naked, bound, blindfolded, crying out in pleasure.

"At your disposal," she said and she seemed more relaxed. "At your command. I seem to recall a promise about harem girls and massages…"

"Oh, that's *right*…" I smiled when I remembered my request. "I do remember something about you being my slave girl and giving me a really sensuous massage, but maybe we should wait until after the nap." I kissed her softly and she seemed to forget about whatever was bothering her.

CHAPTER 19

WE UNDRESSED and slipped under the covers, snuggling together the way we always did at night. Her body was soft and warm against mine and it was so nice and comfortable that I felt my eyelids close and I drifted in a semi-awake state.

Then my cell chimed, announcing that a text message had arrived.

"*Crap,*" I said and grabbed it off the bedside table.

"Ignore it, Drake," Kate said, yawning.

"Can't," I said. "That's someone from the foundation calling."

I took my phone and read the text. It was from Dave.

DRAKE, are you alone? Call me. I have something to tell you... You better be sitting down when I do, buddy.

THAT DIDN'T SOUND VERY PROMISING. What was the problem? Something bad to do with the Foundation? I wracked my

221

brain trying to think of what it might be. Did someone abscond with funds? Did some Foundation money go to arms deals instead of to hospital construction or tools? I couldn't imagine why Dave would want me to be sitting down.

"I'll be right back," I said and left the bedroom, going to the living room where I sat on the couch and dialed Dave's number.

"Hey," I said when he answered. "What's up? What's the crisis?"

"Is Kate with you?" he said, his voice hesitant.

I frowned. "Yes. She's in the bedroom. Why?"

There was a pause. "Have you seen the *New York Weekly*? The Society Page?"

I got up and went to the pile of mail and papers on the table by the door. There was the New York Weekly, under an envelope. I hadn't even had a chance to read it, let alone the Society Page. Did someone write something about me? Had Kate's meddling friend finally got me in trouble by going public with information about my participation in the BDSM lifestyle?

I opened the page and searched through the articles.

And then I saw it.

Ice filled my veins. Kate leaned against a wall with a blond-haired young man leaning over her very possessively, a hand on the wall beside her head. He was standing close as if he was whispering to her or preparing to kiss her. She didn't look happy, but she was there – wearing the dress she wore to the DWB event the other night.

The caption of the photo read *"Kate McDermott and Escort attend Doctors Without Borders fundraiser."*

Escort?

"Do you see it?" Dave said, his voice hesitant.

"I see it," I replied, my face hot with anger. Jealousy burned in my gut.

"She was with some old flame, from what I heard. I spoke with Nigel. He said Kate was hot and heavy with him a year ago. Some former pilot who volunteers for Doctors Without Borders."

"Flyboy," I said, my throat choked with emotion.

"Flyboy?" Dave said.

"That's what they call him. Kate and her dad."

"Is she still with him? I thought the two of you…" he said, his voice trailing off.

"They broke up a year ago. At least, that's what I was told. Did you see them arrive together?" I asked.

"No," Dave said. "I *thought* Kate arrived by herself. I saw her speak with Nigel and then she gave the donation on behalf of her father. Then she left just after six o'clock and he followed her. When I saw the picture, I figured she was still seeing him or something. She never spoke to him at the function and I had no idea he was her escort."

I didn't know what to say. Had she planned on meeting him? It didn't seem at all like the Kate I had come to know – and love. My jealousy was like a coiled snake inside of my chest. I was so upset, my heart was pounding very fast. I fought to keep from throwing the phone across the room.

I did everything in my power not to jump to any conclusions but it was incredibly hard and as each moment passed, it became less and less possible.

"I'll speak with Kate. See what's up," I said, keeping my voice controlled. "Thanks for calling."

"I hate to be the bearer of bad news, but when I saw the photo in the *Weekly*, I thought I should call you and tell you what I knew."

"Thanks," I said and ended the call.

I sat with my head in my hands. Was this why Kate had

been acting strangely? Was she going to break off our relationship? Maybe she didn't really want to go to Africa but didn't know how to say it.

Anger and hurt seethed inside of me as I tried to understand what I had seen and what Dave had said. I sat there, the phone in my hand, considering what I would say to Kate.

That was how Kate found me when she entered the living room. I heard her footsteps and saw her out of the corner of my eye but I didn't look at her – I *couldn't* look at her just yet.

"Drake?" she said, her voice barely above a whisper. She stepped closer to the couch. "Drake," she said, her voice wavering. "I—"

"*Don't*," I said, holding up my hand to stop her. "Don't say anything."

"But I need to explain—"

"Not now," I said, desperately trying to keep control over my emotions.

"*Please* Drake," she said, her voice panicked. "I was going to tell you…" She came over to the couch and was going to sit next to me but I turned to her, frowning.

"Stop," I said. "Leave me alone. I need some time to think."

"Why?" she said, her voice pleading. "There's nothing to think about. I ran into Kurt at the fundraiser, he followed me out of the building and some photographer took that picture when I was telling him to leave me alone. That's *it*," she said, chopping her hand down emphatically. "End of story."

"You never said anything about Kurt being your," I said, trying to control my voice. "*Escort.*"

"He wasn't!" She sat closer to me. "The paper made that up. I wasn't *with* him. He followed me out and they took that picture. That's it."

"What time did you get home that night?" I said and frowned, trying to remember. "When I woke up, it was

almost eight thirty. Dave said you left the fundraiser at six –
with Kurt."

She exhaled in frustration. "I did leave at six. I didn't want
to stay because Kurt was there. He followed me out. I didn't
leave *with* him. He cornered me, I told him I was with you
and was happy, and then I left. I took a cab because the limo
driver was away and I wanted to escape Kurt. I got home
around 6:15 and you were asleep so I didn't wake you up."

It sounded possible but the photo... "So you have no proof
that you were home that early? Dave said you left with Kurt."

"I *didn't*," she said, her face white, her brow furrowed.
"There's the concierge in the entry. You could ask him."

"*God*, Kate," I said, emotion overwhelming me. "Do I
really have to check with the doorman to know if you're
telling me the truth?"

"Why would you doubt me?"

I turned away, my heart pounding. She was right. Why
would I doubt her? Finally, I turned back to face her and the
expression on her face was almost enough to make me trust
her. Almost.

"Why would I doubt you?" I said, exasperated, conflicted.
"Because you didn't fucking tell me the truth right away,
that's why. Dave had to tell me."

"It meant nothing," she said, her voice insistent. "I didn't
want to upset you over nothing. You've been through so
much with Liam and the transplant and being sick. You were
so tired..."

I shook my head, not meeting her eyes. "Is every fucking
woman going to cheat on me?" I muttered. Then I turned
back to face her. "Didn't I pay enough attention to you?
Couldn't you wait until I recovered?"

"Couldn't I *wait*?" she said. "What do you mean?"

She crawled onto my lap, her arms around my neck, tears
in her eyes. I couldn't respond, my jealousy so strong, my

fear of once more being cheated on keeping me from believing her.

"Drake, don't *do* this," she said, her voice breaking. "Kurt means nothing to me. *Nothing.*"

"Did he touch you?"

"What do you mean, did he touch me? He grabbed my arm, he touched my cheek. I didn't touch him. We spoke for five minutes and I left. *Alone.*"

I stared at her, my eyes hungry for her. Even as I sat there feeling betrayed, I couldn't help but love her, desire her – want to fuck her right then and there, hard and fast.

"Did you fuck him? Just for old time's sake?" I asked it, needing to know the truth so I could shut off my emotions. Shut her out of my heart.

"*What?*" she said, pulling back in horror.

"Tell me the truth, *Katherine*," I said. Maybe she needed me to be more dominant. Maybe she needed someone more forceful. "At least tell me the goddamned truth."

"Do you really, *seriously* think I'd just fuck some man?"

"Kurt isn't just some man," I said, thinking back to everything Kate and Lara had told me about him. He was in the Marines, like Ethan and my father. He was alpha, if clumsy in his introduction of kink with Kate. "He was your lover. I know how these things go."

"No, stop for a moment and think," she said, her voice breaking. "Do you *really* think I could fuck Kurt? I need to know."

I shrugged, already closing off my emotions. "I don't know. The paper said he was your escort. You left with him. You were home late. You have needs…"

"Drake, that's *insane*. If you can even *think* that might happen, you don't know me at all. I would *never* do that."

"How would I know? We've only been together for four

months," I said. "You're still so young. Who knows what hidden kinks you might have."

I thought of Kate perhaps liking the idea of multiple partners, polyamory. Who knew what she might desire. If she wasn't being truthful with me about Kurt, there was no telling what kind of kink she might be into.

"It's the *truth*," she said, stroking her hands through my hair, her eyes brimming. "I was back here at 6:15. I was so happy to get away from Kurt and back to you."

"Why didn't you wake me up?"

"You were sick!"

Our eyes finally met, and her tears spilled out over her cheeks.

"Oh, *God*, Drake," she said, almost sobbing. "*Nothing* happened."

"You have to always tell me the truth, *Katherine*," I said, my voice low. "You have to tell me right away. I have to know you're being completely honest with me, completely open. I can't have any doubt *ever*," I said. "I *can't*."

"You don't have to doubt me," she said, her voice breaking again. "I *love* you. More than anything. More than I ever thought possible." She kissed me, her hands on either side of my face. I didn't respond, still not convinced that it was all a mistake. She pulled away, her expression almost desperate. "Drake, I love only *you*." She kissed me again. "*Only* you."

"Why, Kate?" I said, my own voice breaking. "I let you in. I let you *in*."

She glanced away but I stopped her, tilting her chin up so that she was forced to look in my eyes. I pulled her against me, burying my face in her neck and pressed her down on the couch. With her body under mine, listening to the desperation in her voice, the fear in her eyes, I made a decision. I had to trust her, even if the circumstances didn't appear to merit it. But she had to know that she could never keep anything from me again. I couldn't take it. I couldn't stand to doubt her. I had to know for certain that she was mine.

"Why didn't you tell me right away?"

"I knew you were jealous," she said. "You *told* me you were jealous. I was afraid you'd misunderstand."

I exhaled. "Kate, I can't stop men from hitting on you, but you have to trust me completely and tell me when they do. No secrets. It's absolutely necessary for this to work. I've been lied to. I've been cheated on. I can't have it. I *won't* take it."

"You have to trust me, too, " she said and I knew she was right, but trust had to be earned. It was earned by telling the truth right away.

"How *can* I when you didn't tell me right away? Were you hoping it would never come up?"

"Every time I tried to tell you, you'd do something to stop me," she said, raising her shoulder up. "I wanted to find the right time, and well, you read the paper…"

"It upsets me that it was Dave who told me," I said, and that was what really bothered me. I wanted Kate to feel so secure with me that she could tell me anything. A Dom needed to know everything in his sub's heart and mind. It was imperative. He had to *know*. "It hurts that he had to phone me to ask if I'd seen the picture."

She sighed and shook her head slowly. "I was wrong not to tell you right away. I didn't think it was important. It meant *nothing* to me. If anything, it reinforced why Kurt and I broke up. You have no reason to be jealous."

"You have to understand," I said, touching her cheek. "Your father tried to fix you up with Kurt first, before me. He thought Kurt was just your type. He thought Kurt was *perfect* for you. I was around, listening to him talk about Kurt and how he wanted you to get together."

"What?"

I nodded. "You know, Kurt's a Marine like he was and like my father. A veteran. A pilot. Strong. Intelligent. A bit older than you, but still, closer to your age. He's really good looking, on top of everything. You have to understand back then, I was forced to listen to your father's campaign to get you together with Kurt. He told me all about how he thought Kurt was *perfect* for you and that you'd *love* him…"

Kate shook her head. "He's not. I *don't* – he's nothing to me. You're *everything*."

"I was like second best to your father," I said, giving her a rueful smile. "If Kurt didn't work out, there was always me." And that was the truth—Ethan had chosen Kurt for Kate over me.

"You're better," Kate said, her voice a little desperate sounding. "A million times better. And I can't believe my father talked to you about setting me up with Kurt. Why?"

"I asked about you. Frequently," I replied. "He seemed to want to talk about you to someone. He was busy trying to get you together with Kurt when we started to become friends. I figured he didn't consider me because I'm so much older than you."

"I *like* that you're older than me. I've told you that."

"Still," I said, remembering what I had seen of Kurt – young, studly, blond surfer good looks. "You might not always like it." I'd always be twelve years older than her. When she was forty, I'd be fifty-two. I'd be an old man when she was still an attractive middle-aged woman.

She shook her head. "I can't imagine not being with you. Not loving you."

I sighed and played with a lock of her hair. "People stop loving you, Kate. I know."

"Not always. Drake, I'm so *sorry*," she said, her voice

breaking. "This is all my fault. I should have told you right away, as soon as you woke up."

I nodded and touched her cheek with my fingers, unable to keep from touching her, making contact even when I was still upset. "You should have."

"Please forgive me."

I forced a smile. "I do. But I'm going to have to punish you."

"What?" She pulled back, a look of shock on her face.

I nodded, knowing that I had to punish her for breaking the terms of our agreement. She was supposed to be truthful about our relationship and her feelings. At all times. She'd broken the terms.

"You broke the rules about truth. You *know* you're supposed to always tell me the truth. You are *not* allowed to hide things from me. I *have* to punish you or what kind of Dom would I be?"

"I don't want you to spank me."

"Kate. You *intentionally* didn't tell me about Kurt," I said, needing her to understand how serious this was. It meant she didn't really understand what was required of her. This wasn't just some sticking point for me personally. It was a firm tenant in BDSM that the Dominant and submissive had to be completely honest and open about their likes and dislikes, limits and needs. "You intentionally deceived me. I asked you if you saw anyone I'd know at the function. You saw Kurt. A lie of omission is as bad as one of commission."

"I don't want you to punish me," she said, shaking her head, pulling away from me. "I don't want you to spank me again."

"It's not about what you want," I said, holding her firmly. "This is about the rules, *Katherine*."

"That's not fair," she said. "You let the rules fall by the

wayside when it suits you, and enforce them when it suits you."

"I'm the Dominant. I'm the Master," I said, realizing that I had failed in my duty to show her and teach her what she needed to know or else we wouldn't be having the conversation. "It's my prerogative. You should re-read the agreement."

She pushed away from me and finally succeeded in escaping my grip. I let go, telling myself that I shouldn't be restraining her. She had to come to this on her own. She had to *understand*.

"I'll rip the fucking agreement up." She stomped away but stopped at the door. "Look," she said, her fists clenched. "I *was* wrong to hide what happened with Kurt, but as far as I'm concerned, if you spank me, it will be overkill."

I went to her, my arms on either side of her, preventing her from moving. "In case you misunderstood, in our power exchange, I'm the one who decides about punishment. Your breaking the rules about lying was *not* accidental. It was intentional. You have to be punished. I choose the punishment."

I grabbed her arm, then sat on the bed and pulled her over my lap, one of my legs thrown over hers, confining her completely. She could only wriggle, her arms flailing to try to stop me, but I was able to control her, and gripped her hands in one of mine.

"You better not spank me," she said, her voice low.

"You better just take it, *Katherine*. You agreed that I'd punish you if you broke the rules," I said, breathing in slowly and deeply, gaining control over my emotions. "Did you break the rules?"

She said nothing, so I waited. Finally, I repeated my question.

"Did you *break* the rules?"

She stopped fighting but was tense and did not answer.

"Katherine, I *promise* you, I've been doing this now for five years," I said, finally in complete control. "I have more than enough patience to wait for you to reply properly."

"You're very selective about what and when you punish."

"That's my prerogative, as I said and as is spelled out in the agreement. Maybe we better sit down and re-read it." I let that sink in for just a moment before continuing. "I've been exceptionally lenient with you since we've been together, but there are some things I can't tolerate. Lying is one of the things I *will* not tolerate. So once more, did you break the rules?"

She was tense, her breath coming in short gasps. "*Yes.*"

"Yes, what?"

She held back, not answering right away but I waited her out. Finally, she gave in.

"Yes, *Master.*"

"Good girl," I said and hiked up her nightgown above her ass, baring her buttocks. Once I saw them, my dick hardened despite my earlier anger and hurt. I couldn't help but run my hand over them, enjoying their creamy smoothness, their plump roundness. "So nice and creamy white. It's too bad I'm going to have to make them all red."

"You don't *have* to do anything," she said, her voice edged with anger. "You're choosing to do this."

"Yes, I am, Katherine," I said calmly. "A Dom has to have some standards. I've let mine slip with you because I love you so much, but if I don't enforce this rule, our relationship is doomed. I can't lose trust in you or this will fail." I leaned down and put my lips by her ear. "I don't want to lose you." I kissed the skin on her bare shoulder. "I can't lose you. So, I want you to tell me what you did wrong. Complete openness Katherine. Complete honesty. No more hiding things from me."

She said nothing, but covered her eyes. "I saw a video of you with Sunita."

A shock went through me at that. "*What?*"

"Dawn sent it to me."

I breathed in deeply in an attempt not to overreact. She saw a video of me with Sunita?

Sunita had taken a video of our scenes. She liked to watch it over and over again. How had Kate seen the video?

"I told you about our relationship."

"Dawn tried to arrange a meeting between us but I said no."

I tensed, barely able to believe what Kate said. "She *what?*"

"Then, she sent me the video. And because Maureen had said some things when she called that scared me, I…"

Maureen called Kate?

"*What* did Maureen say?" I asked, feeling like all the blood had drained out of my body, my heart pounding.

"She said you were barely under control. That you had a lot of anger bottled up inside. That I should think of that before I went to Africa with you."

Dammit… Adrenaline jolted through me, my cheeks heating. "And you thought watching a video of me with Sunita would help clarify how dangerous I am?"

"I'm sorry I didn't tell you," she said and her voice was truly repentant. "I didn't want to upset you. I couldn't believe Maureen said those things. I was going to tell you, but you weren't feeling well from the shots and then you were sick…"

I fought to control myself, my breathing fast, my heart thumping in my chest. "That's three things, Katherine. Three things you kept from me." Then, I lay my hand over her ass.

"I don't want this," she said, but I could hear the resignation in her voice.

"But you want me to be your Master, Katherine, deep down," I said for I knew it was true. She did want me to be

233

her Master. That's why she went looking and when she met me, she wanted me to be the one. I had no doubt about that. "I've been a bad Master, not controlling you well enough, or this would never have happened. I won't let that happen again. So you see, this is really my fault for letting my control slip. Now, I have to punish you even though I'd rather make love to you. I have to take your anger so that our relationship's re-established. We'll both feel better when it's over."

"Cut the psychobabble and do it," she said, her voice tinged with anger.

"It's not *psychobabble* and you know it," I said, remembering with that one word why I was in love with her. She was smart. She was beautiful. She wanted submission, even if at times it seemed the opposite was true. "Remember your safe word."

"I won't use it."

I wouldn't give in. I'd be a force of nature. An immovable object. That would make her feel safe. "Tell me what your safe word is."

She shook her head, fighting to the end.

"It's *red*, Katherine."

She said nothing, lying across my lap, waiting. She didn't try to wriggle out of my grasp.

Finally, she exhaled loudly, giving in. "Just *do* it."

I smiled to myself while I stroked my hand over her buttocks, lingering over the small of her back, then slipping my fingers between her cheeks.

"When I'm ready."

"I *hate* you."

I stopped my motions, for I knew that she didn't mean it, but still the words hurt and I knew she'd regret saying them later.

"*Don't* say that," I said softy, trying not to sound hurt but failing, my throat choking. "Not even in a moment of anger."

She said nothing and did nothing and neither did I. I'd wait her out, my hand on her ass.

Then, I began to stroke my hand over her cheek once more.

"You *don't* hate me, Katherine. You love me. *Only* me. You said so yourself."

Then she spoke, her voice breaking. "I couldn't help it that Kurt was there. I didn't want to see him. I didn't want to have to deal with him. It's not my fault."

I leaned down, and tucked her hair behind her ear, my mouth beside her ear.

"You didn't have to lie about him. You should have told me about Sunita's video. You should have told me Maureen spoke to you about me."

"I *didn't* lie. I was going to tell you."

"I have no way of knowing if you would have," I replied for I didn't. She might never have spoken about it, hoping to avoid a confrontation or uncomfortable conversation. "Now, because you didn't tell me right away, how can I trust you? Three things, Katherine, that you held back. Three important things."

"You have to choose to trust me when I say I was going to tell you," she replied. "You said that to me once, if I remember correctly."

I said nothing in response and considered her words. She was right. I had to choose to trust that she would have eventually told me. Something kept her from telling me – fear of my reaction. Lack of trust that I could take the truth without overreacting or removing my love.

She sighed. "I guess I didn't trust you enough yet to tell you. I guess I was afraid of what you'd do. I was afraid of you."

I stopped my motions immediately, but kept my hand on

her buttock, hating to break our connection. It was as if she read my mind.

"Why?" I asked, wanting her to be as truthful as she could. "Have I ever done anything to make you afraid of me?"

She shook her head. "No. But maybe you didn't do enough to make me trust you completely. Every time I tried to talk, you shut me up. You'd go into Dom mode and we'd have sex and that was it. You've been under so much emotional stress and turmoil, I was afraid this would be one more thing to hurt you and upset you. It meant nothing to me so I didn't feel it should matter to you, but I was afraid it would and I was right. "

She was right – it did matter to me. I felt incredible jealousy that she'd been alone with Kurt. He was still a threat. She had been attracted to him once but had been afraid of her response to his clumsy attempts to introduce her to kink. Ethan had wanted them to be together and that meant something.

I was incredibly jealous of Kurt.

"That's exactly why you should have told me right away. I *would* have been upset. I would have been very jealous and hurt. But we would have discussed it, you could have reassured me that what happened with Kurt was nothing, and now, instead of me having you over my lap, ready for a spanking, you'd be massaging me like my favorite slave girl and then we'd be making love."

"You don't have to spank me," she said, her voice still petulant. "It's your choice."

"You took away my choice when you didn't trust me enough to tell me the truth right away. It's because I've been too free with you, letting you get away with too much. Not disciplining you when you broke the rules because I enjoy you too much. Now, I have to reassert myself, reestablish my dominance. I *have* to punish you, Katherine."

"You don't need to reestablish anything," she protested. "You don't need D/s to keep me at arm's length. We've been so happy. We don't need an agreement."

"We do. *I* do," I said, exasperated. "I'm a Dominant, Katherine. I was when you met me. I am *now*. I need an agreement to keep myself in control. I loosened my control because of you, I opened up and let you in, and this is what happened. Now, I have no choice."

She craned her neck around. "Did you hear what you said? You confirmed that you use D/s to keep people out of your life. You *let* me in. Don't shut me out now. I'm not *just* one of your subs."

I shook my head. "I have no choice."

I didn't. I had to wait for her to submit and accept my dominance or she'd be testing me endlessly. She wouldn't truly believe I was strong enough to control myself or her.

Finally, her body went limp. She didn't say anything. She waited.

That was the signal that finally, she'd given in and accepted that I would do what I would do and she'd have to take it. I stroked my hand over her ass, filled with such love for her at that moment, I couldn't believe my luck at finding and winning her.

Then I knew I couldn't punish her. I couldn't spank her. I wouldn't hurt her, even if that was in our agreement. I removed my leg from across hers and released her. She scrambled up and stood in front of me, her expression shocked.

I got up and went to the chair where my clothes were folded and got dressed. She followed me when I went to the hall closet and took out my coat.

"What are you doing?"

I slipped on my coat and boots, not meeting her eyes,

needing to escape the situation, take some time to think it through.

"Drake," she said, her voice panicked. "What are you *doing*?"

"I don't know what to do any longer," I said, fatigue overtaking me. "No matter what I do, it'll be wrong. If I spank you, you'll hate me. If I don't, you'll think I'm weak and despise me. I can't win." I went to the door and opened it. "So, I'm going out."

"Where?"

"I don't know."

I left, my body feeling wooden, my muscles tense, my mind in turmoil. She followed me to the elevator.

"Don't go," she said, reaching out for me. "Not now. Not like this. We have to figure this out."

I avoided her hand, knowing that if she touched me, I'd give in. "I don't know what to do," I said, shaking my head, completely defeated. "Don't follow me."

The elevator doors closed.

I was alone.

CHAPTER 20

I GOT in the car and drove to the only place I felt comfortable – 8th Avenue. As I drove though the streets of Manhattan, I thought about the apartment. It was my old place from when I first moved to New York. It had been my father's apartment at one time, and was filled with memories of him.

It was our place – Kate's and my place where we first explored each other. Where I first tied her hands and she knew what it felt like to be helpless and under my complete control.

I parked and walked to the old brownstone, glad to see the dried up, brown ivy creeping up the façade. In the spring, the window boxes would be filled with flowers. When Kate and I returned from Africa, if we did go, we would move in there if I had a say in it.

I went inside and sat in the living room surrounded by my father's boxed and furniture from his place. At that moment, I felt completely at a loss. What was the right thing to do with Kate?

I honestly didn't know anymore.

My cell chimed. I removed it from my pocket and checked my messages.

It was from Kate.

Drake, please, come back. I can't stand this. I admitted I was wrong, and that I should have told you right away. I promise that from now on, I will tell you everything right away and be completely honest with you. I need you. I want only you...

I sent her a single line:

I'm staying at 8th Avenue for the night.

She texted me back right away.

Please don't do this. I can't stand not having you beside me.

I responded after thinking what to write for a few moments:

I need time alone to figure this out. Don't come here.

She wouldn't give up.

Drake, there's nothing to figure out. If you stay away now, you'll put a wall up between us. Don't. We might never be able to break it down and we'll become strangers. Please come back home now and let's see this through tonight. I can't imagine not being with you. I can't imagine not being able to reach out and touch you.

I closed my cell and left the apartment on 8th Avenue, not wanting to be there if she came by. I needed to work things out in my mind, think it through. If she was there, I knew I'd cave and be unable to resist her.

Instead, I decided to go and meet with Ken at the pub.

I drove to the pub and entered through the rear entrance. The kitchen was busy as prep people in white aprons and hairnets worked to get the food ready for the evening meal. I popped into the office and saw Mrs. O sitting at her desk, poring over a ledger, her half-eye glasses perched on the end of her nose.

"Drake!" She leaned back when she saw me and let me kiss her cheek.

"Hi, Mom," I said, warmed to see her smiling face. "I was in the neighborhood and thought I'd drop by."

"That's nice," she said. "It's just me here. Ken is out picking up some supplies."

I shrugged, sad that I missed Ken. I needed his big brother wisdom. "Tell him I was here. Nice to see you."

"Wait," she said and pulled out a chair beside her. "You look like you need someone to talk to. Sit down. How are you doing, Drake?"

Mrs. O was as close to a mother as I ever had. If anyone would know what to do, it would be her. I sat down beside her, my elbows resting on my knees.

"Ken told me about your son," she said, her voice soft. "How is he?"

I recounted the round of meds I'd taken and how Liam had been prepared for the transplant.

"You are so wonderful for doing that," she said and took my hand, squeezing it briefly.

"How could I refuse?"

"People do all the time," she said and crossed her arms. "So, you and Kate..." She smiled at me, pleased. "When are you getting married?"

I laughed, although I felt sick inside. Mrs. O was always pushing for me to get married again.

"You two will be going to Africa soon, right? I hope that's still going to happen."

"I hope," I said. "Liam is doing really well, so we're scheduled to leave soon."

"You should ask her to marry you before you go."

I smiled, amused at her persistence. "We've only been together for five months..."

"Love doesn't run by any schedule but its own," she said, wagging her finger at me. "If you love her, if she's the one,

241

you should snap her up before someone else does. Just think how sad you'd be if she ends up marrying someone else."

I nodded without saying anything. Of course she was right. If Kate and I broke up and I learned she had married someone else, I couldn't imagine it.

I'd feel like a failure.

"So, why are you really here?" she asked, giving me a look that suggested she doubted my earlier excuse.

"Kate and I had a..." I said and hesitated. What did happen? "A disagreement."

"And you want to talk about it." She patted my hand.

"Not really," I said. "I know what I have to do. I just wanted to go somewhere and get away from it all for a while."

She nodded as if she understood. "She sounds like a wonderful girl from what Ken told me. You're very lucky to have found her. Whatever the disagreement is about, keep that in mind."

I smiled at her. "I *am* very lucky."

Then, my cell buzzed. I removed it from my pocket and saw that it was another message from Kate.

Drake, I came to 8th Avenue looking for you. I'm still here. Come to me. I don't want to ever be apart from you. Not one night. I love you.

"Is that from her?" Mrs. O said.

"Yes."

"You better respond," she said. "I'm going to the kitchen for something to drink. You take your time." Then she stood and laid a hand on my shoulder before leaving me alone in the office.

I thought about my response for a long time.

Katherine, I want you waiting for me, blindfolded, naked, kneeling on the floor by the bed. I'm going to spank you. And then I'm going to fuck you. You're going to take it without complaint.

Do you understand?

I knew what she'd write before she even sent the text and when I saw it, I was right.

I don't want you to spank me.

I replied immediately.

Of course you don't but I have to. Trust me on this, Katherine.

She replied in moment.

What if I break up with you because of it?

I texted right back.

We'll break up if I don't. I realize now that this relationship won't work unless we follow the rules we drew up and committed to when we signed the agreement. The rules are there for a reason. Both of us need them. We can't be just a vanilla couple. I can't be a vanilla boyfriend, Katherine. I might try, but I'd fail and you'd eventually be dissatisfied. I'm a Dominant and you want submission in the bedroom, even if you haven't completely accepted what that means yet. We have to follow the rules or neither of us will be happy.

If you love me – if you really love me – the Dominant I am inside – you'll accept this and obey just as I have to accept that you really want submission underneath your uncertainty. You need my dominance to feel free.

After a moment, she replied.

I will obey.

I exhaled in relief, glad that finally, we had come to the right place where we both needed to be. What happened next would decide whether we stayed together or broke up. Both of us could want to be together but if neither of us got what we wanted – and needed – we wouldn't be happy and eventually, we'd start to fight over small things and then break up, resenting each other or feeling dead to each other.

Be waiting for me as I described. Be prepared to be spanked, Katherine. Then, be prepared to be fucked. I'll be there in 15.

I left the restaurant after I said goodbye to Mrs. O and

went to the car, only slightly nervous about what would happen next. I had to handle Kate just right so that she would understand what the relationship meant – and what I needed. Only then would she get what she needed. Once I was outside the apartment, I called her cell and let it right twice before hanging up. That was our signal that I would be up in mere moments and that she was to be ready, waiting as I instructed. As I got out of my car and walked the short distance to the apartment on 8th Avenue, I imagined her on her knees by the bed, wearing her stockings and garters and nothing else, her hands clasped behind her back so that her breasts were jutting forward, her eyes down.

My body responded, my dick thickening, a delicious thrill in my groin despite my concern that this scene must go well.

When I finally entered the apartment, I was rock-hard and ready. I shucked off my boots and coat, then went to the kitchen to get the bottle of Anisovaya, downing a quick shot to help calm my nerves. Then I went to stand in the doorway to the bedroom and I took in the vision of Katherine – her naked flesh glowing in the late afternoon light from the window, her breasts full, her nipples hard in the cool air. Then my heart sunk. Tears slipped down her cheeks from under her blindfold and I knew then she was very upset. I hoped it was regret and not from anger for if it was, it meant she was not ready and had not understood.

Normal vanilla couples could lie to each other to their hearts content – about petty attractions to others, about what they really wanted and needed from the relationship. Couples involved in kink could not. There was too much at stake. Power exchange meant responsibility – the total giving over and taking of power and responsibility to the other partner. When a sub was completely helpless, she had to trust her Dom completely. When a Dom carried out an act on her body, whether it be painful or pleasurable, he had to know that the act would fulfill her and that she was truly consenting to it, or else it was just abuse and violation.

I went to where she knelt by the bed and sighed when I saw her part her lips, her bottom lip quivering slightly. She was regretful, not angry. She understood that this would be for the best.

I picked her up, and sat down on the bed with her across my lap. She slipped her arms around my neck, waiting, open. I kissed her, my lips on her cheek, kissing below each eye, wanting to take her sadness away.

"Oh, *Katie*," I whispered. Then my emotions overwhelmed my resolve and I kissed her deeply, unable to get enough of her, needing to feel her response to me. She kissed me back, pulling her body tightly against me. I ran my hands down her naked body, to her breast, squeezing, pulling her nipple taut between my finger and thumb, my dick hard against my jeans.

I had planned to spank her in punishment, but after seeing her like that, I couldn't do it. I realized that I didn't want to hurt her – not even in punishment. I couldn't imagine hurting her or making her cry. I only wanted her pleasure. Instead of spanking her in punishment, I decided that I would show her a sensual spanking – one designed to give her pleasure.

So instead of spanking her hard, I spent my time arousing her, kissing her. I lay on top of her, touching her, slipping my fingers between her lips to feel her clit, stroking it slowly, sinuously. She moaned when I kissed her shoulder and then claimed her nipple, sucking firmly, teasing it with the tips of my teeth.

I moved lower, my tongue slipping down over her belly to her pussy, finding her clit, and stroking. She responded with a moan, her breath coming in quick gasps as she neared her orgasm. Instead of letting her go over, I pulled off and turned her over my knee as I had done earlier, one hand pressing down on her upper back, the other on the back of her thighs.

"Will you lay quietly and submit? Don't speak," I said. "Nod your head. If you won't submit, I'll have to confine you with my leg."

She nodded without protest.

"Good *girl*," I said and kissed her shoulder.

I ran my hand over her buttocks softly, circling each one, playing with them, outlining them before slipping between them to touch her pussy. I leaned over and kissed her back, my mouth moving lower to the small of her back. I hiked up her ass a bit more, and kissed each cheek.

I was hard as rock.

I hit her buttocks with my right hand using a light rapid touch that was not meant to hurt but was instead meant to stimulate the entire area, get blood to the surface. The pain would be no more than a light tap at first, building up to a slight sting.

When I struck the inside of each buttock, the stroke was intended to arouse, to stimulate the whole area including her pussy. It worked. Soon, she was writhing beneath my hand, groaning with pleasure.

"Spread your thighs wider," I said, for I wanted to make sure I could penetrate her with the fingers on one hand while maintaining the light slapping of her ass with the other.

She gasped when I slipped my thumb inside her, circling over the sensitive ridge of tissue an inch or so inside her body. My other fingers found her clit, and pressed against it. Then, I began slapping her ass with my left hand, continuing with the firm tapping I had begun earlier. I increased the force and maintained the slow circle of my thumb inside of her, my fingers stroking her clit.

"You're going to come while I spank you, Katherine," I

said after a few moments. I stopped my motions for a moment and leaned down, my mouth beside her ear.

"Are you sorry you didn't tell me about Kurt as soon as you got home from the fundraiser, *Katherine*? Are you sorry you didn't tell me about Sunita and about Maureen?"

"Yes, Master."

I began the sensual spanking again, my thumb moving inside of her, my finger stroking her, my hand striking her ass lightly and rapidly. Her thighs began to shake, signaling that her orgasm was near.

"Master, *I*…"

"Good girl," I said, pleased that she remembered to tell me. I stopped the spanking and Kate lay gasping, waiting. "I don't think you're ready to come yet."

I didn't remove my fingers but let her come down a bit, one hand stroking over her butt.

"Oh, *God*, I'm going to come," she gasped.

"No, you're not," I said, pleased she was so close. "Take a deep breath and blow it out. Relax completely."

She complied.

"I *like* this, Katherine," I said, rubbing my groin against her hip. "I love having you lying on my lap like this, your ass up and open, my fingers inside of you. You're so close, your body is about ready to convulse with pleasure."

I kept my thumb inside of her, my fingers pressing on her clit and she fought to feel more pressure, her body clenching around my thumb.

"*No*," I said firmly. "Don't make yourself come, Katherine. I'm the only one who can make you come. Nod your head if you understand."

She nodded, breathing rapidly and I knew she was right on the edge of her orgasm. Any motion on my part would drive her over.

"Maybe a few more smacks," I said, stroking my left hand

over her cheeks. "Just a few love taps and you're so close, I believe I could send you *over*..."

I smacked her several times over her pussy, harder than before, and that did it. The pressure was enough to move her body against my fingers and she went over the edge, her orgasm starting.

"Oh, God, oh *God*," she cried out, her body shuddering. "*Ohh*..."

"That's *good*, Katherine," I said, leaning down so that my face was next to hers. "That's so good..."

I thrust my thumb deeper, my fingers stroking her clit. I bent down to kiss her mouth as she came around my fingers. Then, I lifted her ass up and stood, holding her by the hips, positioning her so that her knees were at the edge of the bed, her face pressed against the covers, ass in the air. I unfastened my belt and pressed the head of my cock against her pussy.

"Now I'm going to fuck you, *hard*." I rammed my entire length inside of her, grasping her hips, pulling her against me with each thrust. "You want to know what being fucked hard feels like, Katherine?" I said, my lips next to her ear. "This is me fucking you hard."

I rose up and thrust even harder and faster, my hands digging into her hips.

Kate began thrusting with me, pressing back greedily each time I thrust inside of her.

"So, you want to come *again*, do you, Katherine?" I said. "I don't think I'll let you."

I was so close, it took only a few more thrusts for my own orgasm to begin and I cried out in pleasure as I ejaculated deep into her, the pleasure blinding. Then I collapsed on top of her.

As we lay recovering for a few moments, I kissed her shoulder, and brushed the hair away from her cheek so I could kiss it, too. Finally, I rose up and pulled slowly out of her, enjoying the sight of my come spilling out of her.

"If you spank me like *that*, you can punish me any time you like," she said. I could hear the amusement in her voice. I leaned back down again, my face next to hers, my mouth beside her ear. "I assure you, that was not a spanking in punishment. That was an erotic spanking and was meant to arouse you."

"You succeeded."

"That I did," I said, smiling.

I turned her over and lay on top of her, my body between her thighs. She wrapped her legs around my waist, pulling me closer. I kissed her, our tongues touching.

"Kate, *please*," I said when I pulled back. "Always tell me everything. Everything you're thinking and feeling. Don't hold anything back. Anything that happens that you find uncomfortable – I want it all. I *need* to know. You can trust me. I won't lose control."

"I thought men didn't want a bunch of talk. That's what you kept saying – enough talk."

"I was wrong to stop you from telling me," I said. "I was just so self-absorbed with everything, I needed to lose myself in you. But normally, a Dominant *wants* to know what his sub is thinking and feeling." I kissed her again, softly. "Power exchange is a huge responsibility. We take it seriously. When you give yourself over completely to me, I have so much power over you. I *want* that power. It turns me on completely. To be a good Dom, I need to know when you're happy, when you're sad, when you're afraid, when you're aroused, when you have doubts. When anything happens that affects our relationship. Do you understand?"

She nodded, and I could tell by the expression on her face that she was finally taking this seriously.

"Yes," she said, her voice breaking a bit. "I'm so sorry I didn't tell you right away. None of this had to happen."

"You didn't tell me for a reason," I said, knowing it was because I failed to make sure she trusted me enough. "You don't trust me to handle the truth and so you hid it from me. Kate, I *would* have been jealous. I *would* have been upset that you saw that video of me with Sunita. I *would* have been upset about what Maureen said. Eventually, I would have accepted it and dealt with it, but not until I fucked you hard and fast and made you come a few times."

Still blindfolded, she couldn't see so instead, she ran her fingers over my face and stroked my cheek. "I *liked* it when you fucked me hard and fast."

I kissed her neck. "You did, didn't you?"

"I did. I could have come very easily, if you'd let me."

"I had to do something to punish you. I figured since you liked the erotic spanking, I'd have to deny you a second orgasm."

"You're so mean," she said in mock anger. "It didn't hurt. It seemed to make the whole area like on big erogenous zone."

"That's the purpose of an erotic spanking. The nerves in your ass are deep under a layer of fat and it takes an erotic spanking to stimulate them. They're so close to the nerves in your pussy and clit that the whole area becomes stimulated when it's spanked. Plus, I love watching your nice round ass jiggle. A woman's ass is so desirable. Delicious. If a woman's body, if her belly and ass are too lean and muscular, it's more like a man's body. I like a womanly ass with a bit of jiggle in it. Makes me hard, in case you didn't notice."

"I noticed," she said, grinning.

"*Vive la différence*, I always say. You're petite and luscious." I kissed her again, smiling against her mouth.

"Are you ever going to take off my blindfold?" she said.

"I don't know. I might keep you in bed all night and day

with that on, doing all kinds of things to your body that you can't see and can only feel."

"*Mmm*," she murmured, smiling. "That sounds very hot."

"It does, does it? Have I created a monster in you, Ms. Bennet? An insatiable sex goddess?"

"*Insatiable sex goddess*," she said, grinning. She reached out and felt my face, slipping her hands behind my head, pulling me down for another deep kiss.

Finally, I pulled the blindfold off and leaned over her.

"Kate," I said, doing my best to keep my voice soft. "I don't want another night like tonight. I can't handle it. You have to follow the rules of the agreement. I'm going to have to be stricter with you, until you do so without thinking. It's not just for your sake, but for mine. If I'm going to control you, I have to control *myself*. If you're going to submit, you have to trust me completely. Only then will you be truly happy."

"I will," she said, her voice breaking from emotion. "I don't want another night like tonight either. I can't handle it." She pushed a hank of hair behind my ear, and stared into my eyes. "I *will* follow the rules," she said. "I didn't think you wanted to, because you never really have been very dominant with me. I thought you wanted a relationship with me that was more than D/s and sex."

"I *do*," I said and stroked her cheek. "But I've been single, for all intents and purposes, for five years. The only relationships I've had with women have been purely D/s. No emotion." I hesitated, not wanting to say too much. "But with you…" I inhaled deeply, my gaze moving over her face. "If I'm going to let you in, I have to trust you. That means you tell me everything when it comes to sex. That means when ex-boyfriends hit on you at fundraisers, you tell me right away. Will you accept that completely?"

She looked in my eyes, her brow furrowed as if she were considering.

"No."

"No?" A shock went through me.

She shook her head. "I want to amend our agreement."

I pulled back a bit, wary now that she still hadn't understood. "What do you mean?"

"I *want*," she said and ran a finger along my jaw. "I want the option to get fucked first thing in the morning occasionally, when I need it and when you can spare the time."

I leaned down to her, relieved. "Consider it done."

I pulled her into my arms and kissed her again, so glad that it was the only amendment to the agreement. We lay together in the darkness, the moonlight flooding in from the window.

CHAPTER 21

I WAS AWAKE EARLY the next morning, feeling invigorated after our night of confessions. After I was finished with my shower, I started to brush my teeth. I went into the bedroom where Kate lay under the covers, a toothbrush still in my mouth.

"I'll be gone all morning," I said around the toothpaste foam. "I have an appointment with the oncologist and then a lunch meeting. I've got things to do at the office. Won't see you until later."

Kate sighed. "I've got to finish the canvas so I'll probably spend the day there and come back here when I'm done."

"I'm glad you're painting," I said and stood regarding her, wishing I had more time and could crawl back under the covers. "If the oncologist says Liam's in the clear, we're free to go to Africa but I'll have to wrap up my work on the board and at the Foundation."

"No, I understand." Kate smiled. "You're not trying to avoid me?" she said, her voice almost a whisper.

"What?" I frowned and pointed the toothbrush at her. "Hold that thought." Toothpaste dripped down my chin, so I ran to the bathroom, rinsing my mouth out. Then I returned and lay on the bed beside her, focusing on her.

"Ms. Bennet, I am not trying to avoid you," I said, my voice firm. "Liam's getting tested this morning to see if the transplant is working and so my mind will be occupied with how it's going. I need to keep distracted all day. I have work to do and that will keep my mind busy so I don't ruminate too much on all the possible things that could go wrong. As a doctor, I already know what those possibilities are and so you can imagine how my mind is working, imagining them all." I touched her bottom lip and leaned down to kiss her.

She pulled away and held a hand over her mouth.

"Morning breath," she said, offering me her cheek.

"Lazybones," I said and laughed. "That's why you should get up when I do and shower with me." I kissed her neck instead of her cheek, and then moved the strap of her nightgown so that her full breast slipped out. I squeezed her breast and took her nipple in my mouth, sucking softly for a moment. Kate groaned in delight.

"If I did, I'd get all aroused and want you to fuck me," she replied, her eyes closed.

"I said I would – on *occasion*."

"I'll hold you to it." She opened one eye, a grin starting on her lips.

I smiled back. "Ms. Bennet, you can hold me to *it* any time you want." I covered her breast once more and gave her a chaste kiss on her cheek, pulling her into my arms.

"Kate, I know this is a big commitment, coming with me to Africa. Giving everything up that you built here, even if only for six months. I know you're concerned about what our relationship will be. I'll tell you what it will be – you're collared. You're my life partner. There's nothing else short of marriage that's as binding or as serious."

"I don't really understand what collared means," she said softly. "I'm so new to all this."

"I know you are," I replied, "but you have to know I'm serious about you. I want you and only you, from now on. I want us to be exclusive. Bound to each other."

"I want that, too."

I inhaled deeply. "Do you think you can trust me enough to tell me everything? Even things you think will upset me? I need you to trust me that much for this to work. I don't think you do yet."

"I want to," she said hesitantly. "But we've only known each other for such a short time…"

"I know, but it's been enough time for me to know you're all that I want."

"You were so willing to think I'd cheat on you, Drake. That upset me."

I frowned, regretting how I responded. "It was foolish. I wasn't thinking straight. I know you'd never do anything like that. I had to work like a dog to get you to even kiss me that first night…" I grinned. "Most men would have already given up."

Kate laughed. "Not you."

I shook my head, remembering back to when we met. "I could feel you were different that night at your father's fundraiser. It was like you could change everything, if I let you in. That scared me, after my first disaster of a marriage. But I can't imagine a life with anyone else but you." Kate buried her face in my neck and at that moment, I felt my heart squeeze. "I love you, Kate."

"I love you."

I leaned down and kissed her, unable to get enough of her. Then I touched her collar and smiled.

"Gotta go," I said. "Or I'll be late for my meeting with the oncologist because of my not-so-small problem." I placed her hand on my erection and her eyes widened. She squeezed me and closed her eyes.

"You sure you don't want to stay?" She opened one eye and peered at me.

"*Katherine*," I said, frowning. "On the days I can stay and you have that look in your eye, I *will* stay. I said I'd accept your amendment to the agreement and I meant it. Today is not a day I can."

"Sorry," she said, her face flushing.

"It's OK," I said and kissed her, pinning her down when she tried to avoid me. "I want to stay. Once I'm done, I'll text you. We'll do something special tonight."

She smiled and so I rolled off the bed and finished dressing. Finally I went to the hallway and pulled on my coat before returning to the bedroom, bending over to kiss her neck once more.

"I'll see you later, Ms. Bennet. Be waiting for me."

She smiled.

I closed the door behind me, eager to get my morning out of the way so I could return to her arms.

I DROPPED by the hospital and checked in with Liam's oncologist, speaking to him between patients. He assured me that everything was going exceedingly well and that the transplant seemed to have been successful. So far, there were no signs of rejection and the team had high hopes that it would be tolerated. More than tolerated – Liam would be cured. On a whim, I broached the subject of visiting Liam once before I left for Africa. Luckily for me, he was agreeable and together, we went to speak to the nurses who would be on staff that night. They agreed to let me slip in and check on Liam once later that night.

Maureen had asked them to call police if I showed up, but none of them agreed with her orders.

Elated from the news about Liam and happy that I'd get another chance to see him before Kate and I left for Africa, I spent only a short time at the corporate offices of my father's surgical implements business, for I had another errand to run that was far more important – at least to my mental state. I'd woken up in the middle of the night and lay awake watching Kate as she slept beside me. Mrs. O's words came back to me and I thought about how I'd feel if Kate and I broke up and I learned that Kate was getting married to someone else.

I couldn't imagine it. The very thought made my chest ache.

I knew what I had to do – what I wanted to do – and so after I signed some papers and made a show of attending to business, I sent Ethan an email asking for a meeting and he agreed happily.

I left the offices and drove to Ethan's Park Avenue apartment. I thought hard about what I'd say to Ethan when I met with him. I was going to ask him formally for his blessing when I asked Kate to marry me. I felt a little knot in my stomach at the prospect of asking Ethan.

He welcomed me at the door and ushered me into his study. I sat down on a chair across from his desk and exhaled.

"So, tell me what you wanted to talk about. I'm all ears."

I took in a deep breath. "Ethan, I'm here to ask for your blessing to ask Kate to marry me."

Ethan had been sitting with his hands steepled, examining me with a pleasant expression on his face.

"Why?"

I frowned, and swallowed hard, not expecting to be asked why.

"Why do I want to marry Kate?"

He said nothing for a moment and then burst into laughter.

"Of course, you have my blessing. Good lord, man. I couldn't be happier." He stood up, extending his hand for a shake. "I've been wondering when you'd get around to this." I stood and we shook hands across the desk.

"Oh, *hell*, this deserves a hug at least," Ethan said and came around the desk to my side. We hugged, clapping each other on the back. I was smiling broadly, relieved that Ethan was taking my question so well.

"Thank you," I said, my gratitude almost overwhelming me. "You don't know how happy this makes me. I'm in love with Kate. I want to spend the rest of my life with her and make her happy."

Ethan pulled away and nodded.

"You will. I have no doubt about it. I couldn't be happier."

After Ethan and I said our goodbyes, I drove down Fifth Avenue in search of my next quarry.

Cartier's Flagship store.

I spent an hour there, speaking with the sales clerk about diamonds, settings and choice of band. I wanted something unique, something a bit excessive, and something that would symbolize our unique relationship. When I finally found the right setting, the sales clerk smiled, obviously pleased with the price and her commission.

I felt sure that Kate would love it and hoped she'd say yes.

AFTER I WAS FINISHED at Cartier, I went to the Chelsea apartment and came in to find a pair of men's boots by the door. The sound of Kate's laughter filtered in from the back of the apartment – in the bedroom.

Kate came out of the bedroom with Keith behind her, a serious expression on his very Byronic face.

"Drake, you're home," she said and came over and kissed me on the mouth. She turned and pointed at him. "Keith helped me with my canvas, bringing it over in his van and then helping me mount it on the wall in our bedroom. Come and see it."

She took my hand and pulled me towards the bedroom.

"That's my cue," Keith said and winked at Kate. "See you later."

She smiled at Keith, and I felt a stab of jealousy that she would smile at another man – especially one who was a potential competitor but kicked myself.

Kate chose me.

"Keith again?" I said when the door closed behind him, unable to keep a note of jealousy out of my voice.

"Come on, Drake," Kate said. "I'd never be able to do it myself and I wanted it to be a surprise for you."

We entered the bedroom, and I stopped in my tracks, my jaw dropping when I finally saw it. A painting of me, naked.

"*Kate…*" I said, letting go of her hand, moving closer to examine it. It was really *really* good and very realistic, right down to my flaccid penis. "I had no idea this is what you were doing."

"I woke up early on a few mornings and sketched you, then I painted from memory. What do you think? Can you understand why I'm so aroused in the morning?"

"It's beautiful. The lighting, the shadows." I turned to Kate and pulled her into my arms. "But no one can see it. I don't want people looking at my *dick…*"

She laughed and pulled me closer. "I did another one with the sheet covering you up. I think I'll do a series of portraits. A collection."

"I don't know what I think about that."

"Don't worry," she said quickly. "None of the nudes will show your face. I'll do some with your clothes on, too, although that's such a waste."

I hugged her, completely baffled and impressed at the same time. "Only if you agree to let me take some photos of you for a book."

She inhaled deeply. "I'd like that. A private book for our own enjoyment. I wouldn't want any pictures with my face to get out there as long as my father is running for office."

"Don't worry. My photographer's very trustworthy and maybe we'll use a mask to hide your identity."

"You look pleased," she said, taking my coat and hanging it up. "You have good news about Liam?"

"The best. The preliminary tests show that his transplant is taking and there's no sign of rejection, either host-graft or graft-host. In a week, if things stay the same, he'll be in the clear. They'll test him every week for the first couple of months, and then, if he's still fine, every month for a year. I can come back to Manhattan if things take a turn for the worse, but as it is, we can leave next week. I've already booked our tickets."

"I'm so happy," she said and wrapped her arms around my neck once more.

I kissed her and then pulled her into the living room. After I sat on the couch, I pulled her down onto my lap.

"I have a mission for us tonight," I said. "I've spoken with the staff on the pediatric oncology ward. They're going to let me visit Liam again while Chris and Maureen are at dinner tonight. I want you to come."

"*Drake*," she said, frowning. "Do you think that's wise? The staff were instructed to call the police if you show up again."

"I spoke with Liam's oncologist and he cleared it with staff on the ward. They agree that as his biological father and as the one who gave him the donation, I have a right to just

pop in – as a doctor – and see how he's doing. I won't identify myself except to say I was the one who gave him the
donation. That's all."

Kate looked doubtful. "Maybe you should talk to my
father first?"

I shook my head. "Don't want to include Ethan in on this.
It's my decision. I've passed it by Liam's doctors. We're
covered." I kissed her and then stood up, letting her slide out
of my arms. "Now, go get dressed. We have a very narrow
window of time to get there, get inside, and get out. Chris
and Maureen are having dinner with her parents so they'll
both be away tonight for at least an hour. One of the nurses
heard their plans and let me know.

"If you *really* want to do this…"

"I *really* want to, Kate," I said. "I want you with me. He's
still in isolation because his immune system is still so new
but we can both go in. I want you to meet him."

Kate nodded and went to get dressed, but I could tell she
was reluctant.

WE DROVE to NYP and went to Liam's ward. I spoke with the
nurses to make sure the coast was clear and was assured that
things were all taken care of. Chris and Maureen were out
and should probably be out for at least an hour.

We had to follow contact precautions before going to
visit Liam. I led the way to Liam's room. From the anteroom,
I could see Liam was sitting up in bed playing with a toy,
watching the television. He wore a hospital gown in blue,
which highlighted his blue eyes. He looked small and frail,
but I could tell he was feeling much better than when I last
saw him.

After we gowned up, we entered his room.

He looked up from his toy. "Hello."

"Hello, Liam," I said and went to the side of the bed. "I'm Doctor Morgan. We met a few days ago. I've come by to see how you're doing."

"I'm good," Liam said. Then Liam turned to Kate. "Are you a nurse?"

She shook her head. "Just a colleague of Dr. Morgan's."

Liam nodded.

"You know, I was the one who gave you the stem cells," I said softly. "I just wanted to come by and see if you were doing better. Your doctors said you were almost ready to go home."

Liam made a face. "*You* gave me the blood cells?"

I nodded. "We're a match so I did what I could to help."

"Thank you." Liam smiled. I extended my gloved hand and Liam took it and we shook like two men. I leaned closer and ran my hand over Liam's head.

"I'm so glad I was able to help." I was filled with emotion to see him doing so well. I finally let go of Liam's hand and pointed to the toy. "What's that?"

"It's Bumblebee," Liam said, and held the toy up for us to see. "A transformer from the movie. Did you see it?"

I shook my head. "No, I never did see that one. What does it do?"

"You transform it into a car, like this," Liam said and demonstrated how to arrange the toy so that it transformed from a robot to a car. "He works for Optimus Prime. He's the head autobot. They're from Cybertron."

"Wow," I said and took the newly-transformed car when Liam handed it to me. "That's amazing." I tried to transform it but wanted to let Liam show me how. "It's too hard for me." I handed it back to Liam, who transformed it back into a robot with a few quick turns of the toy's joints.

"See?" Liam said, holding it back up. "Simple. Even I can do it. My dad taught me how."

I nodded, a stab of regret in my chest at the mention of Chris and the fact it was Chris who Liam saw as his father. Although I knew it was true and right that Liam considered Chris his father, I couldn't help but feel a stab of regret.

"That's cool. Your dad must be pretty smart to show you how to do that."

"He's an engineer. He makes things so this was *easy* for him."

I stood for a moment and watched as Liam assembled the robot once more into a car. He smiled and showed us the transformed robot, proud of his accomplishment.

I glanced at the clock on the wall. "I guess we better go. I'm glad to see you're all better."

Liam nodded, and in a few seconds, we were forgotten. Before we were even out the door, he was watching television. I took Kate's hand and led her into the anteroom to remove our gowns and masks. We didn't stop by the nursing station, but I nodded to the nurse as we passed to let her know I appreciated the help getting in to see my son, despite Maureen's wishes.

I pulled Kate down the hallway, and out of the hospital, wanting to leave as soon as possible so that we didn't run into Maureen and Chris. The sun had set and the sky was dark, overcast. I stopped outside the rear exit where I was parked and closed my eyes, finally overcome with emotion from seeing how well Liam was doing.

"He looks really good," Kate said and squeezed my hand.

"He does," I said, forcing a smile. "He's happy. He has parents who love him."

I pulled Kate into an embrace, needing to feel her warmth. She slipped her arms around my neck and pulled me down. I nuzzled her neck, my lips pressing against her throat and beneath her ear.

Then, I pulled away and sighed.

"Let's go home."

WE DECIDED to stay at my apartment before we left for Africa so we could spend some time alone. Ethan and Elaine understood since we had a lot of planning to do, packing and repacking, and some decisions to make. I sent off boxes to the college for the class I would teach, including textbooks and lecture notes, as well as other paraphernalia I would need to teach robotic surgery. I also packed a few of my father's personal mementos, which I would ship before we left.

"I'm not sending any of this," I said as I sorted through my bondage gear. "Don't want it to be found by curious housekeepers or border security. We'll have to improvise when we get there. No cuffs, no spreader bars, and no butt plugs. Just me." I grinned at her and quirked an eyebrow.

"You're *more* than enough," she said and leaned down to kiss me, her arms threading around my neck.

"I hope so. I'm a very jealous man. Don't want you getting too attached to B.O.B. or Big or anything…"

"With you, Drake," she said and grinned. "Who needs substitutes?"

"I want to ship your painting though," I said and considered one that was propped against a wall. "The one with the sheet covering my … manhood."

"*Manhood*," she said and smiled back.

"The risqué one can stay here. When we come back, I want it moved to our bedroom on 8th Avenue."

"You really aren't going to ship any of your toys and implements?" Kate asked, seeming surprised.

"I can always buy some rope. Leather. I'm handy enough. I could probably even build you canvases for your studio."

"What studio?" she asked and leaned against the table.

"The one we'll make sure to have in whatever house we get." I went to where she stood and pulled her into my arms. "I want you to paint as much as you want while we're there. Do what you want. I'll be really busy at the college and hospital so you have to do what makes you happy."

She nodded. "I'd like my own studio. But you might have to watch out. I've been known to spend the entire day in my pajamas when I get into a painting. No cleaning, no cooking, no domesticity."

"No problem. We'll get a housekeeper and a cook. When I come home from the hospital, I want you ecstatic, ready for me after a long day working on your art."

"Sounds like heaven."

CHAPTER 22

A FEW DAYS before our flight, I picked Kate up from where she was sitting on the couch and carried her into my office. All morning I had been thinking of what I needed to do before we left for Africa. Talking to Kate about our agreement was top on the list.

"We'll be going away in less than a week. I think it's time to do what we've already discussed and renegotiate the agreement. I want you to tell me if anything's changed."

Then, I let her slide down my body. "I'm going to print off a copy and I want us to sit down and go over it once more. Point by point. Anything you want changed, you should say it now. We'll discuss it. Negotiate."

I sat at my desk and opened my laptop, searching through my emails for the one Kate sent with the agreement. I opened the email and printed the document off. I stood up and took her hand, leading her into the living room, where I sat on the couch. I pulled her down onto my lap the way we sat that first night at her apartment, her arms around my neck.

"Now, Ms. Bennet, I want you to tell me exactly what you

want and need from me. A lot has changed since we wrote this up," I said and held up the document. "We'll be leaving Manhattan, living in Nairobi. I'll be working five days a week and will be on call one weekend a month. What do you see when you imagine us together there?"

Kate inhaled deeply and didn't speak for a moment. "I see us as a committed couple," she said, looking into my eyes. "We spend our time together. We do things together. We cook together. We explore together. We sleep together. Of course, we have lots of sex."

I grinned. "Of course."

"But I've never lived with a man before," she said. "The most I've been with someone is a weekend."

"Kurt?"

Kate nodded. "He spent a lot of time at my place. But we only dated for a few months, so... You've been married."

"I have. But I was bad at it. I don't think I knew how to be a proper husband."

She shrugged, her shoulder lifting. "I don't know how to be a proper submissive."

"You're learning," I said, for she was. During our scenes, she was far more responsive to my commands and eager to try things out. "You've got a strong will. I get the sense that as much as submission excites you, it also still scares you. You judge yourself too strongly for wanting it but being happy is more important than being politically correct."

She nodded. "What will you tell people that we meet when we're there?" she said softly. "Your colleagues? Your boss?"

"I'll introduce you as my partner," I replied. I'd thought about it before she asked. We were a collared couple in BDSM terms, and we were definitely committed. "I think that's the going word for people who are committed to each other but who aren't married."

"*Partner*," she said, repeating it. "Sounds like a business relationship. Or sporting."

"It's not perfect, but lover is too blatant. Soul mate sounds too much like Keats."

She laughed and shook her head. "Your colleagues would think you'd gone bonkers if you said I was your soul mate."

"That they would." I leaned in closer and kissed her, threading my fingers in her hair. I was glad she seemed interested in how to define our relationship. When I popped the question, which I had planned out in my mind exactly where and when, I hoped that she would be pleased.

With that in mind, her touch and scent all served to arouse me and I couldn't help but kiss her more deeply, my lips parting hers, tongue finding hers.

I broke the kiss, my forehead pressed against hers. "So," I said. "What in this agreement do you want to change? Anything?"

"Nothing," she said without hesitation. "I want to be with you. I want you to teach me about submission. I want to go where you take me."

I kissed her again. "I want to take you where you need to go," I said. "But I think I want to clarify that we are a collared couple. You're mine, and our bond is as important as an engagement. Some lifestylers see it like a marriage. It's as close as I've come to being in a committed relationship outside of marriage. That means we're completely and totally honest and open with each other. We're completely exclusive with each other. How does that sound?"

She nodded and slid her hand behind my head, stroking my skin. "That sounds perfect."

I nodded, amazed that everything I desired had come my way – Kate as my submissive, my trip to Africa, my position at the college. "I'll revise it and then I think we should sign it again. Make it official. We're Dominant and submissive in the bedroom. We're equals outside of it."

"Are we always going to be doing D/s when it comes to sex?" she asked, tilting her head to the side. "No vanilla?"

I kissed her. "Let's play it by ear. As long as you're honest with me about how you feel, I should be in tune with your needs. Will you let me make the decisions about that? Do you trust me to know what you need?"

"Yes," she said.

"Kate, I don't want anyone but you."

She smiled and cupped my face with her hand. "I don't want anyone but you."

THE DAY CAME for our flight and we spent the morning with Ethan and Elaine at their penthouse, eating a farewell breakfast of waffles, Eggs Benedict, fresh squeezed juice and coffee.

Kate was excited and didn't sleep well the night before and so was both tired and nervous to leave. Once we were finished with breakfast, Kate went to freshen up in her bathroom. I followed Ethan down the hall to his office, wanting to say a special goodbye to him in private.

We spoke in soft voices about the flight and our stay in Italy before we went to Kenya.

"I'll be asking her to marry me there," I said. "I'm pretty sure she'll say yes."

"So am I. She loves you, Drake. Make her happy."

"That is exactly what I want. To make her happy."

Ethan smiled at me from across his desk.

ETHAN AND ELAINE used the limo service and drove with us to JFK to see us off. When the moment arrived for us to part,

Kate was all choked up and tearful, embracing her father again and again, kissing Elaine on the cheek, and generally letting go of them with reluctance.

I stood and watched them after I kissed Elaine, amazed once again at what a great father Ethan was. He gave Kate one final embrace, his own eyes wet.

"I'll miss you, Katie," he said, in his gravelly voice. "But I'm so happy to see you going with Drake. I know it will be a great experience."

"Thanks, Daddy," she said. "I'll miss you. These past few months have been so... So *wonderful*. I feel like I know you better than ever before."

"You're all grown up, Katherine. I'm so proud of you. Take a lot of pictures. Skype me as often as you like."

"I will."

He kissed Kate on the cheek and turned away, and I could tell Ethan was too emotional to say anything else to me so I took Kate's hand and pulled her away.

WE TOOK a direct flight to Naples, Italy were we would stay for a few days, and then rented a car and drove to a tiny resort village named Ravello. The location was famous for being the inspiration for Wagner's opera *Parsifal*.

The hotel in Ravello was in the neoclassical style with white stone walls and columns. Each room had a small balcony that looked out onto the Mediterranean, the rocky shore below and cliffs on either side of us.

That first night, without any of my usual rope or leather cuffs, I had to resort to using my tie to restrain her hands to the ornate headboard of the bed and another to blindfold her.

The bedframe was loose and the screws that held it into the frame rusted and when I began thrusting, it creaked like an old washing machine, completely ruining the mood I was shooting for. We ended up collapsing in laughter, the eroticism of the scene I was imagining lost completely in our mutual mirth.

In the end, each time I tried to resume my movements, Kate giggled, leading to me laughing out loud. Finally, I gave up and moved her to the floor in front of the window. We ended up going pretty vanilla, with Kate on her hands and knees, and me holding her hair and pulling her up for a kiss while I fucked her from behind.

WE SLEPT ALMOST through the morning the first day we were there and then spent time walking the narrow streets, enjoying the village's ambience. After a quiet dinner in our room, we sat on the couch and watched the sunset through the open doors of the balcony. I was waiting for the perfect time to give Kate my ring, wanting to propose to her when the mood was right.

"How are you tonight?" I rubbed her back. "Still a bit tired?"

"A bit," she said. "Nothing I can't manage."

I pulled her closer, so that she sat on my lap. "You've made me very happy, Kate."

"I'm happy that you're happy." She kissed me softly and nestled her head on my shoulder.

"I thought for a terrible few hours that day that I'd lost you," I said, tilting her chin up so I could look in her eyes. "I know it was crazy, but in the back of my mind was this fear that I'd helped you overcome your fear of kink and then, you'd go back to Kurt, who was more your age."

"*You're* more my age," she said. "Besides, I can't imagine being with anyone but you."

"Neither can I."

"*I* was afraid you'd throw me over as being too much trouble," she said after a long pause.

"Never. You know I enjoy a challenge. You do forget to use the proper form of address now and then, and there are times that I know you want to ask me what my plans are, but overall, I couldn't be happier."

"I'm trying to be a better sub."

"I'm trying as well," I said. "Trying to earn your trust."

"I want to trust you completely," she said. "You've never hurt me on purpose. You proved to me that I can enjoy things I never thought I could. You pushed me when I was reluctant, when I was uncertain."

"When you're uncertain about something, it usually indicates ambivalence. You're attracted and repelled at the same time. When you're uncertain, if I can push you a bit, you may discover you can enjoy things you wrote off."

She nodded and then a wicked grin started on her lips. "So, if I *want* you to do something, I should pretend I'm uncertain of it? Would that encourage you to push, so that I'd submit in spite of my reluctance?"

I tried my best not to smile, frowning at her in my best Dom mode. "That would be very bad, *Katherine*. Topping from the bottom and is generally frowned on. Honesty is the best policy."

"I was kidding."

"I'm serious," I said and turned her face to mine. "If you want me to do something, if it brings you pleasure, I'll do it gladly."

She sighed and laid her head on my shoulder.

"There will be a few bumps along the way, Kate. It's inevitable, but as long as we're honest with each other, we'll be happy."

I pulled her more closely into my arms and kissed her,

pushing her down onto the couch, my body between her thighs.

We lay like that for a while in pleasant silence. Finally, I rose up, making an excuse about using the bathroom, where I had hidden the small box containing the engagement ring I'd purchased earlier in Manhattan. When I returned, Kate stood on the balcony watching the ocean below.

I wrapped my arms around her from behind and kissed the top of her head. Kate leaned back against me.

"What are you doing, Ms. Bennet?"

"Watching the stars. They're amazing here, in such a tiny village."

I held her like that for a moment, enjoying the peace and quiet, the serenity.

"We never did have dessert," I said, and kissed her shoulder.

"Mmm, no we didn't," she said. "What do you fancy, Dr. Delish?"

"Dr. *Delish*?" I said and laughed.

"That's what the nurses call you."

"I thought it was *Dr. D.*"

"That, too. And Dr. Dangerous."

"Dr. *Delish*," I said and stroked my hand up her waist to cup a breast while I kissed her neck. "I think I like Dr. Dangerous. Gives me a better ambience, for a Dom."

"Dr. Delish suits you better. You *are* delicious," she said. "At least you were the last time I tasted you."

"Mmm, Ms. Bennet, you are *definitely* giving me ideas…"

"You're never short of ideas."

"No, I'm not." I pulled down the shoulder strap of her dress and bit her shoulder playfully. "Yes, very tasty. Very tasty indeed. I'm going to sample more of your wares."

She leaned back and laid her hands over mine, which held the ring box.

"What's this?" she said and took the box, which was tied with a silver ribbon. She turned around and looked in my eyes. "*Drake…*"

"Open it." My heart was practically bursting while I watched her with the box in her hand. She hesitated for she must have realized what it was – an engagement ring. I felt pretty certain she'd accept, but there was always the chance it would scare her off instead.

When she stood there, unmoving, her mouth open, I decided to take control and took it from her.

"Let's do this properly," I said and opened the box after removing the ribbon. Inside the royal blue velvet ring box was the ring. I opened the box and knelt down in front of her. "See? You've brought me to my knees, Katherine." I smiled up at her. She had covered her mouth, her eyes wide, tears beginning to form.

"I said once that people might think I was your sub, if they saw the way I was with you. But while I'm kneeling down to you now, it's probably the last, so I hope you appreciate it."

She said nothing. Instead, she stared at the ring – a single solitaire diamond, several carats in weight.

"*Katherine,*" I said, my voice emotional. "I know we agreed that you were collared and that it was as good as an engagement, but I've been thinking a lot about this. Finding out I had a son, meeting him, doing what I could to help him made me realize I don't want to go through life without a family. I don't know what the future will hold for us. I only know that I can't imagine not spending it with you."

She still said nothing and then finally, she looked up from the ring to my eyes.

"Drake, are you sure of this? I thought you didn't want to get married again."

"Kate," I said, unable to mask the emotion in my voice. "I

love you so *much*. I didn't realize how much until that night I thought I'd lost you. I said I never wanted us to be parted again, and I meant it."

I took the ring out of the box and slipped it on the ring finger of her left hand.

Then I cleared my throat, my voice thick with emotion. "I believe the proper words are *'I love you, Katherine. Will you marry me?'*" I smiled up at her.

Her eyes were filled with tears but still she didn't speak.

"I believe the desired response is *'Yes, Drake, I love you and will marry you.'*"

"Yes," she said finally. "Yes, Drake, I love you and will marry you."

I stood up and pulled Kate into my arms, unable to imagine life without her, and thanked the heavens that she said yes.

OUR FLIGHT to Nairobi was short and I watched out the window over Kate's shoulder as we flew across the African continent, the thin clouds visible below our plane, the sun shining on the lakes.

"We're almost there," I said, taking her hand in mine, threading our fingers together. "If you look out now, you'll see the city."

Kate watched out the window while we landed and I was filled with happiness that I had scarcely believed was possible only six months earlier. I had been between submissives and felt caught up in the mundane everyday. I wasn't unhappy. But I wasn't happy.

With Kate, I was finally happy.

After we touched down and slowed, I turned to her.

"Well, Ms. Bennet. Here we are," I said, smiling. I pulled her hand up to my lips and kissed her knuckles, remembering that first day at Ethan's apartment and how shocked and thrilled I had been when I realized the hot little brunette with the wide green eyes and nice rack was Katherine.

She smiled at me and turned back to the window while we taxied to the terminal.

In the distance, the Ngong Hills were dark against a perfectly clear blue sky.

THE END

COMING JUNE 29, 2015: *DRAKE UNBOUND,* which tells the story of *Unrestrained* from Drake's point of view.

ABOUT THE AUTHOR

S. E. Lund is a writer who lives with her family of humans and pets in a century-old house on a quiet tree-lined street in a small city in Western Canada. She writes erotic, contemporary romance and paranormal romance. You can find her on Twitter @selundwriter , on Facebook as well as on Goodreads. Look for details and updates on current and new releases at www.selund.com

You can sign up for S. E. Lund's mailing list here and receive free eBooks:

http://eepurl.com/1Wcz5

ALSO BY S. E. LUND:

∼

Contemporary Erotic Romance
  THE UNRESTRAINED SERIES
  The Agreement: Book 1
  The Commitment: Book 2
  Unrestrained: Book 3
  Unbreakable: Book 4
  Forever After: Book 5
  Everlasting: Book 6 (Coming September 2017!)

∼

THE DRAKE SERIES (The Unrestrained Series from
Drake's Point of View)
  Drake Restrained
  Drake Unwound
  Drake Unbound

∼

Military Romance / Romantic Suspense
THE BAD BOY SERIES
Bad Boy Saint: Book 1
Bad Boy Sinner: Book 2
Bad Boy Soldier: Book 3
Bad Boy Savior: Book 4 (C0ming in July 2017)

THE DOMINION SERIES
Dominion: Book 1 in the Dominion Series
Ascension: Book 2 in the Dominion Series
Retribution: Book 3 in the Dominion Series
Resurrection: Book 4 in the Dominion Series
Redemption: Book 5 in the Dominion Series

Coming in 2017
Prince of the City: The Vampire's Pet Part One

84467955R00166